**PR...
O...**

The Readaholics and the Falcon Fiasco

"Laura DiSilverio's first book in her excellent new Book Club Mystery series features an appealingly clever protagonist and her witty group of Readaholics, who dissect great books while solving an intricately plotted murder that kept me turning pages late into the night."
—*New York Times* bestselling author Kate Carlisle

"Engaging characters. Beautiful setting."
—*New York Times* bestselling author Carolyn Hart

"Amy-Faye Johnson and her readaholic friends will leave you wanting more in this engaging new mystery series."
—national bestselling author Sally Goldenbaum

The Mall Cop Mysteries

"An original heroine, a clever concept. . . . Put this series at the top of your shopping list."
—Elaine Viets, national bestselling author of *A Dog Gone Murder*

"One hell of a great novel. This novel will crack you up with DiSilverio's humor and razor's-edge wit."
—Suspense Magazine

"Charming, fun, and refreshing."
—*Seattle Post-Intelligencer*

continued . . .

The **Readaholics**
and the
Falcon Fiasco

A Book Club Mystery

Laura DiSilverio

AN OBSIDIAN BOOK

OBSIDIAN
Published by the Penguin Group
Penguin Group (USA) LLC, 375 Hudson Street,
New York, New York 10014

USA | Canada | UK | Ireland | Australia | New Zealand | India | South Africa | China
penguin.com
A Penguin Random House Company

First published by Obsidian, an imprint of New American Library,
a division of Penguin Group (USA) LLC

First Printing, April 2015

ISBN 978-0-451-47083-6

Printed in the United States of America
10 9 8 7 6 5 4 3 2 1

For my readers
Thanks for thinking books and reading and literacy
and stories are important.
I wouldn't be a writer if it weren't for all of you.

Acknowledgments

As always, thanks to my phenomenal editor, Sandy Harding, who shares my sense of humor and continues to make me a better writer, and my agent, Paige Wheeler, who was the first publishing industry professional to believe in me, and who also challenges me to get better with every book.

Thanks to all the sisters and misters of Sisters in Crime, the most supportive and helpful community in the fiction-writing arena.

Thanks and much love to my husband, Tom, and my daughters. I am greatly blessed.

Chapter 1

The white suit was a bad idea. I knew it when I bought it at the outlet mall, but it was 75 percent off and the A-line skirt disguised the extra ten pounds that tend to cling to my thighs. I knew it when I put it on, but the forecast was for an unseasonable ninety degrees in Heaven, Colorado—the temps didn't usually climb into the nineties until July in our little Rocky Mountain hollow on Lost Alice Lake—and the white linen made me feel crisp and cool. With my copper-colored hair twisted into a chignon, an aqua camisole under the jacket, and nude pumps, I was the image of chic professionalism as I set out to meet my new client. Until the kitten.

It sat at the corner of Eden and Paradise, underneath the four-way stop sign, a tiny ball of bedraggled gray fluff. It had rained hard the night before and the kitten's damp fur convinced me she'd been caught out in it. My windows were down so I could enjoy the rain-washed and still cool air, and I heard a plaintive mew as I waited for a pickup to cross the intersection. The kitten put a paw in the gutter as the truck caromed into a pothole and almost drowned it with a tsunami of muddy water.

"Get back on the sidewalk, kitty," I ordered. I didn't see a collar.

She mewed again and looked at me with big blue eyes. It was my turn to go and I rolled slowly into the intersection. I didn't have time to rescue stray kittens. The bride-to-be was expecting me at nine o'clock sharp at the Columbine, the most upscale B and B in Heaven. Someone else would stop for the kitten; its owner was probably combing the neighborhood for it this very minute. I'd come this way on my return trip to the office and if she was still here, I'd bundle her up and take her to the humane society. I flat out couldn't do it now.

On the far side of the intersection, I hit my brakes and pulled over with a gusty sigh. Slamming my door harder than necessary, I stalked across the street and looked down at the kitten, who tilted her head back and stared at me, unblinking.

"Come on, then," I said, scooping her up. She didn't weigh much more than a wet washcloth, and I carried her balled in my hands, my arms outstretched, to protect my suit from the muddy droplets dribbling off her. She squirmed when we reached the van. Yes, a van. It wasn't the sporty convertible that would have reflected my personality better—I mean, a van doesn't exactly say hot, single, young thirties professional like an Audi TT does—but I'd ended up hauling potted plants, tubs of crystal, and even peacocks for my event-planning business too often to consider a smaller vehicle. With a harried glance at my watch, I put her into an empty champagne box and moved it to the front seat, tossing *The Maltese Falcon*, the book my Readaholics were discussing tonight, into the back. Pulling a yoga top from my gym bag, I tucked it around the kitten, who didn't seem to object to its ripe smell. I couldn't keep thinking of her as "the kitten," so I mentally christened her Misty. There's a law, I'm pretty sure, that requires that all gray cats be named Smoky or Misty.

Hurrying around the van, I climbed back into the driver's seat, flashing a bit of thigh at a young man who honked and grinned as he drove past. I inspected my suit, relieved to see not a speck of mud or one long gray hair. Ha! I'd foiled the forces of the universe that direct their energy at smirching white suits. I hit the gas. The B and B was only two blocks away and I pulled up right at nine.

"Mew." Misty had her front paws over the box's top and her head peeked out. She looked around curiously.

"Don't—" I started as the box wobbled.

I put out a hand and caught the box as it toppled toward my lap. Whew! Another bullet dodged. Misty slumped into a corner as I righted the box. "Mew."

"Don't get snippy with me," I said. "You're the one who tipped the box over." I slewed my lips to the side. I couldn't leave her in the van, even with the windows open. My meeting might go two hours and it would be hot enough to melt asphalt by the time I got back. With another sigh, I tucked the expandable leather folder that held my notes into the box and hefted it. "Kittens are to be neither seen nor heard at important business meetings," I told her sternly, mounting the six stone steps leading to the Victorian B and B's double oak doors. The building dated from the late 1880s, when the town was incorporated, and Sandy Milliken and her husband, transplants from the East Coast, had spent beaucoup bucks fixing it up.

I nudged one door open with my hip, cradling the box in the crook of my elbow. The foyer, graced with wide-plank oak floors, Laura Ashley fabrics, and a Tiffany chandelier, murmured of history and the expensive restoration. It smelled like lemon furniture polish and bacon. Misty apparently liked the latter scent, because her tufty head appeared over the box's rim, tiny nose working. "After we're done here," I promised her, "I'll find you some tasty kibble."

Pushing her gently back into the box, I headed toward the patio, where I was supposed to meet my new client, a Madison Taylor. I didn't think she was a local girl, but I'd been happy to agree to plan her wedding when she called me out of the blue last week. It wasn't unusual to have out-of-town weddings scheduled in Heaven. Brides liked the idea of being married in "Heaven," and the crafty town council had built a lovely wedding gazebo by the lake when they renamed the town fifteen years ago. It used to be called Walter's Ford, but Walter was only a footnote in the town's history, and folks didn't seem to know if "Ford" referred to a Model T or a water crossing no longer in existence, so our elected officials went with a name they thought would attract more tourists and business development. I'd been a sophomore at the time and there'd been something of a kerfuffle when our football team suddenly became the Heaven Demons, but that was resolved by the students voting to adopt a new mascot: the Avengers.

The clinking of cutlery and the splashing of a small fountain drew me toward the patio, where I knew breakfast was served on nice mornings. Wrought-iron tables spaced a gracious distance apart dotted the flagstone patio, which was surrounded by lush greenery and flowers: lavender, hostas, lemon trees, and oleanders in pots, and daylilies just beginning to bloom now that we were into May. They bobbed as flurries of wind, left over from last night's storm, gusted across the patio. A trio of cement goldfish spurted water into a basin six feet in diameter, attracting a sparrow, which sat on the rim. It got a shower whenever the wind blew the fine spray the fish were sending up. Only two tables held guests finishing their eggs, bacon, and Sandy's award-winning cranberry-carrot muffins. Sandy herself refreshed their coffee cups from a steaming carafe. I set Misty's carton in an unobtrusive corner behind the open French doors, extracted some papers from my expandable folder, and arranged it atop the box to keep her inside.

"Stay put," I told her. She blinked at me. I took it for agreement. Rising, I smoothed my pristine skirt, put a smile on my face, and moved to meet my client.

"Here's Amy-Faye now," Sandy said to the petite blond woman sitting closest to the fountain.

The motherly Sandy filled an extra cup for me and I gave her a grateful smile. "Amy-Faye, this is Taylor Madison. She's been telling me all about the 'Heavenly' wedding she wants. I've told her you're the gal can make sure every detail is perfect." She gave a half wink before responding to a request for more marmalade from the older couple at the other table.

"Well, I'll do my best to put together your dream wedding," I said, holding out my hand to the blonde. I knew she was a New York City lawyer, but she looked dainty and unthreatening, more of an angelfish than a shark. In her late twenties, probably. She was no bigger than a minute, with a heart-shaped face, a straight nose, and strong brows that winged up at the ends. She would look ethereal in clouds of white tulle, or maybe a strapless satin column dress, if her taste was as modern as her name. She rose with a smile and shook my hand, hers slim but strong.

"Actually," she said, "it's Madison Taylor. I get that all the time. Two last names, right? I don't know what my folks were thinking. Call me Madison."

"Amy-Faye Johnson," I said. "Pleased to meet you."

We exchanged a few pleasantries about the weather and how beautiful Heaven was before Madison's voice took on a more businesslike tone. "I always assumed I'd get married in Manhattan since that's where I live, but when Doug suggested we get married in Heaven, I figured why not? My family would have to travel from Wisconsin to New York, anyway, so they might as well come here instead.

And Colorado is so . . . refreshing this time of year. New York's all smog and noise and humidity." Her smile invited me to applaud her reasoning. "So I was thinking a morning wedding, with six bridesmaids in carnation pink, followed by a brunch reception . . ."

She'd lost me at "Doug." No, it couldn't be. I began taking notes and offering suggestions, but half my mind worried at that "Doug." There were lots of Dougs in the world. I didn't even know if her Doug was from Heaven or just thought it would be a romantic place to get married. We discussed caterers, florists, and photographers; her three-year-old twin niece and nephew, who would make an adorable ring bearer and flower girl; the pros and cons of an outdoor reception by the lake; and the sticky etiquette of how to involve both her father and stepfather in the wedding. Routine stuff. She didn't say why they were marrying in such haste—three weeks was barely enough time to organize a garage sale, never mind a wedding—but I didn't feel I could ask. Her groom's last name never came up and it was driving me crazy. Doug *who*? I wanted to shout.

When we segued into a discussion of my fees and contract, I couldn't help myself. "Where did you get my name?" I asked.

Madison smiled. "Doug's mother, Elspeth Elvaston. She said you were the best event planner in Heaven, a real perfectionist, and that you'd gone to high school with Doug. She said if anyone could pull this wedding together on such short notice, you could."

Multicolored lights blinked before my eyes and it was suddenly hard to breathe. "You're marrying Doug Elvaston?" My Doug? My former boyfriend and the reason I came back to Heaven after college in Boulder? "I . . . I didn't even know he was dating anyone."

With a girlish laugh, Madison leaned forward. "We met in New York—I'm sure you know he's been spending a lot of time there on a class-action case—and it was kind of a whirlwind thing. Lots of long hours of legal work turned into romantic dinners and walks in Central Park, a weekend at a little B and B on the Hudson." She tucked a strand of silky gold hair behind one small ear. "I knew he was the one for me almost from the moment we met. He said it was the same for him, that he'd never felt this kind of connection with anyone before. You know how it is when you can finish each other's sentences, when you can share a joke just by meeting someone's eyes?" She fairly glowed.

I felt nauseated. Her total lack of self-consciousness told me Doug hadn't even mentioned my name to her. How was that possible? We'd had an on-again-off-again relationship since our junior year in high school. Yeah, we'd been in an "off" phase for almost two years, but I hadn't realized Doug considered us totally off, get-married-to-someone-else off. I'd been so sure that we'd eventually get back together—

"That silly kitten's going to fall into the fountain if it's not careful," Madison said, looking over my shoulder.

I spun in my chair. Misty had managed to clamber onto the fountain's low rim and was stalking the oblivious sparrow. Her concentration was total, her gaze fixed on the bird, her tiny body taut as she moved forward in a slow crouch. Predator mode. How had she gotten out of the box? Caught up in the planning, and obsessing about Doug, I'd completely forgotten about her. I scraped my chair back.

"A cat!" The older woman at the other table sounded like she'd found a cockroach on her plate. Her husband remained semicomatose, even when she said, "William, you remember how I told Mrs. Milliken that I was allergic to cats and she assured me—"

"She's mine," I apologized, moving toward the fountain. "That is, I brought her. Come here, Misty." I held out my hand. She ignored me. Big surprise. We'd had a cat when I was growing up and he'd turned selective hearing into an art form. I was reaching for her when a powerful gust of wind drenched me with water from the spitting fish.

The chill surprised me. "Oh!" I shivered, told myself it was only water, and plucked the disappointed kitten from the fountain's rim as the sparrow flew away. Careful to hold her at arm's length again, I deposited her back in the box and repositioned the folder. "Just a couple more minutes," I told her.

"Mew," she complained, her look saying she could be breakfasting on tasty sparrow if I hadn't interfered. Fat chance. She was so light the sparrow could probably have carried her away without much effort.

I hurried back to Madison, apologizing to her and the other couple as I went, and explaining about rescuing Misty from the roadside.

"Really, it's okay," Madison said, laughing, signing my contract, and handing over a deposit check. "My law firm tried a 'bring your pet to work day,' but it didn't work out too well. One of the partners brought his pit bull and it got hold of my paralegal's ferret. Not pretty."

I hated that the woman Doug wanted to marry instead of me was so dang nice. I wanted to be able to tell him he was making a horrible mistake, but it didn't look like he was. She was younger, thinner, and more successful than I, and a decent human being, to boot. At least my suit was as sharp as her gray slacks topped with a navy linen blazer. We shook hands again and her eyes widened. I thought she was going to say something, but then she shook her head the tiniest bit and told me she looked forward to working with me. We made an appointment to meet at my office on Thursday. "I know you'll make our big day perfect." Her smile outshone the sun.

Unable to choke out an assurance, especially since I was wondering if I could engineer a disaster that would stop the wedding—food poisoning? a tornado? the wedding gazebo burning down?—I nodded and turned away, eager to leave before I embarrassed myself by crying.

The old gentleman at the next table was staring at me, looking a lot livelier than he had earlier. He gave me a once-over and I wrinkled my brow. What was the old guy—? I followed his gaze and saw that the fountain water had rendered the white linen of my skirt totally see-through. I could distinctly make out the lacy pattern of my undies. Really? This morning wasn't miserable enough already? I flushed and fought the urge to run for the door, knowing Madison had noticed, too. I grabbed Misty's box, held it low enough to provide some coverage, and walked with as much dignity as I could muster to the van.

Leaning my forehead against the steering wheel, my arms hanging limp, I looked sideways at the kitten in her box on the passenger seat. "This day has got to get better, right?"

"Mew," Misty agreed.

Chapter 2

"You've adopted a kitten?" my best friend Brooke Widefield asked, arriving early for the Readaholics meeting. She followed me into my small galley kitchen, where margarita fixings waited.

"Not exactly," I said, salting the margarita glasses' rims. Our book club discussions tended to be livelier when we imbibed a bit. It was amazing how insightful we got after a margarita or three.

"Looks like a kitten to me." Brooke bent to pat Misty, who was twining between her ankles. "She's adorable."

Yeah, so adorable I hadn't been able to leave her at the animal shelter where Brooke volunteered. I couldn't keep her, though—my schedule was too erratic, unfair to pets. I was hoping our friend Lola Paget, who owned a plant nursery, might need another cat. I remembered her mentioning that one of her cats had gone to the Great Catnip Patch in the sky a few weeks back. I explained all this to Brooke as I mixed the tequila, triple sec, and sweet and sour in the blender, added ice, and pulsed it.

I poured us each a glassful. "Unless you want her?" I watched Brooke cradle Misty against her cheek. They looked like a magazine ad—Brooke with her Miss Colorado beauty queen complexion, curtain of mink brown hair, and green eyes, and the kitten a powder puff of gray fluff since I'd bathed and combed her when we got home.

"Troy would have a hissy," she said, reluctantly putting the kitten down. "You know how he is. It'd be great if you could place her rather than turning her over to the Haven. We've already got more cats than we'll be able to adopt out."

We drifted into the sunroom, furnished with wicker chairs upholstered in bright floral cotton. Celadon-colored ceramic tile covered the floor. Floor-to-ceiling windows looked out to the front, side, and back-yards. It was my favorite room in the small house, which was 99.9 percent the bank's and .1 percent mine. Moving in two months earlier had made me feel very adult. There's nothing like a mortgage to separate the kids from the grown-ups. This was the first time I'd hosted a Readaholics meeting in my new house. When I formed the group four years ago, we'd originally met in the library but had switched to meeting in one another's homes when it became clear that six of us were going to be the group's mainstays (and library patrons complained about our "too lively" discussions). Misty followed us and pounced on the trailing branch of a spider plant with clearly vicious tendencies. She subdued it with much scratching and hissing and then settled on one of the low windowsills to keep an eye on the front yard.

I set out a plate of petits fours left over from a

luncheon I'd organized for the Episcopal Women's Thrift House the day before, and a bag of tortilla chips with salsa. Martha Stewart, eat your heart out. Gulping down a third of my margarita, I told Brooke about my appointment that morning. She laughed when I mentioned my transparent skirt.

"That wasn't the worst part, though," I said, steeling myself. "Madison—the woman I met with, my client—is marrying Doug. Doug Elvaston," I clarified when Brooke didn't gasp or faint or say, "Oh, my heavens!"

"You knew it would happen one day," she mumbled into her margarita glass.

I narrowed my eyes at her. "You knew!" I breathed.

She looked up and shook her head vigorously, hair swishing her shoulders. "Not to say *knew*. Elspeth Elvaston might have mentioned to my mom that Doug was seeing someone. In New York."

"You knew and you didn't tell me, didn't warn me. You know how I feel about him." This was traitorage on a monumental scale, even worse than when she'd chosen to go to CSU after I was accepted at CU.

Setting her glass down with a click, she said, "C'mon, A-Faye. You guys called it quits two years ago. Time to move on. He obviously has."

Youch. "Calling it quits is our favorite activity. We broke up before senior year of high school and got back together for prom, and then after our sophomore year at CU because I was doing the semester abroad in Italy that fall and didn't want to be tied down, and then three times our senior year." I ticked them off on my fingers: "When Doug thought he was getting that internship in Los Angeles, and then when Giancarlo from Italy came to visit me over spring break, and then—"

"I was there for all the drama the first time," Brooke said. "I don't need to relive it." Before I could reply, the doorbell rang and I rose to let in Ivy Donner. Wearing a shirtwaist dress in a graphic brown-and-cream print, she'd obviously come straight from her job as assistant to Heaven's chief financial officer. Her brown hair was gelled into a spiky pixie that gave her a gamine look and accented her doelike brown eyes. She'd graduated with Brooke and me, gone to the local community college and then immediately into city government. She liked fast reads with lots of action.

"You got a cat," she announced, gaze going directly to Misty, who had followed me to the door. Before I could explain, she asked, "Mind if I make some tea?"

Ivy was an inveterate tea drinker with a different herbal blend for every occasion—sleeplessness, anxiety, a cold. All her brews smelled like algae on Lost Alice Lake on a hot August afternoon. "Water's already boiling." I led her into the kitchen. "Help yourself."

"Love the tile backsplash," she said, pouring boiling water into the mug I'd set out. Mug in hand, she hugged me. "Sorry. It's been a lousy day. A lousy stinking couple of weeks, as a matter of fact. I took a personal day today—couldn't stand the thought of the office. Had some legal business to attend to."

"I know the feeling." I hugged her back, thinking she felt stiff and tense. I got an acrid whiff of cigarettes and wondered if she'd started smoking again. I hoped not. She'd worked hard to quit two years earlier.

She broke away and followed me into the sunroom, greeting Brooke with an air kiss. "This book is pure genius," Ivy said, waving her copy of *The Maltese Falcon*. "Hammett has it exactly right about men. They're scum, all of them. Even our so-called hero, Sam Spade, is having an affair with his partner's wife and ditches Brigid at the end."

"She was a murderer," Brooke pointed out.

Ivy flipped a dismissive hand. "He had no loyalty. He was all about saving his own skin. Coward." She sank into a chair, took another sip of tea, and glowered.

"Do you think he was getting back together with Iva at the end?" Brooke asked as the doorbell rang again.

I let in Lola Paget, a compact woman with espresso-colored skin, a short Afro, and wire-rimmed glasses. She'd been a year ahead of Brooke and me at school and gone off to Texas A&M for a chemistry degree before coming back to Heaven to rescue the family farm by turning it into a plant nursery specializing in flowers and flowering shrubs. I was pretty sure she supported her grandmother and her teenage sister, who lived with her. Her parents had died in a drunk driver–caused accident when she was fourteen. She tended to prefer more literary mysteries.

"You got yourself a cat," she said in her slow, deliberate way. "Here, puss-puss."

Misty trotted right over and sniffed at Lola's work boots delicately. "Mew."

"She can be yours," I said, lifting the kitten and placing her in Lola's work-roughened hands. I explained how I'd gotten her and why I thought Lola might want her.

"That's very thoughtful of you," Lola said. "It's true Tigger-cat passed on last month. She was a fine mouser. Do you think you could catch mice, puss?" She put her nose down close to Misty's.

"Mew," Misty affirmed.

"You'd better come home with me, then, and have a go at it. Thank you." Lola smiled at me. She had a naturally somber aspect, didn't smile much, but when she did, it lit up the room.

I let go a big breath, not realizing how worried I'd been about the kitten's fate if Lola didn't want her. "You're very welcome," I said. "Soda's in the fridge."

Lola set down Misty, who trailed her into the kitchen to get a soda.

"Hey, Lo," Brooke called. "What'd you think of the book?"

Lola joined us in the sunroom, pulled a coaster from a stack to put her Coke can on, settled herself, and looked around before replying. "This is a lovely room, Amy-Faye. The plants look happy here."

That was a huge compliment, coming from Lola,

who had helped me pick out the plants at Bloomin'
Wonderful. I beamed.

"There were lots of villains," Lola observed,
turning to Brooke. "Too many for me to keep track
of. There were Gutman and Joel Cairo and that
Thursby fellow and that boy with the guns— Did
he have a name?"

"Wilmer Cook," Ivy supplied.

"And Brigid, of course. Spade was no great
shakes, either. I can't say I took to anyone in the
whole book . . . What's the point of a mystery with
no good guys?"

"Amen, sister," Ivy put in, nodding as if Lola
had vindicated her.

"Your door's unlocked—anyone could walk
in," came Maud Bell's voice from the foyer.

"In here," we chorused.

Maud strode in, crackling with energy, as always. Around sixty, she was six feet tall with a sin-
ewy build—a lanky greyhound of a woman with a
sharp nose, shrewd blue eyes, and a surprisingly
ribald sense of humor. Her weathered skin testified
to her summer and fall occupation as a hunting
and fishing guide. In the winter, she did computer
repair and Web site design, making use of the computer science degree she'd earned four decades
ago at Berkeley, where she'd really majored in ac-
tivism, she liked to say. When she turned fifty, she
gave up "marching to the beat of corrupt corporate
honchos' bongos," as she called it, to get back to
nature in Heaven. Her hair was an au naturel mix
of silver, white, and iron, and she wore her usual
camouflage pants with a dozen pockets, henley

shirt, and hiking boots. She smelled faintly of pot, which was not unusual, even before Colorado legalized it. Her favorite reads were spy thrillers and the like, which made total sense since she spent more time posting on her conspiracy theory blog, and trying to bring conspiracies to light, than she did at her paying jobs.

"Froufrou." She gave the margaritas a disparaging glance, disappeared into the kitchen, and returned with a beer. "Damn clever fellow, that Hammett," she commented, sitting. "Nice place, Amy-Faye. Feels like you. Conspiracies within conspiracies, everyone on the take or ready to betray someone else—it read like the front page of the *Washington Post* or the *New York Times*." She took a long swallow of beer. "Where's Kerry?"

A knock at the door answered that question. I went to open it, Misty at my heels. Kerry Sanderson, a Realtor and Heaven's part-time mayor, marched in. She was familiar with the house already because she'd found it for me. She'd spent months helping me locate just the right property and walking me through the legal and financial wickets of first-time homeownership, and I would always be grateful. She immediately noticed Misty.

"Cute kitten," she said, "but do you really think you have time to take care of a pet? What with your schedule being so erratic, and you having to take on even more events now that you've got this mortgage—"

I smiled. Vintage Kerry. At forty-eight, she had a teenage son, a grown daughter, and a grandbaby, all of whom lived with her. She'd been the first to join the Readaholics when I came up with the idea of a book club, back when I still lived in my tiny apartment and we held meetings in the library. She came across as brusque and efficient and managing, but her comments on the books we read, and the way she helped people in the community without making a fuss about it, told me she was really caring . . . and efficient and managing. Not bad qualities for a mayor. She was leagues better at the job than the lazy, pocket-lining, nepotistic crook who'd held the job before her.

"Misty's for Lola," I said, pouring her the last of the margaritas and steering her toward the sunroom.

"Hail, hail, the gang's all here," Brooke said.

"I saw you met with the CEO of Naturocorp today." Maud pounced on Kerry. "I'll bet my new Sage fly rod they're trying to get your buy-in on fracking in the area. That's the way these natural gas companies work . . . get a town's leaders in their corner and then screw the small landowners. Did you see that Matt Damon movie? Lola, you'd better watch out."

Kerry was used to ignoring Maud's attacks. She gave a noncommittal smile, sat beside Ivy on the love seat, and said, "Hammett's prose and the way he used dialogue reminded me a lot of Hemingway—almost no interior thoughts or details about what a character was thinking or feeling. Did you all notice that?"

The conversation was even more heated than usual because we all had such strong feelings about the book, the characters, and the prose style.

Ivy continued to talk about how untrustworthy all the men were in a way that made me wonder if she was talking only about fictional characters. Brooke and I exchanged a glance after one angry comment and Brooke shrugged. Maud continued to enthuse about the book's intricate plotting, and Kerry and I had a sidebar about whether Hammett deliberately chose not to share his characters' thoughts for some narrative purpose, or whether that was just his journalism background showing through. Brooke was quieter than usual and I hoped she'd linger after the others left so we could talk. We broke up at nine o'clock as usual, with Kerry yawning and claiming an early meeting and Lola saying she wanted to get Misty home in time to adjust to her new digs before bedtime.

Kissing the top of the kitten's head, I felt a pang as she left with Lola. Maybe someday I'd have a regular schedule that would allow me to get a pet. It would be fun, comforting, to have a fuzzy critter around, happy to see me when I came home, pleased to cuddle with me when I watched TV or read a book on one of my rare free evenings. Maud left next, saying we should get together to watch the movie version of *The Maltese Falcon*.

"I saw it back in the day, but it would be fun to see it again. I never did see what set women swooning over Bogie, though. Altogether too craggy and hound eyed for my taste. No sense of humor. I always appreciated Michael Caine—a lot going on underneath the surface with him, I always thought. Or, these days, that Chris Hemsworth, who plays

Thor. Big, strong, swings a mean hammer. I'll see if it's on Netflix, or rent it if it's not," she promised.

"Sounds like fun."

Ivy walked out with Maud, turning to remind me that we were meeting tomorrow to plan an office offsite. She swayed. "Whoo—a bit dizzy."

She looked pale.

"You okay?"

"Sure. My tummy's a little squiffy; that's all. Nine o'clock okay? My house. I'm working from home tomorrow—I get more done that way," she said. "Clayton"—her boss—"thinks the offsite will improve office morale and efficiency." She shrugged as if unconvinced but said, "Can't hurt. Come with ideas for how we can make it fun—not the usual sit-around-and-stare-at-each-other office drill with trust falls and all that garbage."

"Will do." My mind churned through ideas as I waved good-bye. A team scavenger hunt, maybe? No, a geocaching event would be better. I'd have to get more details from Ivy about the number of people and the budget.

As I'd hoped, Brooke was the last to leave. She was still in the sunroom, grazing on the last of the tortilla chips. I was going to get on her again about not cluing me in about Doug and Madison, but something about her looked beaten down, and I sat across from her. "What's wrong?"

She met my gaze and gave me a tight smile. "Troy and I are finally talking about in vitro. Or maybe adopting."

"That's great!" I knew she and her husband of

nine years had been trying to get pregnant for almost half their marriage.

"Not according to Troy Senior and Miss Clarice. Little Widefields are born naturally, not created in a test tube, and we certainly don't want to contaminate the gene pool by adopting a baby with an unknown but probably deficient pedigree."

She said it semijokingly, but I could tell her in-laws' attitude grated on her. They'd disapproved of Troy marrying her during their junior year in college. Miss Clarice had told one of my mom's friends that Brooke wasn't "the right kind of girl." I took that to mean she didn't turn out like the "Perfect Wife" recipe Miss Clarice probably concocted in her cauldron: one tablespoon Junior Leaguer, a pinch of heiress, two teaspoons hypocrite, a dollop of Betty Crocker, and a half cup of Stepford wife. After the marriage, the Widefields had continued to drip poison about her into their son's ear in a way that made me want to sock the self-righteous smiles off their rich little faces. Brooke had thought she understood what marrying into the richest and most powerful family in town would mean, but she'd been young and naive. Kind of like Princess Diana when she married into the royal family. The Widefields had wanted Troy Jr. to marry a girl with family political connections, not a cheerleader and beauty queen whose father ran a dry-cleaning business and whose mother was a school secretary. The elder Widefields envisioned Troy as governor someday, and they did not think Brooke was Mrs. Governor material, even though she'd tried hard to live up to their expectations by not working, being active on charity committees, and keeping an immaculate house. "Tell them to go . . . take a flying leap off a tall cliff," I said.

She slid a finger under her camisole strap, as if it were too tight. "I wish. It would help if Troy didn't work for his dad."

It would help more if he grew a backbone, but I didn't say that. Her husband worked for the family auto dealership, a swath of shiny new and used cars out 330 on the way to Grand Junction. "You were born to be a mother," I said, hugging Brooke as she stood to go. "So whatever it takes. You're only thirty-two. It's not like time is running out. You've got options. IVF, adoption, screwing like bunnies . . . whatever."

She laughed and hugged me back. "I'm sorry I didn't tell you about Doug. I really didn't know how serious it was."

I saw her to the door, hugged her again, and watched as she drove off in a Widefield AutoPark Lexus. I bused the glasses and ate the last petit four and thought about time running out. Brooke still had plenty of time to have a baby, but I wasn't even married. In fact, I didn't even have a boyfriend, and my last date had spent the entire evening talking about his abduction by aliens. I'd made a mental note to hook him up with Maud (not in a romantic way), who had visited Roswell and firmly believed the government was hiding secrets about aliens at Area 51. It seemed that time had finally run out for me and Doug. The thought made me droop as I washed the glasses and put them in the drainer to dry and wiped down the counters.

I wasn't really a droopy kind of person, though— too optimistic by nature—so I straightened and made myself look on the bright side. I ran a business I loved and owned my own two-bedroom cottage, and engaged wasn't the same thing as married. Not at all.

Chapter 3

I left my office the next morning to meet Ivy Donner, having already coordinated with my assistant, Al Frink, who was off to supervise a breakfast for the Lions Club, chatted with a caterer about Madison and Doug's wedding, and set up a date with a bakery for the happy couple to taste cakes. I would not be accompanying them on that expedition. (A) I didn't need the calories, and (B) I was planning to organize this whole wedding without ever having to set eyes on Doug. Shouldn't be too hard—he'd be busy at the law firm and my mind boggled at the thought of him giving a hoot about table favors or cake toppers. I cruised down Paradise Boulevard, the main drag in Heaven (its name changed from John Elway Avenue after the town rechristened itself), taking mental notes about the exterior of the grand Victorian homes interspersed with smaller cottages and 1950s- and '60s-era homes. Before becoming a homeowner, I never noticed things like sagging gutters or cracks in driveways, but now they stood out. I admired the crimson paint on a two-story home's gingerbread before I turned onto Ivy's street, where new townhomes stood in brick-fronted groups of four.

A maple sapling, orange daylilies, and bushy Russian sage made her front yard stand out from her neighbors', and I wondered if she'd gotten Lola's advice on what to plant. She had an end unit and I'd been there several times, including for a house-warming party three years ago and for book club meetings since. Her door was painted a shiny cobalt blue and I touched it gently with a finger, liking the slickness. Ivy didn't respond to my knock, so I pressed the doorbell and heard it ding-dong deep inside. Still no answer. Standing on the covered stoop, I dug out my cell phone and called Ivy's number. It went straight to voice mail. Unsure whether to be ticked or worried, I wondered if we'd gotten our wires crossed and she was waiting for me at her office. I dialed that number and got a young-sounding woman—an intern, maybe?—who told me Ivy hadn't come in.

"Hm." I tapped my cell phone against my teeth. Maybe Ivy was breakfasting on her back patio or working in the yard and hadn't heard me. My two-inch heels sank into the dirt as I started across the springy patch of grass and around the side of the unit. Birds twittered from a greenbelt that bordered the property, and I heard the distant *beep-beep-beep* of a construction vehicle backing up. Other than that, it was silent. Most of the folks who lived in this community were professionals, like Ivy, and I suspected few people were home on a workday.

None of the backyards were fenced—against the covenants, Ivy had complained—and I turned the corner to see that Ivy's small yard and patio were empty except for a lizard, which skittered away as my shadow draped it. My heels clicked against the cement patio, which was barely big enough to hold a George Foreman grill and a bistro table with two folding chairs. A terra-cotta pot held a water-deprived geranium. I sighed. I'd wasted my time coming over here. On the off chance, I knocked on the kitchen door. Using my hand as a visor, I pressed close to the window adjacent to the back door and peered in.

Breakfast dishes and a teapot sat on the table in the breakfast nook directly in front of the window. No Ivy in sight. I was turning away when a flicker of motion—I couldn't say what—caught my eye. Frowning, I pressed closer to the window, the pane cool against my forehead. Something white and oblong twitched from just inside the hall that led to the front door. Was it—? A foot! Ivy's foot. I froze. Ivy had fallen and hurt herself, or she had had a heart attack. But she was still alive; I was sure I'd seen her foot kick. I simultaneously dialed 911 and tried the door. Locked.

The emergency operator's calm voice answered and I blurted out where I was and what the problem was. She said she was dispatching an ambulance, but I wasn't going to wait. A couple of minutes might mean life or death to Ivy. I looked around, frantic for a way in, and saw the grill. Hefting it over my head, I slammed it against the window beside the door, shutting my eyes against the storm of ash and glass splinters that flew up.

"Ivy!" Did the foot twitch? Careful to avoid slicing my wrist open, I reached through the broken pane and unlocked the door. My heart thumped like a hummingbird's as the door swung in. Pushing through it, I was barely conscious of a variety of unpleasant odors as I raced to where Ivy lay. Sprawled facedown in the hall, blue nightie rucked up around her thighs, she was as still as death. Pools of vomit splotched the hallway. It looked like she'd been trying to reach the small powder room but hadn't made it in time.

"Ivy?" I touched her hand. Her teal nail polish looked ghastly against the pallor of her skin. I chafed her hand. "Ivy, it's Amy-Faye. There's an ambulance coming. Hold on."

Her fingers half curled around mine. It gave me hope, yet made me feel utterly useless. I had no idea what to do. There was no bleeding to stop and her heart was still pumping, so CPR was out. A blanket. She needed a blanket. I spied an afghan draped over the love seat in the living room straight ahead. Stepping around some vomit, I retrieved the afghan and tucked it around Ivy where she lay on the floor. Red welts stood out vividly against her waxy skin. Could this be an allergy attack of some kind? Was she in anaphylactic shock? Her eyelids flickered.

"Ivy? Can you hear me? It's Amy-Faye. Help is on the way." Where was the damn ambulance?

"Can't see . . . blurry. Clay . . . didn't mean . . ."

Her eyes were mere slits, but I thought they were focused on me.

I picked up the faint sound of the siren and almost sobbed with relief. "Just a few more minutes, Ivy, okay? I'm going to open the door."

Her fingers tightened around mine and then let go. Her hand fell limply to the floor. I hesitated, then jumped up, sped down the hall, undid the dead bolt, and flung the door wide. Sunshine flooded the dim hallway and I blinked. A fire truck slewed around the corner, closely followed by a police car. I jumped up and down to attract their attention, and then hurried back to Ivy when the fire truck nosed into the curb.

Kneeling beside her, I stroked her short hair. Her breaths came in shallow, irregular gasps. "You're going to be okay, Ivy. You're going to be okay." I didn't know if she heard me. The first responders surged in and I got out of their way. I edged into the kitchen as they worked on Ivy, loaded her onto a stretcher, and had her out of the house in less than five minutes. One of the EMTs told the lone police officer to "find out what she took—find the bottle." It took a moment to register, but then I realized he thought she'd overdosed on meds of some kind. My hand covered my mouth and my gaze swept the small kitchen.

It was an ordinary kitchen with newish midrange appliances, walls painted cream, canisters lined up on the counter, and bright Fiestaware dishes stacked in glass-fronted cabinets. I'd knocked over small pots of basil and mint when I broke the window, and their dirt mingled with the glass and ash on the floor. The faucet dripped and I turned it off. Nothing jumped out at me, no prescription bottle on the counter or knocked to the floor, no open bottle of vodka or scotch. A half-eaten bowl of oatmeal with walnuts, a slice of cantaloupe, and a teacup and teapot sat on the table with the *Heaven Herald* open to the second page. The rest of the cantaloupe waited on the counter, a piece of cling wrap stretched over it, and the crumpled oatmeal packet lay on the floor near the trash can. A ladder-back chair painted red was pushed well back from the table, as if Ivy had gotten up in a hurry. It was all excruciatingly ordinary. I was sure Ivy sat in that very chair and read the paper every morning while she ate her breakfast. Tears stung and I wiped them away. I couldn't kid myself: Ivy was very, very sick. The scent of the herbal tea mingled with the smell of crushed mint and basil but couldn't overcome the less pleasant odors, and I tried to breathe through my mouth.

Trying to remember what diseases gave you diarrhea and made you throw up, I thought of cholera and food poisoning. I didn't think Ivy had traveled outside the country recently, so cholera was a long shot. Before I could give it any more thought, a suspicious voice said, "Who are you and what are you doing?"

I turned. The young police officer had returned to the house after seeing Ivy loaded into the ambulance. Short and with a reedy build that made me think "middle schooler" rather than "law enforcement professional," he was staring at me suspiciously, brow furrowed and jaw thrust forward. His gaze landed on the glass and grill and traveled to the broken window. "Hey, someone broke in!" His hand went to his gun.

"That was me," I said, raising my hand slightly. "I saw Ivy on the floor and called nine-one-one, but then I had to get in to try and help her, so I broke the window. Is she going to be okay?"

The cop shrugged uncomfortably, wrinkling a splotch on his shoulder that might have been baby spit-up. "That's for the doctors to say, ma'am. How did you come to find the victim?"

I explained about our meeting while the cop rifled the kitchen cabinets and bagged the containers of aspirin and allergy medications he found. He had to stand on a chair to get into the cabinets over the stove. "Wait here," he told me, heading toward Ivy's bedroom and bathroom. I heard the sound of drawers sliding open and cabinets snapping shut and imagined him ransacking Ivy's medicine chest, pawing through deodorant and dental floss and birth control pills, invading her privacy. He emerged five minutes later with more childproof-capped bottles to add to his collection.

"I've got to take these to the hospital," he said self-importantly. "Give me your name, address, and phone number and someone will contact you."

"Okay." I provided the information and left with him. "What hospital is she at?" I asked as he climbed into his patrol car.

"St. Mary's in Grand Junction."

I nodded. Grand Junction, with a population of about sixty thousand, was the largest city in the region, about thirty minutes west of Heaven. It had the closest hospital with an ER. He screeched away from the curb and I stood there, looking around in confusion, arms hanging heavy at my sides. I felt like I'd run a marathon—not that I know what that feels like. Taking a deep breath, I held it for a minute and then blew it out. I needed to let the Readaholics know that Ivy was ill and then drive to the hospital. I wondered if the police had thought to notify her brother, Ham Donner.

My business was all about checklists, and I made a mental one now. Call Brooke and get her to alert the other Readaholics. Call Ham Donner. Call Al and tell him to cover the two meetings with clients I had scheduled for the afternoon. Drive to the hospital. I got in the van and headed for Grand Junction while I used my hands-free device to call Brooke. No answer. I tried Lola's number.

"Bloomin' Wonderful," she answered.

"Lola, something terrible." I filled her in. "Can you let all the Readaholics know? I'm on my way to the hospital."

"Of course I'll make the calls. And I'll pray for her. I thought she looked a little peaky last night."

The call to Al was easier. I merely told him a friend was ill and asked him to take the afternoon's meetings.

"Will do, boss," he said. "Anything I can help with?"

At my request he found Ham Donner's phone number, and I steeled myself and called him next. "Ham, it's Amy-Faye Johnson."

"Amy-Faye!"

The broad smile in his voice told me he'd completely missed the urgency in my voice. No surprise—

Hamilton Donner wasn't exactly tuned in to other people. He might be Ivy's brother, and I might have known him since the Donners moved to Heaven a couple of years before it became Heaven, and even gone out with him once in a moment of total insanity, but that didn't mean I liked him. Almost three years older, he'd been only a year ahead of us at school and had joined the army after graduation. The military had kicked him out—something to do with a bar fight, I'd heard—after five years and he'd drifted around the West Coast for a while before returning to Heaven. I'd heard talk of him dealing drugs and selling goods that "fell off the back of trucks," but I hadn't asked Ivy about it. She was still in touch with him, but she'd quit talking about him after his first arrest.

"I knew you'd come around eventually, sugar. Drinks Friday night at Rollie's? And then we—"

I cut in on his recital of hot date activities, which probably included a monster truck rally and a tobacco-spitting contest. "Ham, Ivy's sick. Really sick. An ambulance just took her to St. Mary's."

"What?"

"I was meeting her at her house and I found her passed out in the hall."

"Drunk? Overdose?"

Sudden fury that he would judge Ivy by his own low standards made me snap. "No. Ill. Ill enough to maybe die. So stop being an ass and get to the hospital. I'm on my way there now." I hung up and pressed the accelerator to the floor.

*   *   *

I swept into the hospital forty minutes later, having been delayed by roadwork. I was sweaty from jogging from the far corner of the parking lot, and the air-conditioned lobby felt like a walk-in freezer. Heavenly. The cool air on my damp skin gave me such a sense of well-being that for a moment I was sure Ivy was going to be all right. I'd gotten myself in a tizzy over nothing. She was probably tucked up in a hospital bed with an IV for dehydration, sleeping off the aftereffects of food poisoning. Her cantaloupe might have been contaminated with listeria—hadn't there been a big problem with that last summer?—so maybe the docs were giving her antibiotics, too. I hurried to the information desk and gave the volunteer Ivy's name, ready to hear that she had been moved from the ER to a room, and hoping she could have visitors.

Brooke hurried in while the volunteer was typing in Ivy's name. "Lola called. Is Ivy okay?" Concern creased her face.

"Oh."

We swung to face the volunteer. Her kindly, wrinkled face was surrounded by a graying halo of crinkly hair. She pursed full lips. "Um. Well, yes. Ivy Donner, you said? Are you relatives?" She looked from me to Brooke.

"Friends," I said tersely, made uneasy by her obvious discomfort. "How's Ivy? Where is she?"

"I'm afraid I can't give out information to anyone other than a family member."

The hairs on my arms pricked up, and it had

nothing to do with the air conditioning. "She's okay, isn't she?"

"I'm afraid I can't—"

"Let's try the ER," Brooke said, pulling me away from the desk. "She might still be there."

The volunteer looked relieved. "It's faster to go around the outside," she said, pointing.

Brooke and I braved the heat, which felt like smacking into a wall. People can talk about it being a "dry heat" all they want, but hot is hot. Sunlight bouncing off the sidewalk partially blinded me and it took me a moment to notice the man standing outside the ER's sliding doors, leaning against the wall, his head in his hands. His shoulders jerked with silent sobs. Something about him . . . the bulky build and military-short hair . . . I recognized him. Part of me knew right then, but I pushed the knowledge away.

"Ham?" I put out a tentative hand and touched his shoulder.

He looked up. His eyes were red rimmed and bloodshot. "She's dead, Amy-Faye. My baby sister's dead."

Dead. The word didn't penetrate at first. I stared at him, confused, and heard Brooke gasp. It finally sank in. The knowledge was a razor-sharp spear that plunged into my gut and sent grief radiating through me, seeming to pull apart my insides. I hugged Ham to me, tears welling. "I'm so sorry, Ham, so sorry."

He sobbed against me for long moments, body juddering, his tears dampening my ear and hair. I murmured meaningless comfort words and Brooke patted his back. Finally, he stepped back and wiped the back of his hand across his eyes. Brooke, always prepared, offered him a packet of tissues. He took them mechanically, blew his nose twice, and stood with his arms hanging limply. He worked his lips in and out and finally cried, "Why? Why would she kill herself?"

Chapter 4

Late afternoon found me back at my office, trying to accomplish the work that I hadn't gotten to earlier, what with finding one of my friends passed out on her floor, getting help for her, learning she had died, comforting her brother and taking him back to his house, agreeing to plan her funeral, and fielding calls from other friends as the news trickled through Heaven. What a horrible, no-good, very bad day, as some children's book said. I sat at the six-foot-long table that doubled as my desk, dropped my head in my hands, and massaged my temples. Sadness seeped through me. I remembered Ivy as I'd first seen her in the middle school lunchroom. She'd been wearing a beret, which I thought was terribly chic, and holding a tray, looking around in a stiff way that said she didn't want anyone to know she was feeling awkward and lonely on her first day in a new school. I'd scooted over against Brooke and beckoned to Ivy. Thus had begun almost two decades of friendship. I'd gone with her to the drugstore to buy an early pregnancy test after our freshman year in college and waited outside her bathroom door while she peed on the stick (negative), been a bridesmaid in peach taffeta at her wedding, and helped her get over the divorce with a judicious mixture of listening, margaritas, and man bashing.

My assistant, Al Frink, appeared in the doorway.

"You okay, boss? You look sadder than Batman fans when Ben Affleck got cast as the Caped Crusader. That was a dark, dark night." He looked at me hopefully to see if I got it.

I groaned and gave him a watery smile. "Been better. And don't call me 'boss.' How many times have I asked you not to?"

"Four hundred twenty-six."

"Really?" He counted?

"Nah, just pulling your leg, bo—Amy-Faye."

He grinned. With a shock of sandy hair falling over his high forehead, Al looked about fifteen, even though he was twenty-two. He thought the sweater-vests and bow ties he habitually wore made him look older; I didn't have the heart to tell him they had the opposite effect. He'd been something of a screwup in high school and didn't have the grades to get into college, so he'd worked in retail and food service in Grand Junction for a couple of years before getting his act together enough to give college a try part-time. The community college had hooked him up with me for an internship one semester and we'd clicked. Now he was at Colorado Mesa University, working on a marketing degree, and he appreciated the flexible schedule I could give him. I appreciated his energy and the youthful outlook he brought to event planning, although his total honesty with clients was occasionally problematic. I was hoping he'd stick with me after he graduated, but I hadn't broached the subject with him yet.

"I could finish up with the Beauman party," he offered, nodding at the folder I had open on the table.

"Thanks, Al, but it helps take my mind off it." It hadn't so far, but maybe if I actually called the rental company to order the bouncy castle, or talked to Nona about baking forty-eight red velvet cupcakes frosted with vanilla icing and decorated with My Little Pony profiles, it would help.

"Okay. Just wanted to let you know that it went fine this morning, and I'm working on the Finkelsteins' fiftieth. Have you heard him clear his throat? Sounds like a cat hacking up a hairball. And the way they quarrel—I'm surprised they made it past their third. They are a *combative* pair."

I recognized the challenge; ever since he took an English class focused on vocabulary building, Al had been hooked on learning new words. "Disputatious," I came back with.

"Belligerent."

"Bellicose."

"The Finkelsteins were as bellicose as cops fighting over the last jelly-filled donut."

I cracked up and he looked pleased with himself. "Anyway, I've got everything set for the party Saturday, except . . . Do you know where I can get a hundred copies of the newspaper issue that ran their wedding photo fifty years ago? Was the printing press invented then?"

"Hm. That's a new one." I sucked on my upper lip. "Try the *Herald*. If they don't have back issues of the *Walter's Ford Beacon*, then maybe you could get it on microfiche at the library and print the copies. They don't want the whole paper, right? Just the wedding announcement?"

Al nodded. "I'll figure it out. Oh, and there's a policeman here to see you."

I knocked my knee against the table leg as I sprang up. "Ow. Why didn't you say so?"

"Just did," Al said, unrepentant. He had a single-minded focus on the events we were responsible for and was liable to forget to give me messages that dealt with "extraneous" issues like a date calling to change our dinner plans, my landlord calling to say the water would be off in my apartment, or once, famously, my sister giving birth.

Brushing past Al, I stepped into the reception area of the office. I rented two rooms in a restored Victorian house in downtown Heaven for Eventful! They had been the dining room and back parlor when the house was a family home and were at the rear of the house, opening onto a garden reached via a brick walkway that came around the side. I hadn't been able to afford office space in the front rooms that faced the street and Heaven's main business and shopping district. I'd rationalized that an event-planning company wasn't going to get a lot of drop-in business anyway and signed the lease for the ground-floor space at the back. A tea shop called the Divine Herb had the primo front space, a small law firm occupied the second floor, and in the three years I'd been renting there, the third floor had housed a nonprofit organization doing something for women in Senegal, a bike repair shop, and now a yoga studio.

A man stood with his back to me, inspecting the framed photographs of events we'd organized that hung on one wall above the love seat, solitary wing chair, and coffee table that constituted our reception area. Al's desk and an overgrown ficus took up the rest of the small room. French doors opened to the garden and walkway.

The man turned at the click of my heels on the wood floors. "I'm sorry to keep you waiting," I said, unable to keep from thinking that he didn't look like he ate many donuts.

About my age or a year or two older, the policeman was attractive without being handsome. He had ever-so-slightly receding curly brown hair, a nose that had clearly been broken at least once, and tanned skin that said he spent time fishing or golfing or playing league softball. He was almost a foot taller than me, maybe six-four, and had a stillness about him that I imagined could be relaxing or intimidating, depending on his mood. His brown eyes assessed me and I worried that the day had taken a toll on my appearance. I ran a hand over my hair, still mostly corralled in its French braid, and hoped my pale skin didn't look too washed-out since I hadn't touched up my makeup or lipstick since before I left to meet Ivy. I knew my nose was red tipped from crying, and I suspected my mascara had melted into raccoon circles under my eyes. Nothing I could do about it now, and it seemed almost disrespectful to worry about my appearance when Ivy was dead. I flashed on an image of her lying naked and blue tinged on a stainless-steel table and forced it from my mind.

"Ms. Johnson?"

At my nod, he said, "Detective Lindell Hart." He had a Southern accent that told me he wasn't originally from Colorado.

We shook. His hand was large and callused, almost totally engulfing mine.

"I need fifteen minutes of your time. In your office?"

I led the way silently into my office and gestured him toward one of the club chairs positioned in front of my table. Upholstered in grass green velvet, a color that made me happy, they added punch to a room that had pale lemon walls and oak floors. Detective Hart's gaze lingered on the whiteboard behind my desk that contained the ever-changing schedule of events we were responsible for, divided by months and extending until the middle of the following year, when we already had two June weddings on the books.

"Looks like you're pretty busy."

"Early summer—weddings—and the holiday season are our busiest times."

We both sat and he rested an ankle on his knee, his slacks pulling up to show argyle socks. "I understand Ms. Donner was a friend of yours?"

I nodded, my throat swelling at his use of the past tense.

"I'm very sorry for your loss." He sounded sincere and I wondered how many times a year he had to say that. "Please tell me how you came to find Ms. Donner's body."

"It wasn't her body! I mean, she was still alive." I took him through the chain of events, ending with my frantic trip to the hospital. I didn't realize I was crying again until he nudged the box of tissues on my desk closer to me. I took one, blew my nose, and apologized.

"Nothing to be sorry for," he said. "I know it's hard." He paused a beat, and then asked, "When was the last time you saw Ms. Donner? Before this morning, I mean."

"Last night. We had a Readaholics meeting. We're a book club," I said, in response to his questioning look. "We read a lot of mysteries and crime fiction, some Oprah kind of stuff, the occasional classic or nonfiction book.

"Our book this month was *The Maltese Falcon*. We were all there." At his request I listed the group members and he wrote down their names. He wrote left-handed and didn't wear a ring. "Ivy liked the book."

"How did she seem last night?" His tone seemed almost too neutral, like he was trying not to influence my answer. "Did she seem different? Maybe depressed or sad about something?"

"Ivy didn't kill herself, if that's what you're getting at," I said angrily. I'd told Ham the same thing this morning, shocked that he would even think it. "She wasn't the suicidal type and she wasn't depressed. If anything, she seemed mad, angry at someone, or maybe something."

The detective nodded noncommittally. "Any idea what?"

I tried to remember what Ivy had been railing about last night. "She said she had a lousy week and talked about men being scum."

"Was she seeing anyone? Was there a ticked-off ex in the picture?"

His questions made me realize I hadn't had a good conversation with Ivy in too long. I felt guilty and took it out on a paper clip, twisting it. "Last I heard, she wasn't dating anyone—not seriously. She was divorced, but it was years ago and her ex moved out of state, to Oklahoma, I think." I supplied his name.

"What did she die of?" I asked the question hesitantly.

Detective Hart's brown eyes met mine. "We won't know for sure until after the autopsy later this week."

"Why would you even think suicide?" I pushed the point.

The detective hesitated, then said, "Her brother says she was depressed recently, that he was trying to talk her into seeing someone—a therapist—and getting medication."

Astonishment and anger flared up. "Ham? She didn't see him more than twice a year. And the kinds of 'medicines' he knows about aren't the sort that are legally prescribed." I was horrified that I'd let myself say something so ugly—even if true—and I bit my lip hard.

My comment didn't seem to faze Detective Hart. "She had a contentious relationship with her brother? Over anything in particular?"

I squirmed, feeling guilty yet again about bad-mouthing Ham. The paper clip broke and I dropped the two bits as if they'd stung me. "I don't know about 'contentious.' They weren't close, although Ivy took him out to lunch on his birthdays and I think they saw each other most Christmases. He hit her up for money now and then, wanting her to fund his 'business' schemes. The last one was an alligator-wrestling attraction off I-70. She said no."

"What did she have to eat at your house?"

His change of direction took me by surprise and I gave an instinctive denial. "Nothing. Well, maybe a chip or two. But we all had some. I don't think she even had a petit four. Ivy didn't have much of a sweet tooth. That's it—no spoiled shrimp or *E. coli*–infected produce or deli meat past its expiration date." Geez, could I sound more defensive? I took a deep breath.

"Drink?"

"Tea. She brought her own. She always does. I remember she said she had an upset stomach."

"Is there anything else you think I should know?"

"No, I can't think of anything." What did he think . . . that I would suddenly remember Ivy handing me a suicide note before she got in the ambulance, or . . . "Wait. She did say something while we were waiting for the ambulance."

He nodded for me to go on, looking a shade more interested than earlier.

"She said everything was blurry and then said, 'Clay didn't mean—'" I shrugged. "That was it."

Detective Hart noted down the words without saying what he thought of them. Then he flipped the notebook closed, stowed it in his sport coat pocket, and rose. "Thanks for your help, Ms. Johnson. If you think of anything else—" He handed me his card.

I ran a thumb over the embossed black lettering: LINDELL HART, CHIEF OF DETECTIVES, HEAVEN POLICE DEPARTMENT. "'Chief of Detectives'? How many detectives does Heaven have?"

He grinned, making the corners of his eyes crinkle in a surprisingly appealing way. "You're looking at him. I'm pretty sure the town council gave me the title in lieu of a larger paycheck when they lured me up here."

"From where?"

"Atlanta. Georgia."

"I know where Atlanta is. Did it take much luring?"

"I was ready for a change."

His tone told me he wasn't going to explain further. His reticence piqued my interest. He *was* attractive in a somewhat reserved way, and single, if the lack of wedding band was anything to go by. Ivy would've thought he was cute. The thought popped into my mind unbidden, and I smiled sadly.

"I'll be in touch," he said, holding out his hand. I shook it and walked him to the French doors, closing them once he was on his way around the corner of the house. I tried to likewise close off my mind to thoughts of Ivy and her death. Bouncy castles, clowns, cupcakes . . . I held those images firmly in mind as I returned to my desk and forced myself to focus on work.

Chapter 5

It was two days later, Thursday, before I heard that Ivy's death had officially been ruled a suicide. Ham Donner called to tell me the police had released Ivy's body and he wanted to get the funeral and reception organized and "over with" on Saturday. His words made me simmer, and when I met him at his apartment, which turned out to be a noisome room in a converted motel, to discuss the reception, he gave me the news before I even made it through the door. Not that I had any intention of actually entering the room once I caught a whiff of it. It smelled like stale beer (courtesy of the listing tower of empty cans arranged on the windowsill), dirty laundry (undoubtedly from the pile of grimy T-shirts and tighty whities piled in one corner), and damp metal and mold (from the rackety air conditioner halfheartedly spitting cool air into the room). A small stash of marijuana was partially hidden by a lamp on the nightstand, and a stack of DVDs—a mix of thrillers and porn—had been knocked over so bare boobs, guns, Jason Statham,

Michelle Pfeiffer, and Clint Eastwood stared up from the cases all which-way near the television. Three flies buzzing around a Cheetos bag on the dresser flew off when Ham set his Budweiser down on it to greet me. It was nine a.m. The boldest of the flies was back before the first drip of condensation rolled off the can and onto the dresser's scarred finish.

"C'mon in, Amy-Faye," Ham said, making as if to hug me. He wore only a pair of running shorts, which displayed his muscular legs, and a short-sleeved Hawaiian shirt, unbuttoned so his hairy paunch hung out.

I stepped back out of hugging range. "I'm hungry. Let's get breakfast. My treat."

Ham gave me a half-resentful, half-hurt look that said he knew what I was doing, but muttered, "Okay."

"I'll meet you at the diner," I said, hurrying to my van before he could suggest we drive together. No way, not even for Ivy's sake, was I getting into the same vehicle as Ham. I'd made that mistake already and barely escaped with my virtue; I was a firm believer in "Fool me once, shame on you; fool me twice, shame on me."

I pulled into the gravel parking lot of the Pancake Pig, with its chef's-hatted pig statue holding aloft a plate of pancakes from atop a silver pole, and pulled open the door. Chrome and white and turquoise predominated in the diner's decor, and a 1950s sound track vibrated through a cheap speaker system. The Pig always did a good business, and I grabbed the last table available, exchanging greetings with friends and acquaintances as I passed. I had time to order two coffees and a short stack of blueberry pancakes before Ham arrived, looking considerably more presentable with his parrot-patterned shirt buttoned and his hair slicked back.

The coffees arrived when he did, and he slumped into the seat opposite me, added two packets of sugar to his cup, and slurped half of it down before saying, "I can't get my head around Ivy's being dead. Honest to God, I can't. It's really knocked me off my game."

I decided to take that as an apology for the apartment and his appearance when I arrived. "I almost called Ivy today," I said, "to ask her if she wanted to watch *The Maltese Falcon* with the Readaholics tonight. Then I remembered."

"Suicide." He shook his head. "I don't know why she had to do that. It's not like she had any real problems. I mean, she had a good job with a steady paycheck, a nice house. Lots of people don't have that."

Meaning him.

"I mean, she wasn't going to prison or anything, and she didn't have some awful disease, or a husband who was cheating on her, so why? She even had plenty of friends and family who'd've helped her out if she'd let us know she was in a bind. She had me, didn't she?"

I didn't respond, merely looking at him over the rim of my coffee cup. Ham was no one's idea of a confidant or port in a storm. If anything, he added to Ivy's troubles.

When I didn't respond, Ham tried again. "She'd

been depressed, you know. Anyone could see it. I'm sure you noticed." He watched me closely, even though he seemed to be scanning the menu.

"I can't say that I did," I said bluntly. "She seemed the same as always Monday night. A little pissed off about something, maybe."

"She was my sister. We had a . . . a connection."

Yeah—her checkbook.

"I could sense her sadness."

"Really?" I put on my politely disbelieving face. It said: *You are lying through your teeth, but I'm too well-bred to call you on it and embarrass us both.* I drizzled syrup over my pancakes. "What was she sad about?"

"I wish I knew," Ham said with a gusty sigh. "I could have helped her, if I'd known."

Uh-huh. "About the reception . . ." I steered the conversation toward business.

He flagged down the waitress and ordered enough food to fuel the Buffs' offensive line. I knew it was because I was picking up the tab. "I've been thinking about the reception, and I think we want to keep it simple—"

Cheap.

"—because that's what Ivy would have wanted. She wouldn't have wanted a big fuss. And for her ashes, I think she'd prefer that I spread them from a spot she loved—remember the old tree house?—rather than have them interred somewhere. You could go with me. Brooke and Lola, too, since they were Ivy's friends since forever."

Ivy loved being the center of attention. She'd dressed like a fairy princess for her wedding and insisted on all the trimmings. She'd thrown parties to celebrate her birthdays and career achievements like her recent promotion and still had the sparkly tiara she'd worn as a homecoming princess—Brooke had been queen, of course. I decided right then that I was going to throw Ivy the kind of funeral reception she'd have wanted, even if Ham chipped in only enough for Ritz crackers and Vienna sausages.

Biting my tongue to keep from commenting on his cheapness, I told Ham I'd be honored to go with him to spread Ivy's ashes, and I was sure Brooke and Lola would, too. I hadn't thought about the tree house in years. We discussed the details of the reception. When I asked Ham for a deposit, he squirmed. "Until I sell Ivy's house, I won't have much cash on hand," he said.

"You're getting Ivy's house?" I don't know why I was so surprised. He was her brother, after all. It wasn't like she had a husband or children to will it to. I wondered if she'd actually left a will or if he was getting her estate because he was her nearest living relative. The latter, I'd bet.

He smiled smugly. "Yep. But my lawyer tells me I can't access the money in her bank accounts or sell anything until probate's done—whatever that is—so I'll have to ask you to wait for your money. You know I'm good for it."

I didn't know any such thing, but since I'd already decided I wanted to throw one last party for Ivy, I merely said, "Sure, Ham."

He reached across the table and trapped my hand under his. "Look, Amy-Faye. Now that Elvaston is off the market, maybe you and I could try again, huh? After we get Ivy buried, I mean," he added as an afterthought, apparently remembering he was supposed to be grief stricken. His lips shone with bacon grease.

I jerked my hand away, appalled that he knew I was still hung up on Doug—did the whole town know?—and offended that he'd hit on me minutes after Ivy had died. "I thought I made myself clear when I kneed you in the balls on our one and only date."

His hand dropped to his lap protectively. "I figured—"

I interrupted him by signaling for the check. To get off the topic while waiting for it, I asked, "Did the police say anything about how Ivy died? What caused her death, I mean?"

"She poisoned herself. Something in her tea."

I gasped. "How awful!"

Ham snapped his fingers. "Oleander; that's it. She drank oleander in her tea. Not the way I'd want to go," he added. "An easy bullet in the noggin"—he made a gun of his forefinger and middle finger, held it to his temple, and mimed pulling the trigger—"and lights out. Outside, in the woods somewhere. The way she did it . . . I'm going to have to get a cleaning crew in before I can list her house."

Too disgusted to answer him, I scraped back my chair and walked away, stopping at the counter to hand Carmela Olivera, the owner, enough to cover our tab and the tip.

"I was sorry to hear about Ivy," she said, her

gaze going from me to Ham. He had apparently decided not to follow me and was using a toast triangle to wipe up the last of the sausage gravy on his plate. "Do you know when the service will be?"

I told her and she said, "I'll be there. I can bring some tamales to the reception."

"That'd be great, Carmela." I gave her a grateful smile, calmer now that I was away from Ham.

She lowered her voice. "Is it true that it was a suicide?" She crossed herself.

"I don't believe it." That very moment, I made up my mind to find out what had really happened. Ivy deserved better than to have people talk about her death in whispers, as if it was a scandal, something to be ashamed of. The Ivy I'd known for almost twenty years would never have killed herself, and I was going to prove it. Somehow.

My next stop was at Lola's nursery, Bloomin' Wonderful. I'd convinced another one of my brides to use potted daylilies in lieu of cut flowers for her wedding, and I needed to confer with Lola about finding a near-white variety to make the bride happy. Going out to Lola's always made me happy. Even though her small farm was only five minutes outside Heaven, it felt like I'd traveled back in time, to a more peaceful era, when I trundled down the gravel road leading to her farmhouse. On one side, a field of daylilies, some beginning to bloom already, stretched out in a haze of spiky green foliage. In another month, the field would be a riot of yellow and orange, cherry red and deep purple, and pinks of all shades.

Greenhouses lined the other side of the road, their panes steamed. I knew they held all sorts of flowering shrubs and potted trees, as well as other perennials. The smells brought back strong memories of high school, of driving out here to pick up Lola, who usually couldn't take the family's only car, to collect her for a football game or soccer practice the one year we both played on the school's new and very, very bad girls' soccer team. Lola was much better than me, faster and more agile. She displayed a competitive streak on the field that I hadn't even known she possessed. The coach used to say that if the team had eight or nine more Lolas, we might have won more than one game.

The farmhouse was small and painted a cheeky lavender with white trim. Old Mrs. Paget, Lola's grandmother, rocked on the veranda, shelling peas, it looked like, and I waved. She waved back. An aging hound, resting at her feet, barked once as I passed and went back to snoozing, guard duty done. I spotted Lola with a hose near the old barn that housed her equipment. She was washing out a wheelbarrow, Misty sitting nearby, looking like she was trying to decide whether or not to attack the fat green snake spitting water. The kitten looked like she'd filled out some already. Lola smiled when I got out of the car and shoved her glasses up her nose with the back of her wrist. "Hey, Amy-Faye. Come to help mulch?"

"I don't think I'm dressed for it, but I *have* come to place an order for a July wedding. Two hundred containers of near-white daylilies wrapped in silver foil. Can you do that?"

"Can I ever," Lola said, turning off the water. A white smile split her perspiration-shined face. Misty moved forward to investigate the now limp hose. The musty but pleasant aroma of wet earth surrounded us. "Thanks, Amy-Faye. I know you pressured another bride into wanting daylilies instead of roses or carnations and baby's breath. I think the Joan Senior blooms will do. The blooms should be at their peak then and they're about as white as daylilies get."

"I don't 'pressure'—I 'persuade.'" I grinned.

"Come inside and give me the details." She stripped off her work gloves as we walked back toward the house, Misty trotting behind us, convinced that the hose's lack of response meant she'd vanquished it.

On the way, I told Lola that Ham said the police were calling Ivy's death a suicide by oleander poisoning. Lola stopped and looked at me, brow crinkled. "I find that hard to believe."

"Me, too," I said, relieved to find someone who agreed with me.

"Did she leave a note?"

The thought hadn't crossed my mind. "She can't have," I said, after a moment's thought, "or Ham would've said so. He inherits her house and everything else, I guess. Seems pretty jazzed about it."

"Oughta take him less than six months to run through it all, 'investing' it in his alligator-wrestling attraction, or . . . what was his last business idea? Edible crepe paper?" She snorted gently and led me in the back door of the house and into her small office, not much more than a closet off the kitchen stuffed with a desk obscured by a phone, MacBook, and in-box, a filing cabinet, and a waist-high stack of farming and seed catalogs. I gave her the wedding details and she wrote them down in her precise handwriting, every letter a tiny capital.

"It's not right," she said, looking up, a line drawn between her brows.

"I'm sure the date—" I broke off, realizing she was talking about Ivy, not the wedding details.

"Ivy never struck me as the suicidal type," she said. "It's not right folks should think of her that way."

"Just what I was thinking." I dug through my purse and came up with Detective Hart's card. "I talked to a detective the day Ivy died. Maybe we should see him together and tell him how we're sure Ivy didn't kill herself."

Pursing her full lips, Lola said, "Of course, that does raise a question: If she didn't drink the oleander on purpose, how did it get into her tea?"

I blinked at her. "Accident?"

She gave it some consideration, in her usual thoughtful way. "Barely possible. Ivy did like those herbal teas. All sorts of plants get used in making them—rose hips, hibiscus flowers, blackberry leaves, chicory, echinacea, hawthorn, and dozens of others. Still, it's not possible a commercial tea blender could have made that kind of mistake."

"I never heard Ivy talk about blending her own tea," I said. "Plants weren't her thing." I'd tutored Ivy through high school biology (and maybe done a couple of her labs and projects for her—I'm admitting nothing) and been thrilled when she'd gotten a C– for the semester.

"Someone could have given the tea to her."

I put my hands on my hips. "Let's just spit it out. If someone gave her the tea, then they were trying to make her sick. It's not like oleander grows wild in Colorado—does it?"

"No," Lola answered slowly. "Most nurseries have some, though—it's pretty and people buy potted oleanders for their patios or sun porches. I've got some in my greenhouse and I've sold six or eight oleanders this spring already."

I nodded. "So no one's going to chop up an oleander flower by accident and mix it into a tea blend. Not gonna happen. So if someone gave her the tea, then they meant to make her throw up, at least. I'd call that a pretty mean prank. With a lot of room for error. Obviously. "

We stood silently for a moment, staring at each other. The chugging and sloshing of a washing machine vibrated the room's thin walls. After a long moment, Lola said, "I hate to even think this way, but it's possible someone meant to do more than make her sick. If you feed oleander to someone, you've got to know they might . . ."

"Die," I finished for her.

Chapter 6

Lola and I discussed the ways someone might have snuck oleander into Ivy's tea. They ranged from breaking into her house and slipping it into her tea stash, to mailing her a "free sample," to sneaking some into her cup while she drank. We voted the first idea unlikely because breaking into someone's house is tricky, thought the second idea was a bit contrived (although doable if someone took the time to create a flyer about the "new" tea and some kind of interesting packaging), and were not inclined to go with the third one because we couldn't visualize someone pulling a Baggie of chopped oleander from their pocket at Starbucks and sprinkling it on Ivy's beverage unnoticed. I suggested someone might have a Borgia-ish ring for administering poison and Lola shot me down with a look. She said she'd research how much oleander it would take to kill a woman. We carefully steered away from any discussion of who might have wanted to poison Ivy.

Feeling weighted down by Ivy's death and the

mystery surrounding it, I left Lola's and headed back toward town. Passing a familiar turnoff, I suddenly slewed the car to the right. Ivy's old house, the one where she'd grown up, was at the end of this lane. I hadn't been down here for ages, maybe not since Ivy sold the family home after her parents died when we were college sophomores. The road turned to gravel after a quarter mile, still corrugated from the winter's frost heaves and lack of maintenance. I supposed the county was responsible for roads out this way. The road climbed a steep incline and then curved sharply before spitting me out in the small neighborhood where Ivy had lived.

Each house sat on at least two acres and was separated from its neighbors by enough distance that borrowing a cup of milk would have meant a ten-minute round-trip hike. That made it sound like the neighborhood consisted of spacious, custom-built homes, but it was actually composed of older houses, most with large garden plots, some with horses, one with a large chicken coop and a noisy rooster I could hear even from inside the car. I pulled over on the grass verge in front of Ivy's former home and got out slowly, not sure why I was here, but going with the urge, probably prompted by Ham's mention of the tree house.

The house had been a dilapidated two-story, weathered gray, when I used to hang out here. Now it sported a vibrant turquoise paint with yellow trim. An entire flock of pink flamingos stood stiffly in the front yard, and garden gnomes peeked from behind every rock and tree. I remembered Ivy complaining, back when the people she eventually sold the house to were only renters and she'd had to visit to replace a lock, that the woman renter had "never met a piece of kitsch she didn't buy." She had vented about doilies and Hummels and cross-stitched pillows and tables made to look like butlers holding trays. We'd laughed about it, but I could tell she'd been a bit sad about all the changes in her childhood home.

Now I avoided the yard and walked around the side of the property to the woods behind it. Unless it had been torn down, there was a tree house back here, far enough not to be seen from the kitchen window, but close enough to hear a mom calling. Ivy's dad and Ham had built it the summer they moved into the house, and Ivy had claimed it as her special clubhouse. Sometimes I was the favored friend who lolled on the beanbags and read fashion mags and giggled about boys with Ivy, and sometimes it was Brooke or Jennifer or Edith. Ivy had been a one-friend-at-a-time kind of girl, for the most part.

My low-heeled pumps were not intended for hiking, and the layers of damp, molding leaves from autumns past were not improving them, but a glimpse of the tree house made me forget about my shoes. I wondered if maybe another generation of kids had claimed it. I kind of liked that idea, although I thought it was unlikely since it was an older couple who had bought Ivy's house. If I saw signs of recent habitation, I'd just take a peek and leave without invading their privacy. In thirty more seconds I stood beneath the tree house, looking up at the broad boards that formed its floor. Gaps in the wood that hadn't been there before suggested that no one was taking care of the place. The ladder was still nailed to the tree and the house, and after a moment's hesitation, I kicked off my pumps and began to climb it, glad I was wearing slacks and not a skirt. Hauling myself upward vertically was harder than when I was a teenager, and I was puffing a bit when my head and shoulders rose through the hole in the floor into the tree house. I swiveled, surveying the interior. To my surprise, two of the beanbag chairs were still there, although something had chewed through them and scattered the pellets so the chairs sagged like mostly deflated balloons. A decade or more of snow and rain and sun had rotted the denim coverings in places. A musty smell suggested that animals—squirrels, mice, weasels, or others—had appropriated the beanbags.

A rustle from above made me jerk my head up, and I almost fell off the ladder. Grabbing at the floor to steady myself, I saw that it was only a wren, busy making its spring nest atop the cupboard in the tree house. It eyed me warily and then flew out the structure's one window.

"I'm only going to be a minute," I called after it. "Then you can come back and finish your nest." I stood gingerly, my head not quite brushing the roof. The tree house was smaller than I remembered, probably only nine feet square. The floor creaked under my feet and I tested each board before putting a foot down as I crossed to the cupboard. I was curious to see if anything remained in it. Back in the day, Ivy had kept nail polishes up here, her journal, cigarettes, love notes from her various boyfriends, and a couple of books and magazines—including a *Playgirl* or two—that she hadn't wanted her parents to find. I suspected now that they'd known all along what was out here. The door stuck, but I jerked hard on the knob and it popped open. Nothing. Well, nothing more than a spill of burnt orange nail polish, as glossy and slick as ceramic. I ran a finger over it.

Crossing my arms over my chest, I moved to the window, an open square cut in the wall. Careful not to lean against it—I could see from the way the wood bowed out around it that the wall wasn't sound anymore—I peered out at the evergreens and just-budding aspens, wondering why I'd come here. The place was filled with happy memories— I didn't remember ever fighting with Ivy here— and it made me melancholy. Even though Ivy probably hadn't been here in a decade, it still made me sad to think that she'd never climb up here again to sneak a cigarette or ogle the smirking men displayed in a *Playgirl* spread. It's possible a tear or two slid down my face as I said a prayer for Ivy and left, glancing over my shoulder once or twice until the trees hid the hideaway from view.

My next stop was city hall, a three-story, square stone building erected in the 1930s as part of FDR's Depression-era construction plan. Intricate stonework prettified the façade, but the interior was a characterless warren of long halls lined by offices.

Even recently applied cream paint—the sharp odor still lingering—couldn't make the structure seem welcoming. Kerry's office was here, as were the offices for other city employees, including the chief financial officer. Ivy had worked there for coming up on seven years and had enjoyed it. The administrative assistant who had taken over Ivy's duties had called Eventful! late yesterday to tell me she was now responsible for overseeing my work on the offsite I'd been going to talk to Ivy about the day she died.

Kirsten Wiggins was in her midtwenties, at a guess, with a lanky build and a long, narrow face made longer and narrower by straight brown hair that fell past her shoulders.

"Clay's going ahead with the offsite," she told me, leading me down a hall lined with offices on both sides of the second floor to a small conference room. "Even after . . . Well, the business of running the city doesn't grind to a halt when one of the small cogs goes 'poof,' does it?"

She sounded like she was quoting someone, probably Clay Shumer, the city's CFO, whom Ivy had worked for. I wasn't sure if I was more offended by the idea of Ivy reduced to a "small cog" or the dismissal of her death with a casual "poof."

I bit down hard on my lip to keep from blurting something impolitic and then said, "Ivy didn't get a chance to give me the details on the offsite. You're only talking about one day, right? July twelfth? I'll need to know how many people you're expecting, what kind of a budget I'm working with, whether you need me to hire a facilitator, and whether you've already got a venue reserved or if you need me to find something."

We settled into the comfy padded chairs at the oval conference table and spent a good hour hashing through the details for the offsite. Kirsten was surprisingly efficient and I thought sadly that she would take over Ivy's duties and slide into her job, and after a week or two no one would notice that Ivy was gone.

"My caffeine-low light is on," Kirsten said, pushing away from the table. "Want some coffee before we finish up?"

"Sure." I rarely said no to coffee. In the hallway, we passed a restroom and I told Kirsten I needed to duck inside. She pointed out the break room, two doors up on the left, and said she'd meet me there. The bathroom smelled heavily of an aerosol "freshening" scent that made me cough. Holding my breath, I peed quickly, barely flicked water on my hands, and pushed out of the two-stall restroom. I was halfway down the corridor before I realized I'd turned the wrong way. The name CLAY SHUMER engraved on a brass strip beside a barely open office door made me recognize my error. I turned. As I did, an angry voice issued from inside the office.

". . . not my fault! I think she copied . . . my . . . assistant, for God's sake. How do you expect—"

Another voice rumbled over Clay Shumer's defensive words. I couldn't make out what the new speaker was saying. The timbre of his voice sounded familiar, but I couldn't place it.

Realizing I was eavesdropping on what might

be sensitive city business, I was turning away when one of the men in the office pushed the door closed. The wooden smack made me jump, and I hurried down the hall to find the room Kirsten had pointed out, feeling like I'd been sneaking around where I had no business, even though all I'd done was get turned around. I took a deep breath before walking into the break room, where I found Kirsten watching coffee drip into a carafe.

"No one in this frigging office ever makes a new pot when they empty the old one," she fumed. "And they must all think their moms work here, or the cleaning fairy, because they never bother to clean up after themselves, either."

She ripped a paper towel from a dispenser and began a furious assault on the coffee spills and grounds on the Formica counter. A shelf sat above it, lined with mugs I assumed belonged to people who worked here, some whimsical, some plain. I made a silent bet with myself that the plain gray mug with "I'll try to be nicer if you try to be smarter" written on it was Kirsten's. A refrigerator hummed from the end of the counter, with a microwave beside it. Two large cans of coffee sat beside a small stainless-steel sink, one regular and one decaf, and a container of nondairy creamer and a bowl of sugar were pushed against the tile backsplash. Beside them was a white ceramic canister decorated with ivy vines.

My eyes fixed on it. "Pretty," I said, sure I knew whose canister it was.

Kirsten followed my gaze. "Yeah, that's Ivy's special tea. Was. Lipton's wasn't good enough for her." I thought I heard a hint of snideness in her voice, but then she said, "Although I will say she was the only other one in this office who bothered to clean up after herself. The only one who wasn't raised by wolves." She said this last in a loud voice, apparently in response to a suited man who had come in while we were talking, slopped coffee into his mug, and not bothered to wipe up the drips from the still-brewing machine. They sizzled on the burner, sending up an acrid odor.

"Lighten up, Kris," he said, slouching out. "That's why we have a janitorial service."

"*Kir*sten."

The byplay was enough to make me glad, once again, that I owned my own business. I'd worked in the English Department office for two years while I was at the University of Colorado, and the pettiness and gossip and complaints about lunch items going missing from the communal fridge had driven me batty. I felt sympathetic toward Kirsten, although I sensed she was the kind of woman who made things harder for herself. My eyes returned to the canister, completely accessible on the counter. Anyone could have doctored its contents. Should I share my suspicions with the police so they could test the tea in the canister? They would undoubtedly pooh-pooh my theory. I had to do something, though, before one of Ivy's coworkers brewed a cup of tea using her special blend and got sick . . . or worse.

"It's really sad about Ivy, isn't it?" Kirsten said, reaching for a pair of mugs on the shelf. "Scary, even. Makes you wonder if you really know someone at all. I mean, I would never have thought she would off herself. Never. Don't get me wrong, she wasn't Miss Sweetness and Light, always perky and happy and everything, but I never got the feeling she was that unhappy, unhappy enough to kill herself, even though it was pretty clear her little office romance had come to its inevitable end." She slanted me a sly look while pouring coffee into a Save the Manatees mug and the gray one I'd pegged as hers. "You were her friend, right, so you must have known?"

"I'm not sure I know what you're getting at," I said, accepting the mug with the partially scraped-off manatee and blowing on the coffee. My fingers tightened around the warm ceramic; I was afraid I *did* know what she was getting at.

Kirsten's raised brows accused me of being disingenuous. "Really? Well, everyone here knew. I mean, you can't screw around with the boss and expect people not to notice. They thought they were being so discreet—"

Unlike Kirsten, who was filling me in on office gossip in the break room with its open door.

"—but people notice when you stay late to 'work' together, and go to conventions in Indianapolis, and call in sick on the same days. Leaving each other little gifts, too—I mean, that's just rubbing it in. Did they think we were all stupid? Everyone knows that's why she got that promotion."

Ah. Kirsten felt slighted, which explained her nastiness.

"Maybe she got promoted because she worked hard, was good at her job, and had been here longer than some other people," I suggested, knowing as the words left my mouth that I should have kept silent.

Kirsten's eyes widened. "I never expected to get that promotion; I only interviewed for the practice," she said, confirming my suspicions. "I was only saying that—"

I didn't want to hear any more gossip about Ivy. There wasn't a woman over fifteen who hadn't been stupid about a man at one time or another— witness the fifteen years total I'd spent hung up on a man who was marrying another woman in two weeks—and I wasn't going to pass judgment on her or listen to this envious twentysomething coworker do so. "Look, I've got another appointment to get to. I think I've got enough to get started with. I can call you if I have questions, right?"

"Uh, sure," Kirsten said, taken aback.

Setting my half-full mug in the sink, I used a paper towel to pick up the ivied canister—I read enough crime fiction to know all about fingerprints. Maybe I should adopt "What would Kinsey Millhone do?" as my new mantra and have it made into one of those rubber bracelets: WWKMD. I tucked the canister into my purse.

"I think Ivy's brother would like to have this," I said, not making it a question. Before Kirsten could object, I made "great to be working with you" noises and said good-bye. My heels clicked on the stairs as I descended, and my mind whirled with memories of Ivy, excited about getting hired into the CFO's office, excited about working on an accounting degree she never quite finished, excited about a budding romance that had started two years ago.

She'd been coy about not naming her partner, calling him "Loverboy," and although I'd suspected his identity, I hadn't challenged her on it. She hadn't wanted him to leave his wife initially; indeed, after her short-lived marriage she'd sworn she'd never marry again and preferred to date married men because they didn't want "permanent." Within the last six months, though, I'd gotten the feeling she was unhappy with the status quo. If Kirsten was right and Ivy and Loverboy had broken up, had she initiated the breakup or had he? Thinking back to her remarks on Monday evening, I suspected the latter.

That thought popped into my head as I reached the small lobby and spotted Clay Shumer—"Loverboy," if Kirsten was to be believed—shaking hands with another man I recognized. Troy Widefield Sr., Brooke's father-in-law, looked even sterner than usual as he gripped Clay's hand. Clay, generally full of the kind of shallow charm and bonhomie I associated with movie depictions of con men and gigolos, looked slightly green as his head bobbed in response to whatever Mr. Widefield was saying. His caramel-colored mullet—dyed, I knew, because Sheena at Sheena's Hair Jungle had a big mouth—stayed stiffly in place, even as his head moved, and I suspected industrial-strength hair spray. Mr. Widefield, who had an equally full head of hair, although his was white and undyed, looked fitter and trimmer than the twenty-years-younger Clay. I hoped Clay's greenish color was a sign of his grief over Ivy's death. She'd loved him. They'd been together for at least two years. He should have the decency to be sad.

"Gentlemen," I murmured in greeting as I edged around them to get to the doors. I didn't feel like talking to either of them.

Mr. Widefield recognized me immediately; he was the kind of guy who could instantly put a face to a name and remember where he met someone. It was a key skill for my business and I was pretty good at it, too, but not in Mr. Widefield's league. Clay Shumer took a bit longer to place me, nodding when Mr. Widefield said, "Hello, Amy-Faye." Civilities observed, he gave Clay a sharp look and left.

"Thanks for the opportunity to organize your offsite," I said to Clay, figuring I should say something politic. It took him a minute to tune in to me, preoccupied as he was by watching Mr. Widefield stride toward the parking lot.

He wiped the frown from his face, replaced it with an insincere smile, and said, "I'm sure you'll do a great job for us. Ivy Donner recommended you very highly."

"She was one of my best friends." My gaze challenged him to make a similar statement, to acknowledge Ivy's importance to him.

"We're going to miss her in the office; that's for sure," he said.

Wow, what an epitaph. If Ivy's ghost was around to hear that lukewarm declaration, she must want to slap him. I considered doing it for her. WWKMD? Probably not slap him and risk an assault arrest, I decided reluctantly.

"She was too young to die, too full of life, too—" He ran a hand down his face. For a moment I thought he would say more, but he only nodded, turned his back on me, and started up the stairs. I fancied he was blinking back tears, and I felt better on Ivy's behalf.

As I made my way to the van, it crossed my mind that he might blame himself for her death. If he had recently broken up with her, and if he believed she'd committed suicide, he might think the two events were connected. Even though I didn't know Clay Shumer well, and I couldn't help but despise a man who was cheating on his wife, he shouldn't have to live with that burden if it wasn't true. Yet another reason to prove that Ivy hadn't killed herself.

I drove straight to the police department. I was going to be late for my appointment with Madison Taylor, but it couldn't be helped. I wasn't walking around with Ivy's tea canister in my purse a moment longer than necessary. I parked and called Al and asked him to apologize to Madison when she arrived and start the meeting without me. Inspecting my teeth in the rearview mirror and slicking on a melon-colored lipstick, I approached the police department. The building was redbrick, separated from the street by the sidewalk, and one block off the downtown square between Mike's Bikes and A World Apart, the new travel agency. Pink and purple petunias frothed from planters outside the building, all part of Kerry Sanderson's plan to make all parts of city government seem appealing and approachable, I guessed.

I pulled open the modern glass door, which didn't go with the building's façade, and stepped into a cool reception area with a counter, molded plastic chairs, and what might have been the building's original tile floor. I'd lived in Heaven all my life and never been in here before. My brother and a couple of buddies had gotten arrested as young teens for vandalizing street signs, but my folks had made me and my sisters stay home when they came to spring him. I guess I'd expected something like Andy Griffith's office in Mayberry, with a jail cell in one corner, but this was more like my doctor's waiting area. Very disappointing.

I approached the counter, behind which Mabel Appleman, who was in her seventies and had been the police dispatcher since before telephones were invented, I was pretty sure, was reading a Tess Gerritsen book. Mabel occasionally came to Readaholics meetings when we were reading a police procedural. I told her that I needed to see Detective Hart. Mabel squinted at me and fumbled for the glasses tucked into her tightly permed gray curls. With the blue-framed specs perched halfway down her roman nose, she looked me up and down.

"Amy-Faye Johnson, what in tarnation do you want with a police detective? You don't look scared enough to have been attacked, besides which it's broad daylight and no one but a total moron like the Yoder boy would try to mug some- one while the sun is shining, and it can't be a do- mestic abuse matter because you're *still* not married, and not likely to be now that the Elvaston boy is in the way of getting hitched to a New Yorker. I don't see any obvious injuries, so you weren't the victim of a hit-and-run—"

I interrupted her litany of the reasons that hadn't brought me to the police department. "It's about Ivy Donner."

"Oh." She pursed thin, fuchsia-painted lips. The lipstick had bled into thin lines around her lips, creating a fuchsia halo around her mouth. "He's out on police business. The chief is here, though. I'm sure he can help you."

I was faintly disappointed that I wasn't going to get to see Detective Lindell Hart. I hadn't been conscious of looking forward to seeing him again, and my disappointment surprised me. Before I could decide if maybe I wanted to wait to turn in the canister until Detective Hart was available, Mabel had pushed an intercom button and noti- fied Chief Uggams that I wished to talk to him.

"CC to see you about the Donner situation," she said. She looked up and explained to me, "CC is my own little code. It means 'concerned citizen.' Much more efficient than having to say con-cerned ci-ti-zen." She drew the words out to their longest possible extent.

"Great idea."

She nodded, satisfied, as Chief Uggams ap- peared in the doorway. About my father's age, he'd been deputy chief until Chief Sanderson, Kerry's ex, gave up the job about three years ago. He was a black man with short-cropped grizzled hair, a barrel chest, and a no-nonsense air. His khaki HPD uniform had sharp creases in the slacks and short sleeves, and his brown belt bristled with heavy-looking police paraphernalia, including a gun. I could see from a groove in the leather that he'd had to let the belt out a couple of notches. He and my dad used to play poker the last Thursday of the month with a group of other guys; maybe they still did.

"Amy-Faye." He approached like he might hug me but offered me his hand instead. My hand disappeared into his fleshy palm. "What can I do for you? Boyfriend troubles? I heard that young man of yours has gotten himself engaged. Want me to harass him with parking tickets and jaywalking charges for not treating you right? Too bad there's no law against stupidity or I could arrest him for not sticking with the nicest, smartest gal in town." He chuckled and ushered me back to his office.

I barely refrained from rolling my eyes. Small towns were like Facebook without an Internet connection; once something got on the "wall" of collective memory, it was there to stay. No delete button. It was enough, sometimes, to make me want to move to Denver, or even out of state. "I appreciate the offer, but—"

"How's Norm? Still cheating at Texas Hold'em? Since I took this job, I haven't had as much opportunity to play as I'd like. You tell him 'hey' for me, okay?"

"Will do. Dad's doing great. Mom, too. What

I'm really here about, though"—I drew the canister carefully from my purse—"is Ivy Donner. I heard she was poisoned with oleander in her tea."

The chief's eyes narrowed and he sank into his desk chair, waving me to a sagging love seat with brown leather cushions scoured over the years to a pale tan in the middle by thousands of butts. I sat, holding the canister cupped in my hands. It felt like an urn and I blinked hard twice to dispel the image.

"Where'd you hear that?"

"Her brother. He said you think she committed suicide." I waited for him to correct me, but he remained silent, regarding me with brown, slightly bloodshot eyes. "She wouldn't do that," I said. "I've known Ivy half my life and she was flat-out not the suicidal type. She was a 'pick yourself up and get on with living' kind of person. Even after her divorce. Even when her folks died in that crash. She wouldn't kill herself over a breakup with a man, if that's what you think."

He didn't tackle my points. "What've you got there?" He nodded toward the canister.

"I was at her office today. I'm setting up an offsite—but that doesn't matter. I saw this in the break room and Kirsten Wiggins told me it's Ivy's special tea. I got to thinking that if someone meant to make her sick . . . well, it would be easier to slip something into her tea at the office than at her house . . ." I petered out under the weight of his stare.

"You got any reason to think someone might want to make Ivy sick?"

Good question. Lola and I had carefully avoided talking about possible suspects, and I hesitated to point a finger now. Ham was going to inherit her estate and he always needed money. Kirsten Wiggins was clearly PO'd that Ivy had gotten the promotion she wanted; she might have thought making Ivy throw up was suitable revenge. Clay? I needed to know more about who had broken up with whom and why. "Not really," I said.

The chief shook his head slowly. "Amy-Faye."

He stopped, gathering his thoughts, trying to find a gentle way to tell me to butt out, I could tell. I clutched the canister tighter.

"Amy-Faye, this is police business. It's not for civilians to be messing with. The pathologist's report said Ivy Donner died of oleander poisoning. We have no reason to suspect foul play and good evidence to suggest the poison was self-administered. That is, that she killed herself. I know it's hard to accept that a friend might be that unhappy and we didn't notice. But it's not your fault. Some people are damn good at hiding their emotions. I've been a cop for more'n thirty years and I can't count the number of times I've heard people say about their loved ones, 'I never knew he was angry enough to shoot,' or 'He was always smiling—I can't believe he slit his wrists.' Take my word for it: It happens."

My fault! That thought hadn't even crossed my mind. Now that he'd planted it, however, it took rapid root. *Had* Ivy been depressed? If I'd made time to get together with her more often, might I have noticed her unhappiness?

"If you could just test this—" I proffered the canister.

"Let your friend rest in peace," the chief said, shaking his head no. "The department has more important priorities—"

A footstep at the door brought our heads around. Detective Hart filled the doorway, gaze going from me to his boss. I'd forgotten how tall he was. "Mabel told me Miss Johnson was here with some information pertinent to the Donner investigation."

"This." I held up the canister, not quite ready to give up. "It's Ivy's tea stash from the office break room. I just want you to test it. What if there's oleander in here? Someone else could have drunk it and gotten sick, which is why I took it. Partly why. If there's oleander in here, it'll prove she didn't kill herself, right?" My eyes searched his face, looking for signs that he believed me, but I couldn't read his neutral expression. "I mean, there'd be no reason for her to poison this batch and whatever she drank at home if she killed herself."

To my great relief, Detective Hart reached out and took the paper towel–wrapped canister from me. His fingers brushed mine.

"Fingerprints," I explained, gesturing toward the paper towel.

"You read too many mysteries," Chief Uggams cut in with a frown. "Hart, I've been telling Amy-Faye—"

"It won't hurt to test it," Detective Hart said mildly. "We don't want anyone saying we weren't thorough with our investigation."

"That Bell woman." The chief worked his jaw back and forth. "Did you see what she had on her blog about the town council meeting? Saying the PTA president and the soccer coach bribed council members to vote in favor of annexing part of the old Duncan farm for a new soccer field. Saying they conspired to undermine the success of Heaven's youth. Hogwash."

Maud had discussed the vote with me and told me she had proof that two council members had been promised their kids would make the soccer team if the field purchase was approved. "That money should have gone to new math textbooks," she'd said. "What are we coming to when the PTA president, of all people, is conspiring to elevate sports over academics? What has happened to our priorities in this country?"

"My wife says I shouldn't read it, that it upsets my ulcer," he said, rubbing his stomach. "I can imagine what Maud Bell would have to say about this: 'Heaven Police Conspire to Bury Truth about Woman's Death.'" He eyed the canister with disfavor. "I suppose we need to test it. All right, go ahead, Hart. And you"—he faced me squarely— "go back to organizing weddings and leave the policing to the police. You hear me?"

Happy to have achieved my goal, I stood and smiled. "Loud and clear. Thanks, Chief. Thanks, Detective Hart." I knew he was the one who really deserved my thanks; Chief Uggams had been on the verge of denying my request when Hart walked in.

"I'll walk you out."

Surprised, I nodded. He stepped aside politely to let me precede him out the door, and I couldn't help brushing against him in the narrow doorway. He had a warm, woodsy smell . . . very appealing. Leaving the canister on Mabel's counter, he walked me out the door and onto the sidewalk. The day was lovely—the unseasonable heat of earlier in the week having receded—and I took a deep breath of the dogwood-blossom-scented air drifting from nearby trees.

"That was good thinking on your part," he said. "Taking the canister. I doubt there's anything wrong with the tea in it, but better safe than sorry."

"Thanks." I smiled, relieved that he wasn't going to chew me out for meddling in police business. That seemed to happen more often than not in most of the mysteries I read where PIs or amateur sleuths got involved in murder cases. Not that the police even thought Ivy's death was murder.

"I was wondering . . ." Detective Hart looked down at me with a smile creasing his lean face. "I was wondering if you'd like to get together sometime. For lunch? I've only been in Heaven a month and a half and I don't know a lot of folks. You seem pretty plugged in—"

"I've lived here all my life, well, except for when I was at CU." My inane comment covered my confusion, I hoped. Was he asking me for a date, or was he merely asking me to be a sort of tour guide to show him around the community? Lunch was neutral territory. A date would be nice, I thought wistfully. It'd been a long darn time

since I'd had a date with someone who wasn't cer-
tifiable, a total loser, or a felon (which, in my de-
fense, I hadn't known when I'd agreed to have
dinner with him).

"Lunch sounds good," I said when I realized
Detective Hart was still waiting for an answer.

"Tomorrow?"

"Sure. The Munchery at twelve thirty?"

"See you there." He lifted a hand in farewell
and reentered the police station. I stared after him
for a moment, a goofy smile on my face. A date
with the good-looking new detective in town was
just what the doctor ordered to help me get over
the shock of Doug's engagement and upcoming
marriage. The thought made me remember my
meeting with Madison Taylor. Scurrying back to
the van, I zoomed the few blocks to my office,
parked, and hurried in.

Al greeted me with raised brows and a minatory look. "Your four o'clock's been here fifteen
minutes."

"Is she in my office?" I strode toward the door.

"Yes, but—"

Pushing open the door, I found myself facing
not Madison, but her groom-to-be, my ex-boyfriend,
the only man I'd ever loved, Doug Elvaston.

Chapter 7

I stumbled on the threshold and caught myself with a hand on the doorjamb. I hadn't seen Doug in several months, and he looked as good as ever. Better, maybe. His hair, which had been wheat blond when we were in high school, had darkened a bit but was still thick and long enough to just graze his ears. His face was paler than I was used to—too much time in New York City—but his green eyes were still the same: fringed with pale lashes and full of laughter. He laughed now.

"Same old Amy-Faye," he said, springing forward with the athletic grace that had won us the state championship when we were seniors. He was tall enough to spot receivers downfield, although I supposed these days his height only made it possible for him to dominate opposing counsel in court. He took my elbow to steady me, even though I was as stable as a starfish, clutching the doorframe like I'd be swept out to sea if I let go. Slowly, I made my fingers unclench.

"It's good to see you, A-Faye," he said with the

smile that always made my stomach swoop. "It's been way too long—what? A month or so, at least?"

Ninety-two days, but who was counting? "About that," I agreed casually, crossing to my table desk and sitting behind it. Safe. The expanse of wood between me and Doug made it harder for me to lurch at him, grab him by the collar, and beg him to ditch Madison and the wedding and start over with me. "Where's Madison?" I asked, flipping through a folder with the intensity of someone trying to locate a misplaced winning lottery ticket. "I thought I was meeting with her."

"You were," Doug said, seating himself in front of me, "but she had to fly back to Manhattan for an unexpected court date. So"—he spread his arms wide—"you get me instead."

I wished. I bit my lip. "Well, uh, great. We were supposed to talk about the guest list and invitations."

"I've got it right here." He drew a page from his jeans pocket—he wore scruffy jeans like nobody's business—and flattened it on my desk. "Mom and Dad wanted a cast of thousands—you know how they are—but Madison and I want to keep it simple. Only a hundred people. And here you are." He put a finger on the neatly printed words "Amy-Faye Johnson + 1." His grin invited me to share his joy in his upcoming wedding.

Plus one. Two of the most pitiful words in the English language. Shorthand for "doesn't have a husband or boyfriend, even though she's over thirty and probably owns a dozen cats." "I'll be there, of course," I said in a businesslike voice, "to make sure things go smoothly, but—"

"No, we want you to come as a guest," he interrupted. "You've got Al—let him do the organizing shtick. You just come and have fun."

Fun, he said. Have fun. I'd have laughed if it hadn't been so painful. What could be funner than watching the man you loved swear eternal fidelity to another woman?

"You're one of my best friends," he said in a more serious voice. "It's important to me—and Madison, of course—that you be there."

"Then I'll be there." What else could I say? I forced a smile I hoped didn't look as stiff as it felt.

"Wonderful! Hey, I haven't eaten since before I let my father-in-law-to-be trounce me on the golf course this morning. What say we get something to munch while we discuss the invitations? Oh, and Madison also told me to get your ideas about table favors—whatever those are—and to ask you to set up a small golf tournament for the guests who are flying in the Thursday before the wedding. There'll be sixteen or eighteen of them golfing, she says." He smiled apologetically. "We're foisting a lot of work on you. Madison was hoping to do some of it herself, but now that her case has heated up, she just doesn't have the time. I don't know how that woman does it. Sometimes I'm amazed she has time to fit me into her schedule."

"It's what you pay me for," I said, rising. "How about the Salty Burro?"

"Great idea. Some nachos and margaritas will

make this wedding-planning stuff practically pain-
less."

Two hours and two margaritas later, I was in that
pleasantly buzzed state where everything is amus-
ing and the impossible seems possible. I couldn't
count how many times in the past Doug and I had
sat in one of the high-backed wooden booths at
the Salty Burro, alone or with friends, with a
pitcher of margaritas between us and a smear of
cheese and one lone jalapeño on a large plate tes-
tifying to our appetites. This felt familiar. It felt
right. We had dealt with the invitations and other
wedding-planning items before the nachos arrived and had moved on to discussing first my
business, then his dissatisfaction with his law
firm. He launched into an imitation of his managing partner, who was originally from Boston.

"'Billable houahs, Elvahston,'" he mimicked in
a wicked Boston accent. "'Billable houahs are ouah
raison d'être. If you so much as think about a case
while youah taking a dump, you bill it to the client.'"

I laughed so hard I snorted, and he grinned,
pleased with my reaction. "I've missed you, Amy-
Faye," he said, leaning across the table to put his
hand over mine. "Why don't we see more of each
other?"

His question effectively quenched my laughter.
Could he really be so clueless? I thought about how
I'd fought to hide my feelings from him, after he
initiated the most recent "off" phase of our on-
again-off-again relationship, saying that although

he still loved me, he wasn't "in love" with me anymore, that he wanted to be "just friends." Maybe it was my fault he didn't know how I felt. Should I tell him before it was too late, before he married Madison and was out of reach forever? I opened my mouth to tell him I still loved him, would always love him, but what came out was "We're both busy, I guess. Eventful! takes all my time, and clearly you can't get away from your job even in the bathroom."

Signaling for the check, he smiled and said, "Well, we've got to make the time."

I nodded my agreement, knowing it would never happen. He'd marry Madison and she'd be in charge of their social calendar. They'd see more of her friends than his . . . A thought occurred to me, a dreadful thought. "Where are you and Madison going to live?" I asked.

A wry look twisted his features. "That's still up for debate. Madison's got a great apartment in Manhattan, and of course that's where her job is. I've got the house here, and I'm a partner in the firm. Madison will undoubtedly make partner at her firm in a couple of years, so it would be hard for her to start over in Heaven or even Denver, although any firm in Colorado would snap her up in a heartbeat. For now, we'll probably keep both places and see how it works out. My work in New York will probably last another twelve to eighteen months, and then we'll see."

He sounded like he was trying to put a cheery spin on a situation he wasn't very happy about. I thought starting a marriage off on a long-distance basis, with no shared home, was a recipe for disaster, but I wisely kept my mouth shut. "I'm sure you'll make it work," I murmured, putting twenty dollars on the table for my share of the check.

"Oh, absolutely," he said. "Love conquers all, right?"

We walked side by side to the restaurant door and stepped into the soft light of a mountain twilight. I didn't want him to go. "Maybe we could—" I started to say, not even sure how I was going to finish the sentence. Go bowling? Walk around the lake path? Go back to my place and see what happened when you mixed a few margaritas, old memories, and a bed in the next room?

"Oh, damn," Doug said, looking at his watch. "I'm late. Mom's going to skin me alive." He leaned forward, brushed his lips against my cheek, and added, "It was good to catch up, A-Faye. Sounds like you're doing great. I wouldn't trust my wedding to anyone else." With a grin, he was gone, half jogging to his car.

My phone buzzed and I checked the display. Maud.

"Aren't you coming?" she asked when I answered.

Coming? I knit my brow. Movie night! The Readaholics were watching *The Maltese Falcon* at Maud's. I'd totally forgotten. "On my way," I said. "Start the movie without me."

"Already did," she said and hung up without saying good-bye.

Half jogging back to my van—no mean feat in my low-heeled patent pumps—I drove to Maud's timbered one-story on the outskirts of town. Her pickup with the boat trailer hitched up was in the yard rather than the long garage-cum-shed, making me think she had a fishing-guide gig lined up for the next day. I gave the doorbell a perfunctory ring and stepped into the small foyer with its pale moss green walls and slate floor. The whole house had the same monochromatic color scheme, and I always felt vaguely as if I'd walked into a grotto when I came over. The air was chilly—Maud kept the AC set low to protect her computers—and I wished I'd remembered to bring a sweater. I hurried into the living room, blurting apologies.

The Readaholics, minus Ivy, sat on the U-shaped charcoal sectional with its too-squashy cushions, facing the huge TV screen. The lights were dimmed, but I could still identify everyone and make my way to a seat without tripping over anything. Maud had her legs crossed under her, bony feet bare, and was leaning toward the TV, elbows on her thighs. Lola had a pillow tucked behind her back. She smiled at me. Brooke half reclined on the chaise and raised a hand when I entered. Kerry sat upright with her feet propped on an ottoman, a bowl of popcorn in her lap. "Finally," she said.

"Work," I replied. It wasn't totally untrue. I'd been discussing the wedding with Doug. Knowing from experience that escaping the couch's embrace was an awkward battle, I grabbed a throw pillow and sat on the ground between Kerry and Brooke, my back supported by the couch.

Bogie and an actress I didn't recognize were having a tense conversation on the screen. "Who's that?" I asked, helping myself to popcorn when Kerry passed me the bowl.

"Mary Astor," Kerry answered. "I think she makes a good Brigid."

The others murmured agreement and we watched the story unwind, inserting brief comments about the actors and the action. The TV's light flickered over our faces and cast shadows around the room. We were quieter than usual, and I knew why.

"It seems strange not to have Ivy here," Lola said during a slow moment.

I knew we'd all been thinking it. Ivy was our resident movie buff; she would've kept up a stream of commentary, telling us who the minor actors were, what movies the major players had made before or after *Falcon*, and critiquing the director's choice of shots and backgrounds.

"People are saying it might have been suicide," Brooke said in a low voice.

Maud muted the TV and slewed to face us. "That's crap," she said.

After a moment's hesitation, I shared what I'd learned from Ham and then told them about taking the tea canister from Ivy's office to the police department.

Maud stared at me. I knew her brows were up, even though I couldn't see her face clearly in the dimness. "So you don't think it was an accident or suicide," she said. "That only leaves one thing."

"Murder." Kerry produced the word grimly.

"No one would want to kill Ivy," Brooke said, at the same time Maud said, "We should figure out who'd want to kill Ivy."

"That's the police's job, don't you think?" Lola asked. Her glasses reflected the moving lights from the TV.

"Doesn't sound to me like they're doing it, not if they've already decided Ivy committed suicide," Maud said. She blew a disgusted raspberry. "As usual, they're taking the path of least resistance. Much easier to say that Ivy killed herself than to conduct an investigation that might lead to important city government officials."

"What are you talking about?" Lola asked.

Maud beetled her brows, then said, "Ivy and Clay Shumer were . . . making the beast with two backs."

Trust Maud to find the most colorful metaphor.

"I'm pretty sure it was over," Brooke said.

We all looked at her.

"I saw Fee at Dr. Kloberdanz's maybe a month ago. She was going in as I was coming out."

"So?" Kerry said, expressing the confusion we all felt.

"He's an obstetrician."

There was a moment of silence while we took that in. "You're saying Fee Shumer is pregnant," Lola said.

Brooke shrugged.

"You're not—?" A bright moment on screen washed Maud's tanned face with light, and I could see her brows raised suggestively.

"No," Brooke whispered.

I surreptitiously squeezed her hand, knowing she'd had a positive EPT a month ago that hadn't been backed up by the doctor's lab test. She'd been crushed.

"Fee didn't look pregnant at yoga the other day," I said. We both attended classes—me, somewhat sporadically—at the yoga studio on the third floor of the building my office was in. "She was still downward dogging with the best of 'em."

"Yoga's supposed to be good for pregnant women," Lola said.

"Well," Maud announced after a moment's thought. "That Clay Shumer is pond scum if he was having nooners with Ivy and then getting it on with his wife after dinner. I'd cut off Joe's private parts with a hacksaw if he did that. Not that he would." Joe was her partner, a nationally known wildlife photographer who spent months at a time on shoots in places like the Galapágos and Papua New Guinea. I thought he was in Uruguay or Uganda right now—one of those "U" countries. Their long separations seemed to work for them.

Kerry snorted a laugh, and then we fell silent, watching Brigid O'Shaughnessy plead silently with Sam Spade on the screen. She clutched at him and he detached her. It made me wonder how Ivy had taken the breakup with Clay, if there'd been a breakup. Knowing Ivy, she wouldn't have made it easy on him.

"You know," I said, "all the backstabbing and double-crossing in this movie is about money, or what they all think is money—that silly falcon statue. What if Ivy's . . . murder"—it was hard to say the word in connection with someone I knew—"is about money? Her brother inherits her house and all her stuff, I think. At least, that's what he says. He's practically panting to sell the house. And a woman at her office gets her job."

"Aren't most people killed for love or money?" Kerry asked.

"Or revenge." Maud ticked motives off on her fingers. "Money. Love-slash-lust. Revenge. Power." She waggled four fingers.

I shifted on my pillow, trying to keep my butt from falling asleep. Realizing I still held the popcorn, I passed it up to Brooke.

"And don't forget wanting to keep something secret or avoid humiliation," Lola put in softly. "Maybe Ivy knew something that her murderer didn't want to get out."

We pondered that for a moment, and then Maud put the volume up again, maybe to distract us. It was unsettling to speculate on what Ivy might have known that could get her killed. Did I know anything that could get me murdered if I revealed it? I didn't think so. Although . . . I'd overheard one of the Ford brothers accuse the other of insider trading when I was setting up for their party two weeks ago, and I'd surprised Victor Ingersoll coming out of the Zooks' house, shoes in hand and shirttail untucked, when I arrived early in the morning to clean up after the Zooks' annual backyard tax-day bash. I knew Peter Zook had left for the airport before the party ended, needing to make an early meeting at his CPA firm's headquarters in Chicago. Victor and I had mumbled embarrassed "good mornings" and never mentioned it again. My job gave me access to people's intimate moments, sometimes, because I was in and out of their houses and interacted with them during times when emotions tended to run high, like weddings, significant birthdays, funerals, and big dos that were important to them. Still, I didn't think my life was in danger.

Bogart's gravelly voice grated from the screen: "I'll be waiting for you. If they hang you, I'll always remember you." The credits rolled and Maud clicked on the lights with a remote. I blinked in the sudden brightness.

"We should search Ivy's house," Maud announced, rising with audible creaks and pops from her knees.

"Whatever for?" Brooke asked.

"The Maltese Falcon," I quipped.

"Clues. A diary. Her computer. A calendar to tell us if she was supposed to meet anyone the morning she died." Maud waved an all-encompassing hand, tanned, callused, and obviously used to hard work.

"She was," I said.

They all looked at me.

"Me."

Maud made an impatient gesture. "*Besides* you."

"We shouldn't invade her privacy like that," Lola said. Her narrow shoulders hunched in as she leaned forward to make her point.

I put an arm around her. "Ivy's beyond caring about that, Lo," I said.

"I guess." She still didn't look happy.

"I'm sure the police have already searched her

house," Brooke said. She twisted a lock of dark brown hair around one finger, a nervous habit she'd had since we were in grade school.

I didn't know if she meant to reconcile Lola to the idea or suggest we shouldn't bother since the police had already covered that ground. Her next words made it clear she was arguing the latter point.

"Besides, what are we going to do—bust a window to get in? We'd end up in jail. I can just see Troy's face if he had to come down to the jail to bail me out. Or Troy Sr. and Clarice's faces if they turned on the news and saw me being shoved into the back of a police car. There really would be a murder then: They'd kill me."

She shuddered and everyone laughed, but I didn't think she was kidding. Not much, anyway.

Maud nodded reluctantly as she took in the logic of Brooke's objections. "It was just a thought," she said. She growled with frustration. "Seems to me like friends ought to do *something* for a friend who's been murdered by some coldhearted jerk."

Kerry, who had been silent up until now, spoke up. "I could get in," she said with a triumphant smile, "without breaking a single window or doing anything illegal."

The four of us goggled at Kerry.

"How?" I asked finally.

"I'm a Realtor," she reminded us. "You said Ham wants to sell the house. I call him, offer my services, tell him I need to see the house before we can settle on an asking price, and he hands over the keys. I've never been one of those ambulance-chasing Realtors who are phoning the next of kin trying to get a listing before a body's buried, but I could do it for Ivy."

"Brilliant!" Maud slapped a hand on her thigh. "Let's do it tomorrow."

"I can't let a whole herd of people tromp through the house," Kerry said, sounding tetchy. Her arched nostrils flared. "I could lose my license. I have to do this on my own."

"What if Ham wants to go with you?" I asked. "How will you search then?"

Kerry narrowed her eyes in thought. "Good point. You can come, Amy-Faye. I'll keep Ham with me while you search. We can say you wanted a couple of photos of Ivy to display at the funeral or something."

"That's good," I said, giving Kerry an admiring look.

"You don't think I got to be mayor based only on my good looks and intellect, do you?" Kerry asked wryly. "A certain degree of sneakiness comes with the job."

I was glad Maud let the comment go without saying anything.

We broke up shortly after that, without even discussing the movie. The death of our friend made cinematic murders almost distasteful. We'd have done better, I thought driving home, to delay watching the movie for a few weeks. Maybe our next book should be something lighter; I made a mental note to ask around on some online forums for a suitable title. It was my turn to choose a book since Ivy had suggested *The Maltese Falcon*.

A slight headache reminded me of the margaritas and happy hour with Doug. I downed a couple of aspirin, but I knew they wouldn't alleviate the sadness I felt whenever I thought of Doug's upcoming wedding (which I had to do a lot since I had stupidly agreed to plan it). *Snap out of it,* I told myself, brushing my teeth hard enough to make my gums sting. *Get over him, already.* WWKMD? Hm, Kinsey wasn't much of a role model in the romance department. I'm pretty sure she last had sex twelve or fourteen books back. Okay, then, what would Stephanie Plum do if Ranger or Joe got engaged? Buy tarty lingerie. Blow up a car. Too expensive to be practical for me with my mortgage and barely solvent business.

I grimaced at my reflection in the mirror and wondered if doing something new with my hair would make me feel like a new me, a Doug-less me. I'd been Doug-less for a couple of years, of course, but my appearance hadn't changed greatly in that time. Nothing in my life had changed greatly. I lived in the same town. I did the same work. I was still pet-less and significant other–less. I still ate with my parents on Sunday evenings. My hair was the same. Weight ditto. I was in a rut. I made a face at my reflection and resolved to do something about it.

Tomorrow I would make a list of things to do to shake up my life. I remembered I was lunching with Detective Lindell Hart and smiled. That would be item one on my list. Item two would be sneaking into Ivy's house and searching it, definitely not a "rut"-type activity. Item three . . . I fell asleep before I came up with a third task.

Chapter 8

I managed to keep my nose to the grindstone all Friday morning, even after Kerry called to say Ham was enthusiastic about listing Ivy's house and would meet us there at two. That would leave just enough time for my lunch with Detective Hart. By noon, I had completed preparations for Ivy's funeral tomorrow, checked fourteen items off my to-do list for the Boy Scout picnic Sunday, resolved a minor catering crisis related to the Finkelsteins' fiftieth, and made an appointment with Sheena to do something new with my hair. I left to meet Detective Hart feeling like I'd accomplished a lot.

We arrived at the Munchery simultaneously and exchanged greetings. His smile warmed me, as did the admiration in his eyes as they swept over me. I was glad I'd worn the moss-colored blouse that made my hazel eyes more green than brown and somehow brightened my complexion. We entered the café side by side to be greeted by the clang of cutlery and the babel of dozens of conversations from the packed room. I turned toward Hart.

"Why don't we get sandwiches to go and take them up to Lost Alice Lake?" I suggested. "It's a beautiful day, and if you're hiring me to be your Heaven tour guide, I might as well start earning my pay." I laughed.

"Your pay is a free lunch," he said promptly. "Excellent idea. I'm hoping you can tell me where the lake got that strange name. It's not a morbid story, I hope."

I merely grinned and said, "I'll tell you when we get there."

To-go bags in hand, we got into his official Tahoe with HEAVEN POLICE DEPARTMENT on the sides and headed up the narrow road to Lost Alice Lake on the southern side of town. On a perfect spring day, exercisers, picnickers, and hardy sunbathers dotted the trail around the lake and the expanse of grass sweeping down to it. A lone kite flier struggled with his kite as we got out of the SUV. A strong breeze created some chop on the lake, roughing up the reflection of the mountains on the blue water. The wedding gazebo where Doug would get married in two weeks shone whitely from the left, surrounded by a copse of aspens. I turned my back on it and headed toward a picnic table occupied only by a pair of scavenging magpies. Their black wings gleamed bluely iridescent against their white chests.

"This *is* heaven," Hart said, drawing in a deep breath of the pine-scented air. "I think I could live here forever and never get used to how clear the air is."

I was pleased by his admiration for my town. "It's a beautiful place," I said. "I can't imagine living anywhere else."

Shooing the magpies off the table, I inspected the seat for debris and sat, opening my lunch. The smell of warm pastrami drifted out and I lowered my nose into the bag, making Hart laugh. He maneuvered his long legs over the bench and said, "So tell me the story behind the lake. Did someone named Alice drown here?"

I shook my head while I finished chewing the first spicy bite of my sandwich. "Nope," I mumbled. "Nothing so depressing. For a start, Alice wasn't a person. She was a goat."

"A goat?"

"Uh-huh. According to local lore, the town's founder, Walter Walters, arrived here in the late 1800s, intending to do a little prospecting. He set up camp on the lakeshore. His letters home—you can read them at the historical society—make it clear he wasn't having much luck and was planning to move on to what's now Nevada come the spring. Apparently, he had this goat with him—depended on her for milk, I guess—and she was in the habit of wandering off. One day, she was lost as usual, and he followed her bleating until he found her stuck in a crevice halfway up that mountain." I nodded toward the nearest mountain peak. "Some people say there was a cougar about to pounce on her and that he fired his rifle to chase it away. At any rate, as he dug Alice out, he noticed a glint of silver and realized he'd found what he'd been looking for. They mined silver from his strike until the mid-1970s. They still give tours of the mine. It's interesting."

"But the name?"

"Oh, yeah. In his last letter home, when he summoned his family to join him, he said something like, 'If I hadn't lost Alice, I'd never have found the treasure,' and so his family—his wife and ten sons, if you can believe it—christened the lake Lost Alice Lake when they arrived to help with the mining. The town itself, when it grew up, was called Walter's Ford. That's what it was until fifteen years ago when the council voted to rename it Heaven, hoping to attract more of the tourists who tended to pass us by as they zipped between Denver and Grand Junction and some of the ski areas. It worked, too."

"That's quite the story," Hart said, his tone saying he suspected at least part of it was fiction.

"Don't you go dissing our local legends," I said with a mock glare.

He held up his hands in a surrender gesture. "Wouldn't dream of it."

"Do you miss Atlanta?"

He gave it some consideration, and I was struck again by his quality of stillness. No fidgeting fingers, jiggling foot, or facial tics. A man who was comfortable in his own skin. *Or a hunter in a blind, staying still so as not to startle his prey*, I heard Maud's voice in my head. *He is a cop, after all.* I told Maud to shush.

"I miss some things about living in a big city, and about the South. I can't get a decent biscuit anywhere in this state, and I'd like to be closer to a major airport, but all in all, I like the pace of life here better and I sure as heck don't miss the traffic or the gang problems."

We crumpled up our lunch bags and rose to dump them in the bear-proof trash can. Without talking about it, we turned and strolled toward the lakeside trail. Close to the water, I could see the pebbled bottom and spot fingerling trout lurking in the waving lake grasses. A border collie running with her master galloped up to sniff at us and we patted her. She loped away when her master whistled.

"Leave anyone important behind?" I asked casually. Just because he didn't wear a ring didn't mean he hadn't left a live-in girlfriend behind. Or worse, had a live-in girlfriend planning to follow him out here as soon as she sold their place or found a new job.

"My folks moved to Montgomery, Alabama, when my sister's husband died in a fire. He was a firefighter. She was pregnant with her second and they moved to help her after the baby was born."

"How awful!" I said, almost unable to imagine how horrible it would be to lose a husband that way.

"It was grim, but it's three years ago now and she's doing better. The boys keep her too busy to think about it much, as far as I can tell. Other than that, I've got a brother in England with the air force, and that's it. No other ties." The look he slanted me told me he knew what I'd really been after. "You?"

"You haven't looked me up in some police database?" I kidded, half hoping he had, because that would show he was interested. My record was clean, other than a parking ticket or two.

He laughed. "I prefer getting to know my friends in person. Our computers don't have any of the good stuff, anyway, like what you majored in and why, or who your favorite band is, or why you live in Heaven, or what you'd do if time and money weren't factors."

"Wow. All that on a first da—lunch? Let's see. English, because I didn't know what I wanted to do, and I've always loved books. It was a default major, mostly. I added up my credits when CU told me I had to declare a major and I had more English classes than anything else, so voilà." I shrugged one shoulder, feeling a bit sheepish about not having been more focused, not having more of a plan. "Favorite band: Maroon 5. Yours?"

"Garth Brooks."

"That's not a band."

"Performer, then." He stooped to pick up a stone, drew back his arm, and skipped it. It hopped six times before sinking.

I clapped lightly. "I live in Heaven because it's home. I did a semester in Italy, and I tried working in Chicago right after college, but I felt . . . alien. I lasted nine months with an ad agency before coming back here. I don't think I could live anywhere else.

"Mom and Dad live here in town and I see them regularly, although I have my own house." I didn't want him to think I lived in their basement and mooched off them. "Three sisters and a brother.

One sister here, one in Grand Junction, and one in Denver. My brother, Derek, brews beer. He and a partner just bought a building that's been about fifteen restaurants over the past ten years and they're going to open a brewpub." I'd invested in it and I was keeping my fingers firmly crossed that it wouldn't fail as quickly as the other restaurants had. I'd have to declare bankruptcy—okay, not quite—and Derek would be crushed. "Grand opening's in August. I'm in charge of the party. You're invited. Actually, everyone in town's invited."

"Wow, I felt special there for a moment." Hart grinned down at me.

"You are special," I assured him, returning his grin. "You've got a personal invitation from the master brewer's sister. Most other people will just get the announcement in the *Herald*." I looked at my watch and realized I needed to get going if I was going to meet Kerry at Ivy's place. Suspecting Hart wouldn't be pleased to hear I was headed to Ivy's house, I said, "I've got to get going. Appointment."

"Yeah, me, too," he said. "Duty calls."

As we walked up the hill to his SUV, I asked, "Anything new on Ivy's case?"

His face tightened and for the first time I felt him draw back. "That case is closed."

"But the tea I brought you!"

"Is being tested. It's not like we've got access to a lab that can turn things around in a day. This isn't New York or Atlanta. Not that we got results quickly there, either"—he grimaced—"but that was due to backlog, not lack of facilities and experts. Anyway, the case—I'll call it dormant instead of closed. We're not actively working it. Everything points to suicide."

Hart opened the door for me and touched my arm as I got in. "I'm sorry, Amy-Faye. I know it's hard."

I nodded. We didn't say much on the drive back down to town. Hart pulled to the curb outside my office and said, "I enjoyed it. Any chance you'd like to be my tour guide again sometime?"

I shook off my sadness about Ivy and smiled. He was easy to be with and attractive in a way that was growing on me. "Sure. Heaven's bigger and more complicated than you would expect," I said, acting all serious, like he was in danger of wandering into gang territory or a red-light district, neither of which existed in Heaven. "It's best to have a reliable tour guide."

"Exactly what I was thinking. I'll call you." He smiled as I closed the door and stepped onto the sidewalk.

I watched as he drove off and then dashed for my van, parked around back. If I didn't hustle, I'd be late. I might have exceeded the speed limit a tad, but I arrived at Ivy's town house in time to see Kerry emerge from her old Subaru Outback. There was no sign of Ham. Kerry held up a key ring as I approached and explained.

"Ham dropped these by my office. Said something came up and he wasn't sure he'd be able to get here."

"Hot damn," I said. I hadn't been looking forward to another encounter with Ham Donner. "Let's get to it."

We approached the blue door and paused on the stoop. Shoving her sunglasses atop her head, where her short, gray-flecked brown hair kept them secured, Kerry gave me a doubtful look. The skin at the corners of her eyes crinkled. "I'm not so sure about this, Amy-Faye."

In truth, I was having doubts as well. Still, we were here. "We're not going to hurt anything," I said. "It can't hurt to look."

"I guess." Kerry fitted the key in the lock, turned it, and pushed the door open. She gestured for me to go first.

I froze for a moment, remembering the scene when I was here last. Would someone have cleaned up the vomit? Holding my breath, I stepped into the hallway. A pile of mail, mostly advertising circulars, had been swept aside by the door. At first, everything looked normal. No sign of Ivy's last moments marred the hallway. A faint odor of disinfectant stung my nostrils, and I realized Ham had hired someone to clean up. Thank goodness. I moved farther into the hall and Kerry entered behind me, pulling a clipboard from her tote. Something in my peripheral vision caught my attention and I turned to my right. The living room–dining room combo looked like a yeti had run amok.

All the couch and chair cushions were on the floor, their stuffing spilling out where someone had slit them open. I tried not to think the word "intestines" and vowed to quit reading serial-killer books. The furniture was shoved out of place and the drawers of the buffet hung drunkenly. A pile of table linens and place mats mounded in front of the buffet testified to what the drawers had held. A splatter of cranberry glass from a broken candy dish winked redly in the sunlight slanting through half-drawn blinds. It looked too much like blood and I took an involuntary step back, bumping into Kerry.

"What in the world—?" Kerry surveyed the chaos.

"I'd say either Ham needs to get his money back from the cleaning crew, or we're not the first people to think of searching Ivy's house."

"It is just criminal the way people take advantage of other people's tragedy," Kerry said, her voice hard with anger. "Look at this! Some low-lifes heard about Ivy's death and took the opportunity to break in and rob the place. And they didn't even have the decency to do it neatly. They had to wreck the whole place. What is it with people these days? I'll bet the kitchen's a disaster."

Before I could say anything, she bustled off in the direction of the kitchen. I followed. She was right. We stood on the threshold and looked at the mess. The cupboards and drawers hung open with their contents scattered around the room. Shards of colorful Fiestaware mingled with shattered glass and dented pots. Worse than that, all the canisters had been dumped on the floor, along with the food from the fridge. Open cartons of ice cream and containers of yogurt oozed onto the floor, mixing with flour and sugar and cornmeal to form a gelatinous mass. A bruised apple rested by my foot. A sour odor suggested that the mess had been there for at least a day. It was going to take a keg of Lysol and an army of cleaners wielding shovels, mops, and scrub brushes to muck this place out.

Kerry balled her hands on her hips. "Criminal," she repeated. "Believe it or not, though, this isn't the worst I've ever seen. Once, I got a listing on a house for a bank that had foreclosed on it, and the owners had knocked holes in the walls, clogged all the toilets, and spread the contents of the cats' litter trays all over the carpets. They had four cats. It reeked. Disgusting!"

I noticed a trail of flour-coated footprints leading from the kitchen toward the stairs. "Look," I whispered. I didn't know why I was whispering since the smell of spoiled dairy products told me this hadn't happened in the last couple of hours.

"We need to call the police," Kerry said. "I doubt they'll be able to catch the kids that did this, but at least they can try." She pulled out her cell phone.

"You think it was kids?"

She shot me an impatient look. "Who else? Professional burglars wouldn't bother to make this mess. They'd have been in and out. It was probably teenagers, looking for cash or electronics or prescription meds, who got off on vandalizing the place when they were done looting."

She was probably right, but something about the whole scene gave me the creeps. I didn't believe in auras or any of that nonsense, but I shivered. "Wait a minute before you call the police. Let's check upstairs first," I said.

"Why?"

I shrugged, not really sure. "Just to see where they went." I pointed at the flour footprints.

"I'm telling you they went straight for the medicine cabinets," Kerry said, following me to the stairs. "When I hold an open house now, I tell the owners to make sure they take all the meds out of their cabinets because people come through and steal them, hoping to find oxycodone or Percocet. Even Valium and antibiotics have street value."

I had no idea being a Realtor provided such a diverse education. Careful to avoid stepping on the flour footprints, we hugged the wall as we climbed the stairs. The flour prints had faded by the time we reached the top. We poked our noses into the first room on the left, a guest bedroom, at a guess, which had received the same treatment as the living room. Feathers lay in drifts where they'd been liberated from the pillows. The next room was a bathroom, and Kerry gave an "I told you so" "Hah!" when we saw the mirrored medicine cabinet gaping open and empty.

"The police took some of her meds," I told Kerry. "They thought Ivy overdosed on something."

She sniffed, annoyed at having her theory discounted.

The last room at the end of the hall appeared to be Ivy's bedroom, and it was untouched except for a nightstand whose drawer had been upended on the bed, dumping condoms, pens, lotions, and a couple of suspense novels onto the crocheted bedspread. The rest of the room was pristine.

"Huh," Kerry grunted. "They must have gotten tired of wreaking destruction."

"Or they got scared away," I suggested, edging toward Ivy's dresser while Kerry poked through the nightstand.

"Could be."

Careful not to touch anything—I'd read enough mysteries to be wary of fingerprints—I studied the framed photos resting on the polished cherry surface. There was one of Ham and Ivy as teens and another of a couple I thought might be Ivy's parents. A third showed a group of girls lined up near a tennis net and I remembered Ivy played tennis in college. I was trying to spot Ivy in the photo when I thought I heard something from downstairs. It wasn't a distinguishable sound like a creak or a door closing, but there was a change in the house's atmosphere. I froze.

Chapter 9

Kerry noticed it, too. "Ssh," she hissed, even though I hadn't said anything. We stood as still as ice sculptures, listening hard. I heard a heavy footstep and a muttered curse. Someone was definitely in the house.

"Now would be a good time to call the cops," I whispered to Kerry.

"You think?" She had already dialed the number.

As she spoke to the 911 operator, the hall floor creaked and someone began ascending the stairs.

"Oh my God," Kerry said, eyes wide.

"What do we do?" I asked. "Hide or fight?"

"He might have a gun. We have . . . a clipboard." She held up our only "weapon."

Of one accord, we dashed for the closet. I slid aside the mirrored door and we groaned. The closet was so stuffed with clothes that a paper doll couldn't have squeezed in there. How did Ivy ever find anything? I wondered pointlessly.

"Bathroom!" Kerry pointed and we scurried across the room to the open door of the master bath.

Whoever was in the house had reached the upper level. I heard a strange crunching, shuffling noise from down the hall and puzzled over it until I realized the intruder was stepping on or through the debris on the hall bathroom floor. A sharp ping sounded, like he had kicked something that banged against the tub. He was angry.

Ivy's master bathroom was small. It held a toilet, a vessel sink on a single cabinet vanity, a medicine cabinet, and a tub shrouded by a ruffled *Little Mermaid* shower curtain with a flame-haired Ariel, a cranky-looking Sebastian the crab, and a host of other fishy characters. A green towel was draped over the shower curtain rod. No linen closet or big hamper to hide in. Since neither Kerry nor I was likely to fit in the vanity under the sink, we both stepped hastily into the tub and pulled the shower curtain closed as quietly as possible. I winced at the muted jangle of the curtain rings sliding across the rod. To my nervous ears, it sounded like clanging cymbals.

"*The Little Mermaid?* Really?" Kerry whispered.

We fought off a fit of the giggles, more a reaction to our scary situation than to the odd shower curtain.

The sound of the bedroom door being slammed back so it smacked the wall shut us up. Hardly daring to breathe, we listened as the intruder stomped into the bedroom, muttering curses. It seemed to be only one man. If he didn't have a knife or gun, maybe Kerry and I could take him.

Kerry held the clipboard with both hands at head height. Her face was grim.

The man stepped into the bathroom, brushing against the door. His shoe slapped the tile. The odor of stale cigarette smoke filled the room. Could it be—? The cigarette smoke made me think it could be Ham, and it made sense that Ham would be here, but I wasn't sure enough to step out of hiding.

Before I could decide if I should risk peeking around the shower curtain, the unmistakable sound of a zipper froze me. The toilet seat smacked against the tank and the man began to pee. Kerry and I exchanged horrified looks. After a long, embarrassing thirty seconds, the man sighed, flushed, and began running water in the sink. That made me doubt it was Ham—he didn't strike me as a hand washer. I was beginning to think we could outwait whoever it was, but then the towel over the shower curtain rod jumped.

As he tugged at it, the shower curtain slid aside three or four inches. Not waiting to find out if he'd seen us, Kerry sprang from the tub and brought the clipboard down on the man's head. She got tangled in the shower curtain, so the blow wasn't too hard. Ham Donner staggered back, eyes wide with surprise, and put his arms up to ward off another blow. I grabbed for Kerry's arm, saying, "It's only Ham; it's only Ham," but I tripped on the edge of the tub and jolted forward, knocking into Kerry and Ham. The three of us went down in an ungainly pile, half-covered with the shower curtain. My knee slammed into the tile floor and I yelped.

"What the hell—?" Ham bucked and twisted to wriggle out from under us.

I grasped the counter edge and pulled myself up, offering a hand to Kerry. She shucked the shower curtain and stood, still clutching the clipboard. She looked from Ham to me to the toilet and back to Ham. "I might have known you wouldn't put the seat down."

"You hit me," Ham complained, rubbing his forehead. A lump was already rising and I suspected he'd have a lovely bruise.

"We thought you were the burglars who trashed the place," I said.

"Sorry," Kerry said in a noncontrite voice. "You shouldn't sneak up on people." She ran her fingers through her hair to straighten it and twitched her blouse into place.

"It's my house. And I wasn't sneaking. I showed up to meet you and found that mess downstairs. I was hoping the bastards who did it were still in the house so I could rip their heads off and stuff them up their—" He cut himself off. "This is gonna damage the value of the house, isn't it?"

Ah, dependable Ham. More concerned about the bottom line than anything else.

"It doesn't look like they did any permanent damage," Kerry said, reverting to her professional Realtor voice. "You might have to replace the refrigerator—"

An approaching siren cut through her words. The police. Finally.

We all trooped downstairs to explain to the same Boy Scout–age officer who'd been here when

I'd found Ivy that there was no immediate threat. As he toured the house, making notes and taking photos of the damage, Ham turned to me, suddenly suspicious. "What are you doing here anyway, Amy-Faye?"

I was glad Kerry and I had come up with a cover story. "I thought it would be nice to have a few photographs to display at the funeral. Don't you think so?"

"Ah, um, sure," he said.

"Do you have any that would work?" I asked sweetly, 99 percent sure he wasn't the sentimental type who would cherish family photos.

"Uh, I'm sure you'll get better ones here," he said, hitching up his jeans, which his paunch had pushed down. "Ivy was more into family keepsakes than me. Of course, she had all this space to keep them in"—he gestured broadly—"while I'm lucky to have a roof over my head most of the time. Not anymore, though." He smiled with satisfaction. "Soon as this place sells, I'm gettin' a condo, one of those nice ones going up on the north end of town, or maybe in Grand Junction. I've got plans. Big plans. I could tell you about them over dinner."

His usual leer was absent. He actually seemed eager to share his ideas with me, maybe with anyone, and I felt a twinge of guilt as I turned him down. "I don't think so."

"Suit yourself." He wandered away to keep tabs on either the cop or Kerry.

I was on the verge of leaving, ready to consider the whole "search Ivy's house" thing a bust, when the brass mail slot suddenly opened and the mail carrier thrust circulars and an envelope through it. They plopped to the floor, the envelope sliding almost to where I stood. The address was written in what looked like it might be Ivy's handwriting, and there was no return address. From out of nowhere, I thought about Sam Spade mailing himself the locker key in *The Maltese Falcon*, and without stopping to think about it, I bent and scooped up the letter. I didn't have time to look at it. I heard footsteps behind me and barely had time to slip the letter under my shirt before Officer Ridgway reappeared. Pretty sure that tampering with the mail was a felony that could land me in federal prison until I hit menopause, I plastered a look of total innocence on my face and turned to face him.

"Are you okay, ma'am?" he asked. "The bathroom's just there." He pointed.

Apparently, my "innocent" look came across as "queasy." "I'm fine," I assured him, edging toward the door. "But late. Yes, late. I've got an appointment. With . . . someone." I was absurdly conscious of the envelope's corner pricking my skin. Could he see its outline through my blouse?

His brows drew together. "I could get you a glass of water."

Stop being nice and let me out of here, I wanted to scream. "Uh, thanks, but no time." The envelope crackled as I turned. Had he heard it? I kept walking, pulled the door open, and stepped onto the stoop. Realizing I'd been holding my breath, I sucked in air. I'd make a terrible spy. Hurrying down the sidewalk, I made it to my van without being stopped. Kerry might wonder where I'd disappeared to, but she was deep into Realtor mode and wouldn't miss me immediately. I'd call her later to explain. Leaving the envelope inside my blouse, I started the van and drove off.

Al was at class when I got back to the office, so I had the place to myself. Pouring myself some iced tea from the pitcher we kept in the mini fridge, I went into my office and shut the door. *Paranoid.* I pulled up my blouse and peeled the envelope from where it was now sticking to my damp skin. It was a garden-variety business-sized envelope. Nothing special. I studied Ivy's name and address, written sloppily—in haste?—in black ink. I wasn't sure, but I thought the handwriting was Ivy's. I flipped the envelope over and my finger traced the V of the sealed flap. It gapped slightly on one end and my letter opener fit easily into the space. Last chance. I could drop the envelope in the nearest mailbox and no one would ever know I'd taken it from Ivy's. It was probably only a come-on from a dentist's office or mortgage broker—one of those ads they tried to get you to open by making it look like an actual letter.

Don't be such a ditherer. I sliced the envelope neatly along the top seam, laid the opener on my desk, and withdrew a single sheet of folded paper. Impatient now, I unfolded it and found myself looking at what was clearly a Xeroxed ledger page. The paper was lined and slightly askew, as if the book it was copied from wasn't aligned quite right with the copier. An orderly series of numbers made up each entry. At first, I thought the numbers were dates, because they were grouped in threes and separated by slashes. The first two groups read 1/26/10 and 8/14/43, but then the third group was 51/2/2, which couldn't possibly be a date. They weren't telephone numbers or social security numbers. Lock combinations? Nobody had this many locks. As I puzzled over the page, I realized the numbers at the ends of each line didn't fit the pattern. They weren't separated by slashes. The last numbers on the first line were 10000 and on the second line 1550. That pattern continued down the page. *Huh.*

It dawned on me that maybe the entries were written in a code of some kind. The thought made me drop the page, and it wafted to the floor. Retrieving it, I tried to think why Ivy would have a ledger page with coded entries on it. If I was right about the handwriting, she'd mailed it to herself. From where? I picked up the envelope. The cancellation stamp said it had been mailed from right here in Heaven the day she died. I shivered involuntarily. How could that be? Ivy had been home on the day she died. It made no sense that she'd mail herself something from her house.

My office door opened suddenly and I gave an involuntary shriek and dropped the page again.

Al poked his head in. "Jumpy today, huh, boss? Anyway, I'm here. Anything you need me to do for the Boy Scout picnic? I think I've got the Finkelstein event under control." His gaze fell on the paper, which had landed near his foot. "I'll get it."

"No!" I lunged for the page and snatched it up as he reached for it.

He eyed me warily. "What is that, anyway? A bill? You're not late with the rent again, are you? Mr. O'Donnell's not kicking us out, is he?" Worry sharpened his tone; he depended on what I paid him to pay his tuition.

"I was only late with the rent once," I said with dignity, "and Mr. O'Donnell completely understood. Sometimes clients are slow paying up." I folded the page and tucked it into a file on my desk. "It's nothing. Did you manage to get a copy of the newspaper wedding photo the Finkelsteins wanted?"

We talked business for a few minutes and my pulse gradually returned to normal. By the time Al returned to his desk, I knew what I was going to do. The idea should have come to me immediately. Surely Maud, my conspiracy-obsessed friend, would know something about codes. Didn't codes and conspiracies go together? I left the office at three thirty, telling Al he should leave, too, since we'd be working at Ivy's funeral and the Finkelsteins' party tomorrow, and the Boy Scout picnic on Sunday, and drove the short distance to Maud's.

Chapter 10

Maud was happy to abandon the Web site she was building for an architecture firm when I told her why I was there. We were in her office, a former bedroom at the back of her house that held two powerful computers, three large monitors, a scanner, a shredder, and her political campaign button collection. A framed collage of photos showed a young Maud stabbing an IMPEACH poster into the air outside the White House, celebrating with college friends after the *Roe v. Wade* decision was announced, shoveling ash from a family's roof in the wake of the Mount St. Helens eruption, and laying a single daisy atop a mountain of tributes left for John Lennon outside the Dakota building. Later photos showed her with Joe in Nicaragua, South Africa, the Galápagos, and what looked like Antarctica. There was not a piece of paper, writing implement, or filing cabinet in the place. Despite being almost thirty years my senior, Maud was way ahead of me on embracing technology. She prided herself on doing everything digitally and constantly hectored me to make my office a paperless environment. I wasn't as evolved as she was; I couldn't imagine not being able to cross items off my lists with a satisfying slash of my pen.

She was completely unconcerned about my possible incarceration on mail-tampering charges. "Ivy's not going to complain about you swiping her mail, is she? Fuhgeddaboutit. You don't think the police or the FBI hesitate to read people's mail when they want to, do you? They do it all the time, probable cause be damned. Watergate was our wake-up call—I circulated a petition calling for Nixon's impeachment—but we rolled over and forgot about it. Now there's the NSA collecting our metadata, which we know about courtesy of that weasel Snowden."

"I'd have thought he'd be your hero," I said.

She shook her head. "On balance, he did this country a service, but he's a coward. If you believe in what you're doing, you stand pat and face the consequences; you don't turn tail and suck up to a psychopathic cretin like Putin. Did Daniel Ellsberg run off to Moscow after leaking the Pentagon Papers? Did Sherron Watkins head for the hills after outing Enron?"

"I'm guessing 'no'?" I wasn't going to admit I didn't recognize either name.

"There is no such thing as privacy in this country anymore. Big Brother is alive and well and lurking in spy satellites and traffic cams," she said. "It's even worse online. The government spies on your credit card spending, your mortgage activity, and even your medical status. Doctors aren't converting to digital records because they want to, you know. No, the government is forcing them to so they can mine those records and know what kind of mental issues you have, what kinds of drugs you take, and whether or not you use birth control. You running off with a letter is small potatoes by comparison."

I wasn't sure two wrongs made a right, but I knew she wasn't going to turn me in, so I handed over the ledger page.

"Ah, code! Lovely, lovely code," she said. "I think I know you," she told the numbers. She swiveled to face her computer. Her short-nailed fingers danced over the keys as she searched various Web sites faster than I could have typed in the URLs. Her booted foot tapped constantly. Her concentration was total; I was pretty sure she'd forgotten I was in the room. Knowing she wouldn't miss me, I wandered to the kitchen for a drink and returned with a glass of water just as she said, "I knew I was right."

Spinning the chair to face me, she announced, "I am a genius, and you are pretty bright yourself for bringing this to me."

I smiled at her completely inoffensive, because totally accurate, self-assessment. "So what is it? The numbers."

"It's a code, of course. Do you want the good news or the bad?"

I hated that game. "Both."

She nodded. "It's one of the simplest codes ever, a book code." At my blank look she continued.

"Blindingly simple. Look." She pointed to the first trio of numbers. "The first number is the page of the book, the second is the line on the page, and the third is the letter on the line."

I studied it. "So, each of those groups of numbers adds up to one letter?"

"Exactly."

"That *is* easy. So what does it say?"

"Ah, there's the tricky part. Unless you know what book the coder is using, there's absolutely no way to break this code. That's the bad news. The coder can use any text. The Beale ciphers used the Declaration of Independence. Benedict Arnold—slime-bag traitor—created a book code using *Blackstone's Commentaries on the Laws of England*. Chances are, whoever put this together didn't use either of those. The codebook could be the *Kama Sutra*—"

"I thought that was just pictures."

"—*The Joy of Cooking*, or the Harry Potter books. Anything. Do you think Ivy wrote this?"

I shook my head. "I don't think so. I'm pretty sure the handwriting on the envelope is hers, but this seems different, although it's hard to tell with just numbers. But see how the zero on her address is fat and round and the zeros on the copied page are narrow and have kind of a tail at the top?" I used my forefinger to underscore the difference.

"You're right. Well, that makes it all the harder. If it was Ivy, you know her well enough to at least guess at what book she might have used to create the code. When you don't even know who the coder is, you don't have a prayer of deciphering it." She handed the page back to me.

"Do you think this might be related to her death?" I asked.

"Absolutely."

Her certainty both amused and dismayed me.

"Think about it," she commanded, reading my skepticism. "Ivy makes a copy of this page somewhere and mails it to herself, which is strange to start with. Then, probably on the day she mails it, or the day after if she missed the mailbox collection time and it sat in the box overnight, she keels over dead from oleander poisoning. How could it be possible that two such unusual events are *not* related?"

"It's got to be theoretically *possible*," I argued halfheartedly. I didn't want the page to be linked with her death, because if it was, I had only one course of action open to me.

She gave me a look.

"Fine," I conceded grudgingly. "Fine. That means I've got to take this page to the police." And tell them where I got it. Which would land me in jail, where the flower of my youth would bloom and wither in the presence of tough women named Big Mama or Nina the Knife. *Flower of my youth?* I really needed to be choosier about what I read.

"Why would you do that?" Maud asked.

I knew Maud didn't trust any uniformed person, with the possible exception of a Girl Scout, but this was too much. "Come on. They're the ones who can find out where the page came from and who wrote it. Maybe they can get fingerprints off it." Mine and Maud's—yikes. "We don't have the resources to do that."

"Balderdash," Maud said. "We know far more about Ivy's life and habits than the police do. We've got a much better chance of figuring out where she got this page. Besides, the police aren't even investigating anymore, are they?"

"The case is . . . dormant," I said, supplying Detective Hart's word. "But I've still got to give this to them." I couldn't see a way around it, even though I didn't want to have to confess to purloining Ivy's mail. "Maybe this will kick-start the investigation again."

Maud snorted. "Let's at least make a copy. We can see if the other Readaholics have any idea where Ivy got this." She twitched the page from my slack grasp and ran it through the scanner. It appeared on the monitor moments later.

I had to admit it was pretty slick. "I suppose I should get this over with," I said glumly. It was four o'clock. The police department would still be open.

"Want me to go with you?" Maud offered.

I was touched since I knew she'd rather bathe in bat guano than willingly engage in civil conversation with a member of the government's legitimized forces of oppression. The thought that she might not keep it civil made me say, "I got this. Thanks, though."

Ten minutes later I stood outside the police department for the second time in two days and the second time in my life. I'd come straight from Maud's, not wanting to give myself an opportunity to chicken out, but I hadn't figured out what to say. Part of me wanted to stuff the page in a manila envelope and deliver it with an anonymous note saying it was Ivy's. However, the police might not take it seriously, might think it was a prank, if I just slipped the envelope under their door in the dead of night. Sucking in a deep breath, I pulled open the door.

I expected to see Mabel at the counter, but her shift must have been over because Officer Ridgway sat there, filling out forms. A coffee maker sputtered behind him; other than that, the building was quiet.

"Hey," he said when he noticed me. "Are you feeling better?"

His unrelenting niceness grated on me. "I need to see Detective Hart about Ivy Donner's case," I said.

"No need." He gestured at the forms spread on the counter in front of him. "I've written up the whole thing. Probably kids. They might brag about it to their buddies, though, and then we'll catch 'em."

"It's not about the break-in," I said. "Is Detective Hart here?"

"Nope. Off-duty. Said he was headed to Grand Junction."

"Chief Uggams, then."

Ridgway shook his head again. "Nope. He's gone, too. I'm in charge." He sat straighter and puffed out his chest.

I chewed on my lower lip. Actually, this might be the easy way out. Ridgway was less intimidating than Hart or the chief. I'd give him the letter with a minimum of explanation and let him pass it along. I pulled the envelope out of my purse and put on my helpful citizen face. "When I was at Ivy's house this morning, the mail came through the slot. This envelope must have stuck to the bottom of my shoe because I found it when I got to my van." I studied his face to see how he was reacting to my story. He'd scrunched his brows inward, but wasn't yet expressing outright disbelief, so I plowed on. "When I read it—"

"Accidentally?"

Okay, so he wasn't as naive as I'd thought.

I nodded. "Well, not really accidentally, but kind of automatically. Anyway," I hurried on, "it looks like it might be some kind of code, and I figured it might be related to Ivy's death, so I thought I should bring it to you. To the police." I thrust it at him.

He took it and looked at the envelope.

"That's Ivy's handwriting," I offered helpfully. "She must have mailed it to herself. You'll make sure Detective Hart gets it, right?" I turned to go, but of course it wasn't that easy.

"Wait a minute, ma'am."

I turned back, expecting to see him removing the handcuffs from his belt, ready to slap them around my wrists, but he held up a form. "There's a form to fill out for stuff like this. Can you spell your name for me?"

Almost drowning in relief, I hurriedly gave him the data he wanted, thanked him for his help, and walked quickly from the police department. I knew my reprieve would be short-lived; when Detective Hart got hold of the report, he was likely to ask tougher questions than young Officer Ridgway.

Chapter 11

I entered the small room at Ellory Funeral Parlor Saturday morning, the day of Ivy's funeral, feeling edgy and sad. The source of my sadness was obvious, but I didn't know why I felt nervy and anxious, like I could dissolve into tears or erupt with anger equally easily. The room was window-less, carpeted in a somber wine color and wallpapered with a discreet floral print that somehow conjured graveyards rather than a happy summer garden. Maybe it was the scent of lilies and carnations from the two small bouquets on either side of the wooden urn where Ivy's ashes reposed that gave me that impression. Ham Donner sat in the front row, shifting back and forth on the padded folding chair, which squeaked every time he moved. His hair was slicked back with gel, and a white shirt and black slacks had replaced his usual Hawaiian shirt and shorts. Ivy's friends and co-workers were scattered about, most leaving at least a chair's distance between them and the next mourner, as if not wanting to connect with anyone.

Kerry Sanderson and some city employees, including Kirsten, sat near the front on the side opposite Ham. Kerry looked crisp and professional in a navy suit, her wash-and-go hair just brushing the jacket collar. As I watched, she patted Kirsten's shoulder somewhat briskly, consoling the younger woman, who had her face in her hands. I hadn't thought Kirsten was that attached to Ivy. I spotted Brooke, sans Troy, sitting with Maud and Joe. Brooke's curtain of silky brown hair spilled across the back of her chair. Maud and Joe sat with their shoulders touching, heads of amazingly similar white, dark gray, and silver hair—Joe's curling around his ears and Maud's in a fishtail braid—tilted toward each other as they whispered. Lola, her grandmother, and her sister sat behind them, all three of a height, all three with the same erect posture. It almost made me smile. There were no seats open near them, or I'd have joined them. Clay Shumer and his wife, Fiona, came in just before the service started, holding hands, and sat across the aisle and one row up from me. Fee rested her head on his shoulder. Surely they wouldn't be here together like this, all snuggly and affectionate, if Fee knew about Clay and Ivy?

Craning my neck around, I saw Detective Lindell Hart seated on the aisle in the back row. I knew from reading police procedurals that the cops frequently attended the funerals of murder victims, hoping to spot someone or something related to the case. Did Hart's presence mean he now believed Ivy had been murdered? I shivered. Moments before the service started, the door opened again and

I turned to view the latecomers. A thin woman wearing a black hat entered, followed by Doug. He looked around, spotted me, and made his way to the chair beside me. Kerry happened to turn around just then and raised her brows at the sight of us together. I couldn't tell if she was astonished, disapproving, or amused. Doug's thigh brushed mine as he sat, and I caught a whiff of his familiar aftershave, which made my abs clench. He looked good—better than good—in a black suit, white shirt, and somber charcoal-and-silver-patterned tie.

"I didn't know you were coming," I whispered.

"I've known Ivy as long as you have," he pointed out. "We all went to high school together. I wouldn't miss her funeral, even though I didn't keep up with her the way you did."

His words made me realize that as far as I knew, Ivy was the first of our graduating class to die. I wrapped my arms around myself at the thought, even though it was stuffy in the small room. The minister stepped forward then, cleared his throat, and began the service by talking about "our dear, departed sister Ivy." Not wanting to cry again, I tuned out, hoping Carmela had remembered to deliver the tamales she promised, and that Al had picked up the black napkins and black utensils we were using. Since Ham didn't really have a home, the reception was here at the funeral parlor, in a room at the back that looked out over the columbarium. I felt a little bad for not concentrating on the brief service, but thinking about the catering issues kept the tears at bay.

At the minister's invitation, Ham stood up and

made his way to the front, where he stood with his hands clasped. I wondered if anyone in the congregation attributed his bleary eyes and the slightly greenish cast to his skin to grief rather than a bender. *Not charitable, Amy-Faye.* He could be both grief stricken and hungover. Ashamed of myself for my unkind assessment of Ham, I made an effort to listen.

He cleared his throat twice with a harsh, phlegmy *hrah-hrarr.* "Ivy was my sister." Having delivered this line, he stood for a moment, chewing on his lower lip. He shifted from foot to foot and finally continued, "She was two years younger than me, but smart as all get-out. I remember a time . . ."

He launched into a rambling story about their childhood, which became a story about his run of bad luck with investments. Rustling sounds arose as people wiggled in their seats or surreptitiously looked at their watches. "I know the roadside gator attraction would've been a hit—when was the last time you saw gator wrestling in Colorado?—if only Ivy would've loaned—" He broke off, coughed into his fist, and finished, "She was a good sister, probably the best sister she could be. I'm gonna miss her." He shambled back to his seat, head bowed.

Really, when it came right down to it, was there a better epitaph than to say you'd been the best spouse, friend, or sibling you could be, and that you'd be missed? Had I been the best friend I could be to Ivy? Was I the best sister or daughter I could be? Sniffling, I resolved to visit my parents this weekend and call my sisters. Doug shifted beside me and reached for my hand, giving it a squeeze. I shot him a quick, startled look, but he was facing straight ahead. His palm was warm against mine. Comforting. Familiar. I let my hand rest in his briefly before pulling it away. As the minister wrapped up with a few solemn words and a recorded hymn began to play, I rose and edged past Doug, muttering something about needing to set up for the reception.

Outside the room, I took a deep breath and held it a moment before blowing it out. Ivy. Doug. *Get a grip.* I made myself focus on a different list: tamales, punch, black napkins, utensils, flowers, balloons . . . Ivy loved balloons. Striding toward the reception room, I mentally clicked through my to-do list. Stepping through the door, I inhaled the spicy scent of Carmela's tamales and felt some of my tension drain away. The room was small, but it had windows on two sides, and the sunlight poured in, glinting off the brass of the chandelier over the table and the dull silver of the chafing dishes. One window framed the columbarium, a peaceful garden with brick walkways, gurgling fountains, and naturalized landscaping. One hundred white balloons bobbed against the ceiling, curlicues of ribbon dangling from them. Al Frink, wearing a black argyle sweater-vest and a black bow tie, filled plastic cups with pink punch from the foaming bowl.

He greeted me with a cheery "Hey, boss. Everything's under control." As if remembering the occasion, he lowered his voice and said, "I mean, how's it going with the . . . the service?"

"They're just wrapping up," I told him.

"When I die," he said with the cheerful optimism of someone young enough to think of death as something that happened to other people, "you can put me in a flaming longboat and launch me across Lost Alice Lake, like the Vikings did it. Might as well go out with a bang, instead of surrounded by people in their dreariest clothes listening to music that would make anyone want to slit their wrists."

"What music do you want? 'Ride of the Valkyries'? The Rolling Stones?"

He thought about it a moment. "Pharrell's 'Happy.'" He started snapping his fingers and singing under his breath, "'. . . room without a roof. Because I'm happy—'"

A good choice.

I shushed him as a murmur of voices preceded the entrance of the first mourners. I was busy for half an hour, making sure the punch bowl stayed filled, helping blot up a glass of punch spilled on the carpet, and fetching more ice from the funeral parlor's kitchen. I ripped the bag open and let the cubes plop gently into the punch. Pink fizz bloomed around each cube. I should have hired a caterer to do this, but since Ham wasn't paying me much, and I didn't expect a large crowd, and Carmela had promised the tamales, it had seemed to make more sense to do it myself.

Kerry approached as I was collecting used glasses from around the punch bowl. "Where did you disappear to yesterday?" Her nostrils worked in and out. "I went to make some notes about the kitchen, and when I got back you were gone. Ham took off, too. The cop hung about until I left; from the way he trailed me around, I think he expected me to try to make off with a coffee table under my blouse. Did you know he and his wife just had twins? He doesn't look old enough. It made it hard for me to do any real searching. Did you find anything interesting?"

I nodded and looked around. No one was within hearing distance. "A letter Ivy mailed to herself."

"You stole her mail?" Kerry's brows climbed. "Isn't that a federal offense?"

"Ssh! You let us in under false pretenses."

"That's different. "

I dropped the argument about who was on soggier moral ground. "Maud says the letter—it wasn't really a letter; it was a page copied from a ledger—is in code."

"Really? What—"

Before she could finish her question, the hatted woman who'd followed Doug into the service approached and asked if I knew where the bathrooms were. By the time I'd finished directing her, someone had claimed Kerry's attention. I glanced around for Doug but didn't see him. Just as well. The Shumers weren't here, either. Detective Hart, likewise, seemed to have left directly after the service. I was sorry not to get a chance to talk to him. Before I could wonder if he was really going to call me like he'd said he would, I noticed Ham hunched over the punch bowl. Strange. I studied him, wondering if he was feeling ill, and then realized he was doctoring the punch from a flask. I rolled my eyes. Did he think he was at a stag party? There were kids here, like Lola's sister, drinking the punch. I caught Al's eye and signaled for him to remove the bowl. It looked for a moment like Ham was going to wrestle Al for the punch bowl, and I scrunched my eyes shut momentarily in anticipation of disaster, but Al prevailed with a quiet word in Ham's ear. I clapped my hands silently and Al grinned. Ham, disgruntled, took a defiant swig from the flask. I turned my back on him. I'd felt semisympathetic toward him during the service, but the feeling was wearing off quickly.

Lola and her grandmother and sister were filling their plates at the buffet table, and I joined them, chatting easily with Mrs. Paget and asking Axie—short for "the accident"—about school. Her name was really Violet, but when she came along more than fifteen years after Lola, so many people referred to her as an accidental baby that the nickname stuck. She didn't seem to mind it, refusing to answer to Violet, which she said was an "old-lady name." She and Lola were going shopping in Grand Junction for a prom dress that afternoon, and by the time she finished enthusiastically describing what she was looking for, and Mrs. Paget had intervened to amend details about hem length and décolletage depth, the crowd had started to thin out.

I drew Lola a little aside and told her about the break-in at Ivy's house and finding the ledger page. She listened intently, eyes unblinking behind her glasses, drawing in a sharp breath when I told her how Maud had identified the code type.

"I'll bet that made Maud's day," she observed. "Codes and conspiracies right here in Heaven." She grew thoughtful. "You don't sound convinced that it was kids that broke into Ivy's."

I shook my head slowly, a little startled, as usual, by Lola's perceptiveness. "I can't help thinking whoever it was, was looking for the ledger page. I mean, it could have been teenagers, of course, or druggies looking for something they could sell or pawn easily, but . . ."

She gave a "just a moment" finger to Axie, who was hovering suggestively near the door. "Look, I've got to take Axie to Grand Junction, but maybe we—and Maud and Kerry and Brooke—should get together and talk this over. We started out wanting to honor our friend and make sure folks knew she hadn't committed suicide, but now— Well, I didn't bargain on invading her home and stealing her letters and mixing it up with house-breakers."

"We didn't—"

"I don't want you to get hurt," Lola said. "I care about you."

The simplicity of the statement made me swallow my words. I hugged her. She was sturdy and warm and smelled faintly of eucalyptus-scented shampoo. She hugged me back fiercely. I told her about Ham wanting us to help him spread Ivy's ashes around the tree house and she said of course she'd join us. As Axie came toward us with a determined look on her face, I said, "Let's meet when you get back from dress shopping. No, wait . . . I've got the Finkelstein party tonight and the Boy Scout picnic tomorrow. How about tomorrow night at my house? After dinner. Eight? I'll tell the others."

The rest of the mourners dribbled away within half an hour, taking balloons with them at my urging, leaving only Ham, Al, me, and a couple of funeral parlor employees. Al had carted the remains of the food and drink into the kitchen and washed up the service items that belonged to a rental company. The funeral director had shucked his jacket and was efficiently placing the folding chairs on a dolly. Another employee ran a vacuum. Ham sat morosely, staring out at the columbarium, occasionally refreshing himself from his flask. There was no point in hitting him up for his share of the reception expenses right now. He probably couldn't even hold a pen, much less make out a check, in his soused condition. Should I offer to drive him home? Ugh, no. Pour him into a taxi? I was debating approaching him when a woman's voice spoke at my elbow.

"Ms. Johnson? Do you have a moment?"

It was the woman in the black hat I'd noticed earlier, who came in just before Doug. Its rolled straw brim shadowed her face, but when she tilted her chin up, I saw that she was young—definitely under thirty. Her face was narrow and pale, with thin lips and brows. She wore a navy wrap dress and navy-and-white spectator pumps. A possible client, I deduced, attracted by how efficiently the reception had been run. I put on my professional smile.

"Call me Amy-Faye. What kind of event are you planning?"

It took her half a beat. "Oh no, I'm not looking for a party planner. Although if I were, I'd definitely hire you. Everything went like clockwork with this reception." Her flattery made me wary even before she added, "I want to talk to you about Ivy Donner. You were her best friend, right?"

"She and I were friends from high school," I said, not sure I merited the title "best friend." I remembered I had no clue who this woman was. "Who are you?"

"Oh, sorry." She offered her hand. "Flavia Dunbarton with the *Grand Junction Gabbler*. I'm a reporter."

"Ah." I didn't try to hide my confusion. "Why is a Grand Junction reporter interested in Ivy Donner?" I asked.

"She came to me, a week ago, said she had— Look, can we sit down somewhere and talk? Somewhere that's not here."

She tipped her head toward Ham, and I got the impression she didn't want him intruding.

"Uh, sure. Here." I handed her a box with leftover plates and napkins. Picking up a similar box containing the serving dishes, I said, "Help me carry these out to the van. Then we can find someplace to talk."

With the boxes loaded into the back of the van, I suggested we grab a beverage at the Divine Herb. Flavia followed me in her car. The lunch rush had passed by the time we arrived and found a table tucked into a corner near the back. We could glimpse passersby on the sidewalk, but they wouldn't spot us back here. The Divine Herb was a cozy spot with artwork by local artists on the walls, a pressed-tin ceiling original to the building, and violets planted in tea mugs on every table. The chairs were dark wood with floral cushions tied to them. Flavia took her time over the tea menu, and I ordered tomato soup and a grilled cheese sandwich, suddenly realizing I was starving. I hadn't eaten one bite at the reception, and I'd skipped breakfast, unable to face food on my way to Ivy's funeral.

When our order arrived, the aroma of Flavia's tea, an herbal blend, reminded me so strongly of Ivy that I swallowed hard and couldn't speak for a moment. Luckily, Flavia took up our conversation where we'd left off at the funeral parlor. She was more self-possessed than your average twenty-something, I thought.

"So," she said, taking a noisy sip of tea, "Ivy came to the *Gabbler* offices a week before she died and asked to speak to me. She said she'd read an article I did about corruption in the city council and she thought I was the right person to talk to."

"About?"

"A story. A big story. Something too big for the *Heaven Herald*. She said she had proof—would soon have proof—of a scandal that would 'lead to indictments of bigwigs from government circles to business leaders.' Her words, not mine. She said the story involved people in Heaven, but also in Mesa and Grand Junction."

"So what was the scandal?"

Flavia *pfft*ed air in a frustrated way. "I don't know. I was actually hoping you might know."

"You don't know?" I stared at her blankly.

"Ivy died before she could give me the proof she was talking about. She said she didn't want to give me any details until she had something to back up her story. We were supposed to meet the afternoon of the day she died."

An icy finger traced my spine. I was pretty sure I knew what Ivy's proof was, even if I didn't have the slightest idea what it meant. The ledger page.

"I already asked her brother about it. He made a pass at me and tried to get me to write an article on his latest business idea—something to do with reptiles—and I think he might have already had a couple of brews, even though it wasn't ten o'clock in the morning. Anyway, it didn't take me thirty seconds to figure out that he had no idea what I was talking about. He didn't strike me as anyone's idea of a confidant, not even a sister's, and I've since figured out that he and she weren't all that close, right?"

She smiled and I found myself nodding in confirmation without meaning to. "I should have done more research before I approached him—I'll know better next time. He offered to help me find Ivy's 'proof,' whatever it was, for a fee."

"Of course." An image of Ivy's ransacked house came into my mind. Had Ham gone through the house, looking for the mysterious proof? That put a new spin on things.

"Have you asked anyone else about this, mentioned that Ivy was onto something big?"

"No. I learned my lesson with her brother."

"Yet you're talking to me." I cocked one brow, waiting for her to explain.

"I've been doing a little discreet investigating. It's what I do." She smiled the disarming smile. "I found out you and she were good friends, that she was at your house the night before she died and you were with her when she died. I'm hoping she said something to you." She gave me a questioning look.

"She didn't," I said. "Didn't even hint at anything like what you're talking about."

Flavia gave me a skeptical look. "Nothing? I find that hard to believe."

Her doubt annoyed me, and I voiced a thought I'd been toying with. "You didn't happen to search Ivy's house, did you, looking for whatever she was going to show you?"

A guilty look flashed across Flavia's face.

"You did!"

"I did not." For the first time, she sounded as young as she looked. "But—"

"But what?" I didn't believe her denial.

"I was there. At Ivy's house. The day after she died. I didn't hear about her death until the morning after she died, and I drove right over to Heaven. The police hadn't yet decided it was suicide, and I thought—" She broke off.

"You thought someone had killed her because of whatever she was talking about, the story she was giving you."

Flavia nodded. "I thought it was possible. If it's really as big as she suggested . . . Anyway, I parked a bit down the block from her house, with some thought, I admit, to having a look around. But the place was Grand Central Station—I didn't get a chance."

"Grand Central Station? You mean you saw people at Ivy's house? Who?"

"Cops."

I waved that aside. Of course cops were in Ivy's house the day after she died, probably collecting the remains of her tea or looking for a suicide note or something. "Anyone else?"

"A couple of men and a woman."

"Together?"

"No, all separate. One of the men came first, then the woman, then the other man."

"Any idea who they were?"

"No." A mischievous smile curled Flavia's lips. "But I've got photos. Want to see?" She pulled a small camera from her purse.

I scooched my chair around until we were side by side and I could view the photos with her. The first one showed a man from the back, his hand upraised to knock. Even from the back I had no difficulty in recognizing Clay Shumer.

"Clay Shumer. Ivy's boss." I identified him for Flavia. I couldn't see any reason not to—she could get his name by showing the photo to almost anyone in town. "Did he go inside?"

"Oh, yeah. I'm pretty sure he had a key. Were they . . . you know?"

The way she licked her lips was slightly off-putting and I only shrugged. Ivy's love life was no concern of hers. After a second, she clicked to the next photo. Aha, this was interesting. I studied the photo of Fee Shumer turning away from Ivy's door. She wore a nice blue dress and pumps; she looked like she was on her way to church or a lunch party. I guessed that pretty much answered the question of whether or not Mrs. Shumer knew about her husband's relationship with Ivy.

Flavia looked a question at me.

"Fiona Shumer," I said reluctantly.

Flavia made a note. "I wonder why she was there."

"No idea." I literally had no idea why Fee Shumer would be at Ivy's house the day after she died. She must have heard about Ivy's death, so she wasn't there to confront her about sleeping with Clay, or invite her to a baby shower (if she was really pregnant, as Brooke suspected), or hit her up to contribute to some charitable cause. "Did she go inside?"

"She walked around to the back and was gone about ten or twelve minutes. I don't know if she got in or not."

We puzzled over Fee's presence and motive in silence for a moment, and then Flavia clicked past a couple of photos of cops—I caught a glimpse of Chief Uggams and the Boy Scout–aged cop and Hart and a couple of uniformed cops I didn't recognize—and stopped on the photo of someone I did recognize. I put a hand involuntarily to my mouth.

Flavia caught my reaction and her eyes gleamed with interest. She reminded me of a squirrel—no, a mink or a pine marten, weaving its way sinuously toward a fat gobbet of suet. "Who is it?"

She had to ask me again before I could make myself answer.

"He's a lawyer. His name's Doug Elvaston." Why in the world was my Doug—okay, Madison's Doug—lurking about Ivy's home the day after her death? I bit my lip. It was possible, I supposed, that he didn't know she had died . . . in which case, why was he going to see her? I remembered I'd been a bit surprised to see him at the funeral service. Was there something between them I wasn't aware of? With dismay, I realized they might even have dated after Doug and I broke up. Ivy had always been a bit cagey about her romances; still, it didn't seem possible that they could have dated for long in Heaven without someone mentioning it to me. Heaven's gossips had certainly found a way to let me know about every female over twelve and under eighty-seven seen in Doug's company. I remembered some of the conversations, the sly eyes watching for my reaction: "Guess who I ran into at the Salty Burro, Amy-Faye? Doug Elvaston. With a very attractive redhead. Probably a colleague, right? Although they didn't look like they were discussing torts or contracts, if you know what I mean." Wink, wink, nudge, nudge.

Flavia interrupted my thoughts, which had veered way offtrack. "I'm pretty sure he didn't go in the house, at least, not then. He knocked a couple of times, tried to peer in a window, and then left. He's hot."

"If you like that type," I said, feigning disinterest. "So is that everyone you saw?"

Flavia tucked the camera back in her purse. "Yeah. There might have been more—like I said, Grand Central Station—but I had to leave. Ortho appointment." She grinned broadly to display her almost invisible braces. "They come off before Christmas, thank God."

"Are you going to share these photos with the police?"

"The police?" Flavia's expression suggested I'd asked her if she was going to tattoo the likeness of Kim Kardashian on her backside. "Why would I do that?"

"Someone broke into Ivy's place and trashed it. The police think it was kids, but maybe it wasn't." I nodded in the direction of the camera. "Maybe someone was looking for something other than drugs or electronics." Like the ledger page.

"In general, I don't believe in sharing with the police," Flavia said, slurping the last swallow of her tea and collecting her bag. "They're too likely to confiscate stuff or try to keep me from publishing. However, if they have something to offer in return . . ." She looked thoughtful. "If you think of anything else, let me know, okay? I'll be around for a while—I'm not one to let go of a story once I sink my teeth into it. Thanks for your time. And I really will call you if I need an event organizer." Adjusting her hat, she flashed a smile and left.

Sure she would. I absently tasted my soup, which

had grown cold during our conversation, and thought about the unexpected encounter, working through the implications of the photos. Clay, Fee, and Doug rolled about in my head like marbles, clinking against one another and then caroming away. I found myself sketching on the paper napkin and looked down to see I'd drawn a Ham Donner– ish figure (pudgy and with short hair, which was as close a likeness as I could manage) pouring booze into a punch bowl with a coffin in the background. In small capitals, I printed, "Funerals that really pack a punch." *Blech.* I balled up the napkin and chomped a big bite out of my sandwich.

By the time I had finished my grilled cheese, I was no closer to figuring it out. As I stood and left money to cover the bill, I considered telling the police myself about the trio of visitors to Ivy's house. It felt a bit low—like I'd be siccing the po- lice on Flavia by doing that, because they'd surely call her and ask for the photos. Not that I owed Flavia anything, but still. Another idea popped into my head: I could talk to each of them, casual- like, and see if I couldn't figure out why they'd gone to Ivy's. *Yeah, right.* Like I could march up to Fee Shumer and say, "What were you doing at Ivy Donner's house the morning after she died?"

I needed another idea. A workable idea.

Chapter 12

Sunday dawned clear and sunny, although a cold front had blown in overnight and it was a good twenty degrees colder than it had been Friday. All to the good, I thought as I readied myself for the Boy Scout picnic. At least I didn't have to worry about any of the boys—or their parents—collapsing with heatstroke. Wearing jeans and a striped rugby shirt, and with my hair ponytailed, I got to the park shortly after nine to start setting up. The packs or clans or whatever would arrive at eleven; I had planned for eighty Scouts plus leaders and parents. Between now and then, I needed to decorate the picnic pavilion, set up stations for the games they'd be playing, greet the caterer and make sure he had the right amount of brisket, pulled pork, and other barbecue items, and coordinate with the troop leaders to make sure we were all still on the same page.

Event organizing is a funny job. You'd think anyone can put a party together, and for the most part that's true, if all you want is two-liter bottles of soda and box wine served in plastic cups, a deli tray or cake from the grocery store, and a handful of friends standing around chatting. If you're having an *event*, though, a party or meeting or wedding that runs on a schedule, where the activities of a variety of professionals (caterers, bakers, rental companies, musicians, speakers, etc.) have to sync up, where there are lots of moving parts and big bucks involved, well, then, you're smart to have an event organizer like *moi*. I describe myself to prospective clients as a cross between the general contractor they'd hire to make sure their house gets built right and a cruise director, with a touch of therapist thrown in.

The day started off on the right foot because the picnic pavilion was posted with the RESERVED sign I'd requested when I booked it with Heaven's parks and rec office, and the grass on the field had been recently mowed, also as I'd requested. Some sort of white box sat at the far end of the field, and I wondered if the grounds crew had forgotten something. No matter. The park had three main recreation areas, including a playground with jungle gyms, an area with a couple of softball fields, and this pavilion with the football field–sized grassy area for all sorts of running games. All three areas shared a central parking lot, and paved walkways led from the lot to the various picnic pavilions. A mix of conifers and aspens bordered the field on three sides, and I breathed deeply of the piney smell as I pulled my dolly laden with boxed decorations up the slight incline.

By the time Al arrived to help at ten, I'd completed the decorating, including making center-pieces of balloons; discussed where to put the inflatable slide with Bowie Hines, who owned Take a Bounce, the inflatables company from Palisade; and patted the ponies who would be giving rides to the youngest kids. Their owner, whom I'd worked with numerous times, set up on the far end of the field to minimize odor and flies near the eating area. Al's arrival coincided with the caterer's and everything was chaos for half an hour, the good kind of chaos that meant stuff that was supposed to be happening was happening. I didn't even want to think about the bad kind of chaos.

By the time the first boys started arriving, everything was under control. The mouth-watering smell of pulled pork was heavy on the air, and the day had warmed up enough that mothers were smearing or spraying sunblock on their reluctant Scouts. Parents chatted in small groups while the Scout leaders organized and ran games out on the field. The bulk of my job was done. The Big Cheese Scout Leader, the one who'd hired me, had already told me he was pleased with all the arrangements. I could expect more business from the Boy Scouts, I thought happily. Hands on hips, I observed to Al, "Looks like it's going smoothly."

"Knock wood." He rapped his knuckles against one of the columns holding up the pavilion roof.

He was surprisingly superstitious for someone so young. "Were you ever a Scout?" I asked.

He shook his head. "I was never into uniforms, not even as a kid. A couple years back, before I started college, back when I wasn't doing much with my life, my dad suggested I join the military. They've got great educational benefits, and it might've been fun to get stationed in California or Florida, near Disney or a beach, but I couldn't do the uniforms. Or the guns," he added as an after-thought. "Or the rule following, or the respect for authority, or—"

"I guess now's not the best time to mention the uniforms I just bought for us to wear when we're on-site for events? Black slacks for you and a black skirt for me, with a pale pink shirt with Eventful! embroidered over the pocket—"

"You'd better be kidding, boss," he said.

I grinned and he whooshed out a relieved breath. "Had you going," I said.

Al nodded and then made a visor of his hand and peered toward the makeshift corral, where three ponies plodded in a slow circle. "That pony seems to be going a little fast."

Indeed it did. A fourth pony, fat and white, was trotting across the field, tossing its head up and around, with a small girl clinging to its brushy mane, wailing. *Oh no.* Al and I started jogging toward the pony, now being chased by its owner and a handful of enthusiastic Scouts. I was hoping to intercept it before it barreled into the rows of Scouts lined up for three-legged races and egg tosses. As I got closer to the runaway steed, I heard screams. Looking up, I saw eight or ten kids wind-milling their arms and running from the corral area. They were yelling something and it took me a moment to understand what they were saying.

"Bees," they cried. "Bees!"

The pony neared and I lunged for the loose lead rein trailing from his bridle. I snagged it, planted my feet, and pulled. Thanking my lucky stars that the pony was fat and already winded, I brought him to a halt and swung the little girl out of the saddle. The pony stood docilely, smelling like horse sweat, and lowered his head to munch the grass.

"Are you okay, honey?"

"The pony scareded me." She clung to me, blinking wet lashes. "And the bee stinged me." She pointed to an angry welt on her arm. The sight of it made her tear up again. "Mooommmy!"

This was definitely the bad kind of chaos. Al skidded to a stop beside me and I handed him the little girl.

"Find her mom. Get the first-aid kit from the van." I always carried a first-aid kit to events, and it was stocked with EpiPens in case of allergy emergencies. I'd once had a guy keel over with anaphylactic shock after eating shrimp dip. This little girl seemed fine, but I didn't know the state of the other kids trying to outrun the bees. "And tell everyone there are bees. Maybe they should get in their cars."

As Al ran back to the pavilion, I intercepted the group of kids running toward me, most of them still swatting at the air. Several bees buzzed around the last boy in the group and I flapped at them. They flew off toward the white box sitting not far from the corral. I had a sinking suspicion that I knew what the box was. On the thought, a sharp burning pain erupted on my neck. I clapped a hand to it and accidentally smushed the bee that had stung me. Dang, it hurt.

"I think they're gone, now," I told the boys through gritted teeth. "Did anyone get stung?"

Six of the seven raised their hands. "Three times," a boy with glasses said proudly.

"It's a good thing you're tough," I said, scanning them all and seeing no signs of distressed breathing or all-over redness or welts. I herded them back toward their parents and the pavilion, saying, "Isn't there a Scout badge for camping and stuff, or first aid? Did you learn what to do for bee stings?"

"Don't try to pull out the stinger," a short boy with a welt on his knee said. "That makes it worse. Did you know bees die after they sting you? When they stick the stinger in, it pulls out their guts." He said it with eight-year-old relish and looked pleased when I said, "Ew."

The parents had organized by now and quickly checked their offspring. One mother pulled ice cubes from a cooler and applied them to the stings. I gratefully accepted one and held it to the welt on my neck. It helped a little. The hubbub gradually died down, but several of the younger kids were crying, from fear or overstimulation, and some of the parents began packing their offspring into SUVs and minivans. The event was breaking up prematurely, but there was nothing I could do to stop it.

I headed back toward the corral, hoping Reina, the pony wrangler, might be able to tell me what had happened. However, I was only halfway there when the Big Cheese Scout Leader hailed me, coming from the direction I was headed.

"She says there was a swarm of bees," he said, indicating Reina with a jerk of his head. "They stung the pony." His rubbery lower lip jutted out. "We're lucky no one was seriously hurt."

I nodded fervently.

"They came out of that hive." He jabbed a finger at the white box I'd noticed when I first arrived. "What kind of moron," he continued, "sets up a beehive in a park where kids play games?"

I shrugged, preparing to admit that I didn't know what kind of moron that would be and was already planning to call parks and rec, but he forestalled me with a more pointed question: "And what kind of moron doesn't check the field for hazards when she's expecting a hundred young boys to be running around *and* has been paid to make sure things go right?"

That would be my kind of moron, I guessed. It wasn't totally fair to blame me for the bee invasion, but if I'd checked out the white box when it caught my eye, we could have avoided this fiasco. "I'm sorry," I said. "I can't imagine why or when someone put—"

"I can't imagine why someone would hire you to organize dinner for two," he said and strode off without giving me time to reply.

I guessed that meant I wouldn't be organizing next year's Scout picnic. Too bad. With a little heads-up, I could maybe have arranged a killer piranha infestation for everyone's amusement. Shoot. I'd talk to the Big Cheese in a couple of days, when he'd cooled off. Right now, he was probably still suffering from the adrenaline rush of realizing dozens of parents might have sued the organization and him personally if any of the boys had reacted badly to the stings. I couldn't blame him for fearing litigation; people had tried to sue me for the "mental anguish" associated with not having centerpiece flowers the exact shade of blue as their bridesmaids' sashes, for a freak July snow shower ruining an outdoor commitment ceremony, and for the dry-cleaning bills associated with being spat upon by an annoyed camel (long story). Even in Heaven, too many people were willing to drag their neighbors into court for the most trivial slights and wrongs.

Squaring my shoulders, I continued on to the corral and made sure the ponies and Reina were all right. Learning they were, I helped her load the stolid beasts into her trailer and then cautiously approached the hive. As I got closer, a humming seemed to vibrate the air. I could tell, somehow, that the humming was bees happily going about their bee business, not preparing to go on the warpath. A few bees left the hive, crossing paths with a similar number returning to it. I wished I could peer inside, but I didn't want to incite the bees again.

A splash of chartreuse some feet in front of the hive caught my eye, and I stooped to retrieve a tennis ball. Odd. I tossed it in the air, figuring one of the Scouts must have brought it. Leaving the bees behind, I returned to the pavilion in time to watch the inflatable slide hiss and sag when Bowie pulled the plug on it. That was kind of how I felt—like someone had pulled the plug on me. I took Al up on his offer to finish supervising the cleanup and headed home for an ibuprofen, a salve of vinegar and baking soda on my bee sting, and a phone call to parks and rec.

Parking the van in my driveway fifteen minutes later, I descended wearily. I tucked the expandable file holding receipts for the day's vendors and supplies under my arm and walked to my front door. As I fitted the key into the lock, a yellow paper spiraled to the ground, loosed from the piece of tape used to stick it to my door. I picked it up and almost crumpled it without reading it, figuring it was an ad for a roof inspection or a Realtor begging for a listing. It looked homemade, though, so I scanned it after laying my folder on the kitchen counter.

"QUIT BUZZING ABOUT IN THINGS THAT AREN'T YOUR BEESWAX," it read in printed capitals. "NEXT TIME THE STING MIGHT BE FATAL."

Chapter 13

Brooke tried to soothe me. Scared by the threat and by the fact that someone had been to my house to deliver it, I'd dashed out, not even grabbing my purse, and driven straight to Brooke's. We sat in her kitchen, the only room in her house that wasn't formal and expensive and intimidating. Well, it was expensive—acres of granite, appliances with foreign names I couldn't pronounce, and extras like warming drawers and a second oven and a walk-in wine cooler—but it was homey, too, with red brick around the stove and floral cushions on the chairs. We sat at the table in her breakfast nook, which looked out on a backyard so *designed* that it looked like it'd been imported rock by rock and plant by plant from the Denver Botanic Gardens.

Troy stood at the stove in running gear, reheating last night's stew for lunch, while Brooke fetched me a glass of cranberry juice.

"Drink," she said when I started to talk.

The glass chittered against my teeth as I drank.

The sugar washing into my system made me feel more stable. "Thanks." I swiped my mouth with the back of my hand.

"Is it girl stuff?" Troy asked. "Do you want me to go away?" Tall and slender, he had slightly droopy posture and seemed younger than thirty-two. His pleasant, open face and light brown hair, which waved around his ears, could have gotten him cast in any high school movie as the hot girl's loyal guy friend who would turn out to be her true love.

"Not girl stuff," I said, shoving the threatening note across the table to Brooke. Troy came to peer over her shoulder.

Brooke read it and looked up, puzzled. "It sounds vaguely nasty, but I don't get it. 'Buzzing'? 'Sting'?"

I explained about the mysterious beehive and the Boy Scout picnic fiasco.

"So now you think someone put the beehive there on purpose?" Troy asked. He returned to the stove and ladled rich-smelling stew into three bowls, inserted a spoon into each one, and set them on the table.

I began to eat automatically, not realizing until the first savory bite hit my tongue how hungry I was. "That's exactly what I think. Furthermore, I found a tennis ball not far from the hive."

This revelation only confused them further.

"I think someone was hiding in the woods and threw the tennis ball at the hive to agitate the bees." The thought had come to me on the ride over here, when the tennis ball rolled off the passenger seat and under the gas pedal. "Someone deliberately pissed off those bees, hoping they'd ruin the picnic. And that's exactly what happened."

Brooke and Troy exchanged a glance.

"Exactly why would someone do that, honey?" Brooke asked.

They didn't know about Ivy's house being vandalized or the coded ledger page. I quickly filled them in, ending with how I'd dropped the ledger page at the police station Friday evening and talked to Flavia after the funeral. "Someone's trying to scare me away from looking into Ivy's murder," I announced, scraping my spoon against the bowl to get the last of the gravy.

"How would they even know?" Troy asked. "I mean, who have you discussed it with?"

That was a darn fine question. I sat up straighter and thought about it. "Well, all the Readaholics. And Ham Donner knows I was at his sister's house Friday. Maybe Kirsten at her office, because I took the tea canister. And the police know, obviously." The shortness of the list made me uncomfortable. "And I suppose any of those people could have told other people."

Troy nodded, unconvinced. "I think you're paranoid, Amy-Faye." Picking up our bowls, he carried them to the sink and ran water into them.

I could hear Maud's voice saying, *Just because you're paranoid doesn't mean they're not out to get you.*

Brooke watched her husband. "Remember, your mother's coming by later to talk about the gala."

"I forgot." Making a face, Troy transferred the bowls to the dishwasher, sponged up a spot of stew on the range top, scrubbed out the sink, and folded a dish towel precisely, talking while he worked. "Isn't it more likely someone at the picnic wrote this note, maybe as a prank? Or maybe it was an angry parent—pissed off because little Johnny or Janet got stung—who wanted to scare you a little bit."

"I don't see how the line about 'mind your own beeswax' fits in that scenario," I said. "Someone's telling me to butt out—of something—or else. The only 'something' I can think of is Ivy's murder."

An impatient look flitted across Troy's face. "Come on, Amy-Faye. It's probably not even a murder—the police said she committed suicide. You're just bored and upset about Elvaston getting married—"

Brooke's guilty look told me she'd discussed it with him.

"—and looking for attention. You need to get out of here for a bit, get a fresh outlook. Take a little vacation, say, a long weekend in Denver. Brooke could go with you. You could do the spa thing"—he mimed painting his nails—"and do some shopping."

Brooke looked from her husband to me, half-embarrassed (presumably because he'd called me an attention hound) and half-hopeful. "It'd be fun. We could—"

I rose, hurt and angry. "I don't think so. I am not acting out because Doug's getting married. I am not making any of this up. It may turn out that Ivy wasn't murdered, but I owe it to her to make a serious effort to find out, bees and threats and skeptics"—I included both of them in my angry look—"be damned." I stalked toward the front door.

"Amy-Faye—" Brooke started to follow me.

"Thanks for the stew," I said, closing the door oh so gently and dignifiedly behind me.

I drove off and parked around the corner to pound on the steering wheel. Troy and I had never been best buddies—I'd thought he was stuck-up and snotty in high school, and the way he knuckled under to his parents on every important issue since he and Brooke got married drove me batty—but I'd thought he respected me, a little, and my friendship with Brooke, and I'd always respected their relationship. Saying I was making stuff up about Ivy because I craved attention, implying that Doug getting married had caused me so much stress I needed a vacation— *Ooh!* I banged the steering wheel one more time, took a deep breath, and resumed driving.

I drove for a couple of blocks before realizing I didn't have a destination in mind. I was a little bit nervous about going home, although obviously I'd have to do so eventually. I could go to Maud's. She'd believe me about the note—she'd be *eager* to believe me, and immediately start spinning conspiracy theories to account for it. I wasn't in the mood. Should I take it to the police? It was a threat, after all. I shook my head. No. I wasn't going to run the risk that the police would think as Troy did, that I was some sort of unbalanced woman, looking for attention. I'd already been to the police station twice in the last forty-eight hours; I wasn't going back.

I realized that while I was thinking, the van had steered itself toward my parents' house, a rambling two-story on the east end of Heaven, and I remembered my new resolution from the memorial service to connect with my folks this weekend. The house had flaking gray paint, an overgrown yard with apple trees, and a detached two-car garage. Neither Mom nor Dad was much for home maintenance. Mom thought of it as man's work, and Dad was so engrossed in trying to solve unsolvable mathematical equations that he wouldn't notice if a meteor hurtled into his study, never mind if the driveway was more green than black due to the weeds growing through cracks in the asphalt. I pulled into the sprouting driveway with a feeling of relief. At least being with them would take my mind off my troubles.

Not bothering to knock, I opened the screen door and let it slap shut behind me. The noise called to mind my mother's constant reminders of "Don't let the screen door bang" from my childhood.

"Hey, guys, it's just me," I called. The air smelled faintly of books from the shelves lining every wall—and I mean *every* wall—and more strongly of corned beef and cabbage in the slow cooker. I decided I would stay for dinner.

"Out here, dear."

As if I didn't know where my mother was. In the summer, she spent approximately 90 percent of her waking hours at the patio table in the backyard, stack of books in a chair beside her, and a laptop and a bag of corn chips on the table. In the winter, she had the same setup in a small craft room off the kitchen. She'd been a librarian for years, and a voracious reader, and when online sites for booklovers popped up eight or ten years ago, she'd begun posting book reviews . . . by the thousands. She was both revered and feared in book circles and had been interviewed by national publications and even CNN about her reviewing.

I cut through the kitchen and out the sliding glass doors to the patio, where Mom sat in a webbed chair whose seat bowed ominously. She had naturally curly hair that she still wore almost shoulder length. Sheena at Sheena's Hair Jungle was responsible for dying it back to its original chestnut every month or so. She had a complexion like a magnolia, the envy of every woman north of forty in the entire town, which she attributed to her religious use of sunscreen and the hats she'd worn from childhood on. Today's was floral cotton with a floppy brim. Her eyes were hazel, like mine, and she had a wide mouth that was always slicked with bright lipstick. When my sisters and I were little, she used to let us pick out colors for her at the drugstore: Cherries Jubilation, Coral Splash, Neony Peony. She'd always had a tendency to put on weight and she'd ballooned since retiring from the library. Dad and I were seriously worried about her health. We were not alone— Mom worried about it, too, but since her worrying took the form of researching every new skin rash or cough and determining she had black lung disease or leprosy, she wasn't doing much about her real health problem: obesity and its nasty side effects. She was the reason I watched my weight so carefully.

"Hi, Mom." I kissed her soft cheek as she typed at the keyboard, and moved a stack of category romances so I could sit. "Writing a good review or a bad one?"

"Actually"—she looked up—"I noticed a red spot on my calf this morning when I got out of the shower. I'm trying to determine if it's Chagas or maybe Lyme disease. Do you think it looks like a bull's-eye?" She bent with an effort to pull up the hem of her cotton skirt.

I peered at her calf but could see nothing more than a reddened patch of dried skin. Knowing it was useless to downplay her concerns, I said, "Look, I've got a welt, too." I lifted my hair so she could see the bee sting.

"Oh, Amy-Faye. I hope it's not contagious."

I laughed. "It's a bee sting, Mom. Not to worry."

"It's my job to worry about all you kids," she said, finally shutting down the computer and giving me her full attention. Worry clouded her eyes. "Have you talked to your brother lately? He's fussing about the pub not opening on time—something about inspections? And I think he and Gordon have quarreled again, although he didn't say anything."

Gordon was Derek's business partner, a venture capitalist in his fifties who had financed restaurants, nightclubs, and bars in Texas and Colorado. He and Derek frequently argued because Gordon thought his investment gave him the right to make all the important decisions and my brother, the creative force and brewmaster behind the venture, disagreed. Frequently. Loudly. When he was mad, he called Gordon "Gekko" after the *Wall Street* character played by Michael Douglas.

"I'll call Derek," I said, "or maybe stop by. I've got some questions for him about the opening-night party, anyway."

"Thank you, dear," Mom said. "You're such a comfort." Her gaze strayed to the pile of books.

"The Readaholics just finished *The Maltese Falcon*," I said.

That got her attention. "Brilliant book. The way Hammett made it seem as if the book was about the falcon, when all along it's about Spade and his relationships, his failings, his character. The falcon is just a device. What did Hitchcock—I think it was Hitchcock—call it? A MacGuffin. No, the heart of the novel is Spade. It gives me chills every time I read his soliloquy about how when a man's partner dies he's supposed to do something about it." She shivered. "Ooh."

I looked at her, struck. *When a man's partner dies, he's supposed to do something about it.* Ivy wasn't my partner, but she was my friend and I suspected the principle applied. I felt better, suddenly, less worried about whether Troy or the police thought I was a headline-grabbing nutcase, and more sure that I was doing the right thing by looking into Ivy's death. Somehow, whether she meant to or not, my mom always made me feel better. I hugged her. "Thanks, Mom."

She beamed. "You're staying for dinner, aren't you? Go and bother your father until dinnertime. I've got to finish this book." She picked up the top book on her stack and turned to a bookmark at the halfway point. I laughed, kissed her again, and went to bother my father, as directed.

He was standing in front of the whiteboard in his study, making incomprehensible notations, and I snuck up and hugged him from behind. He started, and the marker fell to the floor.

"Amy-Faye!" He swept me into a bear hug, which was easy for him to do since he was roughly the size of a grizzly. He looked more like a mountain man than a mathematician, with his broad shoulders, bushy beard, now mostly gray except for a few reddish streaks, and lumberjack shirts. He squeezed me again and released me.

"Any progress?" I nodded toward the whiteboard.

He rocked his hand. "Maybe a little. We'll see where it leads."

He knew better than to go into more detail with me. It was a great disappointment to him that none of his children had inherited his mathematical abilities, not as related to abstractions and theories. I was orderly and logical, but numbers meant nothing to me. I could comprehend my accounts receivable and payables, but that was about it. My sister Natalie played competitive chess and was a grand master or some such but had refused to take any math classes past geometry. Derek could calculate any equation having to do with brewing beer at lightning speed in his head, but theoretical mathematics left him cold. Ditto for my other two sisters.

He checked the time. "How did it get to be five thirty already? Let's get an adult beverage and sit on the porch."

Beers in hand, we settled on the swing on the front porch and I told him about my week, not mentioning the threatening note. He listened carefully, like he always did, and patted my knee once or twice. "I was sorry to hear about Ivy," he said. "A bit flighty, but I always liked her." After a pause, he added, "So you're planning Doug Elvaston's wedding?"

He kept his voice casual, but I wasn't fooled. I was not going to get drawn into another discussion of Doug. Deliberately focusing on a small beetle crawling along the porch railing, I said, "Yep. It was nice of him and Madison to throw some business my way."

I felt his gaze on my profile but refused to meet his eyes. After a moment, he made a comment about a church function he and Mom had been to, and I relaxed. We chatted for half an hour and then moved inside to set the table and summon Mom for dinner. I left a bit before seven, feeling much better than when I arrived.

As I approached my house in the gathering dusk, though, my uneasiness returned. I sat in the van after I parked it, staring at the house. *This is stupid.* Someone had left a note taped to my door. It wasn't like they'd been inside. I got out of the van, slammed the door, and marched up my front steps. No ugly note on the door. I yanked off the piece of tape that had secured the earlier threat. Taking a deep breath, I put the key in the lock, pushed the door wide, and flicked on the lights. Nothing moved. The house looked just as it had when I left. My purse was on the kitchen counter where I'd set it, and my expandable folder was on the floor where I'd knocked it after reading the note. I knelt to pick up the receipts that had spilled from it. The fridge compressor kicked on and I started. Feeling faintly foolish for getting so worked up, I scooped up the rest of the receipts and stuffed them willy-nilly into the folder. I'd sort them tomorrow.

Crossing to the sink to wash my hands, I heard a click and the faint sigh that told me the front door had been opened. *Oh my God.* I jerked open the nearest drawer and scrabbled for a knife. My fingers closed around a handle.

Chapter 14

I whirled and brandished my weapon. "Stop right there or I'll—"

"Take on all three of us with a spatula?" Maud asked. Lola's and Kerry's heads poked from behind her. Something brushed against my ankle and I squeaked and dropped the spatula.

"Mew?" Misty looked up at me, hurt by my reaction.

I scooped to pick her up and cradle her against my cheek. "I thought you guys were . . . Well, I was afraid . . ." Dang. That stupid note on my door had upset me more than I'd realized. I'd completely forgotten the Readaholics were coming over to discuss our next steps, or even whether we should continue looking into Ivy's death. I was glad I'd been armed only with a kitchen utensil. What if I'd had a gun handy and shot one of my friends by accident?

"Spatulas are the latest advance in nonlethal home-protection devices." I tried to sound like an infomercial as I retrieved the "weapon" and tossed it in the sink.

"'I've got a spatula and I'm not afraid to use it,'" Maud quipped, going along with my relief-induced silliness.

The other two stared at me with concern. "You did say eight, didn't you?" Lola asked.

"I brought donuts," Kerry added, waving a bakery bag. "On sale at City Market when I stopped in for a deli chicken. Are you okay? You look a little pale."

"I'm fine," I said, setting Misty down to explore and helping myself to a donut. "I just lost track of time."

Apparently Brooke had, too, because she wasn't here. Taking care to lock the front door, I led the women into the sunroom. Misty trotted after us, tail held high.

"Brooke called to say she couldn't make it," Lola said, seating herself. "Something about her mother-in-law."

It stung that Brooke hadn't called me. She must still be upset about the way I'd left today, or maybe she believed, like Troy did, that I was involved in this investigation for the wrong reasons. I pushed my hurt aside and filled my friends in on what had happened the past couple of days.

"So," Maud summed up, no-nonsense gaze fixed on me, "you discover that Ivy's house has been ransacked and find the coded ledger page, which you—for some damn fool reason—turn over to the police. Within hours—*hours*—someone booby-traps your picnic with a beehive and leaves you a threatening note. Too cutesy by half, but still threatening. I mean, 'fatal' isn't something to mess with." She tucked her chin and looked at us meaningfully.

"What?" Kerry said with some asperity. "You're saying the police are involved? Just because Amy-Faye gave them the ledger page and two days later a beehive turned up at her event? Puh-leeze."

"I don't believe in coincidences," Maud stated.

"No, you believe everything is a conspiracy," Kerry shot back.

"I don't think the beehive was a coincidence," Lola said slowly, "but I don't think there has to be a connection between Amy-Faye going to the police and the bees. What about that reporter?"

"There's no telling who she might have mentioned me to," I said. "She's really gung ho about tracking down the story Ivy was supposed to give her. For all I know, she went straight from our meeting to Clay and Fee and Doug to ask them what they were doing at Ivy's house."

"I wonder what they were doing," Kerry mused. "Seems a little strange."

"Seems a lot strange," Maud corrected.

"If we knew where Ivy got that ledger page, it would help us sort through it all," Lola said, stroking Misty, who had settled into a purring ball on her lap.

"You're sure it wasn't Ivy's handwriting?" Kerry asked.

"Pretty sure," I said.

"Here, why don't you take a look?" Maud pulled an iPad from her purse, tapped the screen a couple of times, and held up the screen so Kerry and Lola could view the ledger page.

Lola took the iPad. She peered at it and said, "I don't recognize it. But then, I don't know whose writing I would recognize, outside of Mom's and Axie's. You never see anyone's handwriting anymore, do you? I mean, we don't get letters and such—everything's digital." She passed the iPad to Kerry.

Kerry squinted at the screen and then took out a pair of reading glasses. "I hate these things," she said, slipping them on. "It seems like yesterday I could read the fine print on an aspirin bottle, and now I can't read anything smaller than a billboard at close range without these cheaters. Getting old sucks. You'll be here before you know it," she said, shooting Lola and me a look over the top of the glasses. Satisfied that we were properly cowed by the thought of advancing infirmity, she tilted the iPad to read the screen. "It's just a bunch of numbers. How—? Oh, I don't believe it. I know who wrote this." She looked up, eyes troubled behind the magnifying glasses.

The doorbell rang. We all started. Misty jumped off Lola's lap and skittered to the door.

"Hold that thought," I said, following the kitten. I approached the door a bit warily, but then told myself not to be stupid. No one who wanted to deliver a "fatal sting" was going to march up to the door and ring the bell. Nevertheless, I inched the blinds aside on the narrow window beside the door and flicked on the porch light. Brooke stood there.

I swung the door wide. A gust of wind almost banged it out of my hand. A front was coming through.

"Sorry I'm late," she said, hugging me and dropping a gym bag on the floor. Her mink-colored curls tickled my cheek. "Clarice." She delivered her mother in-law's name as if it explained not only her lateness but also the proliferation of nuclear weapons and the cancellation of *Firefly*, one of my all-time favorite shows.

"I thought you weren't coming," I said, returning her hug. "I wasn't sure—"

"Yeah. That. I'm sorry about earlier. I was stupid. Troy was stupider. I know you're not in this for the attention."

"It's not like *I've* ever entered a beauty pageant," I said.

"Ouch." The former Miss Colorado laughed.

"What's the bag for?"

"I'm staying. My best friend has been threatened by an unknown nutter—she's not spending the night alone. I'm your new bodyguard. You'll find my rates very reasonable: pancakes. I want pancakes for breakfast."

Acting like it was no big deal, she picked up Misty and headed to the sunroom. I followed, feeling warmed by her concern but sensing a little tension under her insouciant manner.

"Brooke's here," I announced.

"Who is it?" Maud asked impatiently.

It took me half a sec to realize she was talking to Kerry.

Kerry licked her lips and said, "It's Clay Shumer's handwriting. I see it all the time on financial reports, notes . . . daily."

We were all silent for a moment, absorbing the implications. Ivy had copied a coded ledger page written by her boss and mailed it to herself. Why?

Brooke looked bewildered. "I'm lost."

We gabbled at her, filling her in on the happenings of the last two days. She already knew some of it from my visit after getting the threatening note, but she listened as everyone talked at her.

Maud finally ended the recital. "This is a good thing," she said. We stared at her. "Now that we know who wrote the coded page, we can figure out what book he used and break the code."

"How do we do that?" Brooke asked.

"Simple," Maud said. "Someone gets into his office—he has to be keeping the ledger in his office because Ivy couldn't Xerox a page from a book he kept at home—and makes a list of all his books. Then we try the code against all of them until we find the right one. The book's got to be there—this kind of code isn't something he could do from memory."

We all looked at Kerry, whose mayoral office was in the same building.

"Uh-uh," she said. "I am the mayor. It may be only a part-time, piddly-ass job that pays less than a Walmart greeter, but I owe this city some dignity and integrity—I cannot be caught rifling through the office of the city's CFO. I could, however, keep him tied up in a meeting if one of you wants to catalog his books."

Everyone's eyes shifted to me.

"Aren't you planning a waste-of-time-and-city-funds offsite for his office?" Maud asked.

I wouldn't have described it quite like that. "Ye-es."

"So you've got a reason to go there."

"I suppose I could tell him I need to talk to him about it," I said, warming to the idea. "While I'm there, Kerry could call down and say she needs to see him. That would give me a chance to take a look at his books."

Kerry nodded. "Easy."

Easy. Famous last word.

When the others had left, Brooke and I changed into our pajamas and made up the futon in my small second bedroom/office. I made hot cocoa and popped a quartet of freezer cookies into the oven. The scent of melting peanut butter and chocolate filled the kitchen. Brooke busied herself sponging the counter off and moved the canisters to clean behind them. "What's this?" she asked, holding up a baggie of what looked like potpourri.

It took me a second. "I'll bet Ivy left that," I said. "Her tea."

We stared at it, both of us wondering, I was sure, if the Baggie contained oleander. "I'll give it to Detective Hart," I said, taking it from Brooke with two fingers.

The discovery was a little sobering, and we were silent for a few minutes. Brooke picked up the used glasses from the sunroom, wiped down the microwave, and had started alphabetizing the spices lined up on the back of my stove when I observed, "I'm not expecting Clarice anytime soon."

"Oh!" She dropped the cumin bottle she was holding, then slotted it between the cilantro and the curry. After a half second, she pulled it out again and defiantly placed it after the paprika. "That woman makes me—" She growled with frustration. "I don't know what she makes me. Batty. Bananas. Suicidal."

"Don't say that."

"Kidding."

"Not funny." I topped the cocoas with whipped cream and handed her a steaming mug. "Is Troy okay with you spending the night here?"

She ran her forefinger around the mug rim and licked off the whipped cream. "We might have had a little . . . spat after his mother left."

Clutching my mug and a plate with the cookies, and with the whipped cream can tucked under my arm, I led the way into the small den. I set everything down and turned on the gas fireplace. It was chilly tonight, with a cold front expected before morning. The wind was already picking up, rattling loose screens and whipping tree branches so they scraped the roof. Colorado weather was always changeable; if you don't like the weather, wait twenty minutes, the natives said. Brooke settled into the cozy chair and a half and tucked her bare feet beneath her.

"Tell me," I said, seating myself in the recliner by the fire. I bit into a cookie. *Um.* Nothing like warm, crumbly cookie.

She sighed, coiling a lock of hair around her finger. "It's nothing new. Just her usual attempt to manage every detail of our lives. Troy mentioned to his sister that we had an appointment to talk about IVF, and Bev—of course!—told Clarice and Troy Sr., so Clarice hotfooted it over to tell us how unacceptable that was. By the time she left, Troy was wavering and I . . . I just lost it, Amy-Faye." Misery dragged down Brooke's lovely mouth. "I told him he wasn't married to his mother, he was married to *me*, and that he should be more concerned with my happiness, *our* happiness, than with her happiness. I said something about how wives could offer benefits mothers never could—just trying to lighten things up a bit, you know—and he came back with 'We never have sex for fun anymore—it's just for trying to conceive.' Oh, A-Faye, he's right. I can't remember the last time we fooled around without timing it around ovulation or thinking that we *had* to do it."

She drank down half her cocoa and I could tell she half wished it was a bottle of vodka. Getting out of the recliner, I padded over and gave her a big hug. "Brooke. There's nothing wrong with wanting a baby. And nothing wrong with wanting your husband to put you and your relationship first." I paused, considering my next words. No one, not even best friends, wants unsolicited advice. "Have you ever thought about seeing someone? You know, a counselor?"

"Troy says we don't need a third party poking his nose into our marriage."

"Of course not—you've got Clarice."

Brooke made a sound somewhere between a burp and a laugh. Tears trickled down her face.

"Maybe you could take the advice Troy gave me—get away. Take a long weekend somewhere—Denver, Salt Lake, Vegas. Don't tell anyone where you're going. Promise each other you will not make love, no matter what, but take that Victoria's Secret teddy you got for your last birthday just in case."

Brooke gasped and then laughed a real laugh. "You are so perfect, Amy-Faye. That's why I love you. I'll do it. We'll do it. I'll talk Troy into throwing a change of clothes into a bag and driving to the airport. We'll decide when we get there where we want to go." She wiped away her tears and hugged me. "Do you have any schnapps? This hot chocolate could use some livening up."

We finished the cocoa, a quarter bottle of peppermint schnapps, and the whipped cream, taking turns squirting it straight into our mouths, while watching an *Iron Man* marathon on TV. By the time we went to bed, we'd both forgotten the threatening note, which was the reason for the sleepover in the first place.

Chapter 15

I had butterflies in my tummy as I approached Clay Shumer's office just before three o'clock on Monday. Kirsten, his new administrative assistant, had said he could squeeze me in. She'd seemed a little miffed that I wanted to go over her head to talk about the offsite, but I mollified her by saying I needed Clay's "vision" of what he hoped to accomplish. I'd dressed carefully in a nubby cream sweater and dark red wool pants to offset the chilly temps, and my hair swished loose, held back from my face by a tortoiseshell headband. I tried to channel Brigid O'Shaughnessy and her devious noir sisters, readying myself to lie and deceive and peek into places I had no business peeking in pursuit of my ends. The ends, in this case, justified the means, I tried to convince myself, knocking on Clay's half-open door. A twinge of guilt told me Brigid probably told herself the same thing.

"Come."

Pinning a smile to my face, I pushed into Clay's office. As befitted a city government office, it was utilitarian rather than luxurious. White walls and gray carpet that needed a good vacuuming. A basic desk piled with folders and papers. The desk also held a computer, a phone, and a bowl with a listless Siamese fighting fish. Two small frames had their backs to me. I bet they contained photos of Fee. A window beside the desk looked down on the side of the building to a small park where a pair of mothers watched their preschoolers swing and push a merry-go-round. Behind the desk stood a nightmare, however: a glass-fronted bookcase filled with books. I seated myself on a black, faux leather love seat and stared at them in dismay until Clay's voice brought me out of it.

"Ms. Johnson?" He sounded impatient, like he'd said my name more than once. He sat behind the desk, having risen when I entered and reseated himself, and the glare from the window beside him ruddied one side of his face. His tawny hair was gelled back from his low forehead, making his somewhat bulbous nose seem even more prominent. He was handsome enough, if you liked your men on the fleshy side, but he didn't appeal to me. I tried to study him objectively, to see what had attracted Ivy, but it escaped me.

I took a deep breath. "Thank you for making time to see me. I know you must be busy, that things must be unusually hectic without Ivy."

"She kept things running smoothly, certainly. We all miss her," he said, his gaze shifting from the photos on his desk to something outside the window. Obviously feeling he should say something more, he added, "She worked here for a long time."

"I saw you and your wife at Ivy's funeral. It was wonderful to see so many people from city hall there."

He flushed slightly. "Ivy was well liked. Even beloved."

With an effort, I kept my brows from soaring. I was pleased on Ivy's behalf that he'd used the L-word, even in such a vague context.

Clay leaned in, fixing his blue eyes on me. "I heard you found her the morning she . . . got sick."

I nodded.

"Did she . . . did she go peacefully? I wouldn't want to think of her being in pain." There was strain in his voice as it dropped to a whisper.

"She was pretty ill," I told him without mentioning the sordid details. "But she was almost unconscious when I got there and by the time the EMTs arrived, I think she was out of it." A memory surfaced. "She mentioned you."

He jolted back as if stuck by a cattle prod. "What did she say?" It came out louder than he intended, and he asked it again in a lowered voice.

I tried to remember it exactly. "Something about it not being your fault."

"What wasn't my fault?"

I shook my head, "No, that's not it. She said something like 'Clay didn't mean . . . ,' something, something. At least, that's what I think she said. She was really sick and I could barely understand her. I'm sorry."

Looking shaken, he ran a hand across his fore-head. "No, it's okay."

Taking advantage of his discombobulation, I asked, "What took you to her house the day after she died?"

"What? How did you—?" A thick tongue swiped his lower lip. "She had papers from the office, important papers, time-sensitive papers. I had to—" Apparently recollecting that he didn't owe me an explanation for anything, he stiffened, looked at his watch, and said, "I'm running short on time. Kirsten said you needed to talk about the offsite?"

I went into some rigmarole about how the boss's vision was vital to planning the offsite. "The activities need to reflect the boss's personality and leadership style," I babbled, trying desperately to memorize book titles. An impossible task. There must have been forty books. They ranged from dictionaries and other reference books (including a baby-names book) to public administration tomes and finance snoozers. I willed Kerry to call and say she needed to see him immediately.

Clay leaned back in his chair and laced his fingers together over his chest. "My vision? Well, I guess you could say I'm all about inclusiveness and efficiency. I take my job as Heaven's CFO seriously—very seriously—and I insist that those who work for me remember we really all work for Heaven and its citizens."

Cue patriotic chorus. I nodded.

"We work for you, Ms. Johnson."

He expounded on this theme for another ninety

seconds while I wrote down book titles (real page turners like *Reinventing Government: How the Entrepreneurial Spirit Is Transforming the Public Sector*), pretending I was taking notes. He was winding down and I was trying to think of another question when the phone rang. *Yay, Kerry!*

He answered it with a brisk "Shumer." Fifteen seconds of monosyllables and listening later, he hung up. "I'm afraid I have to see the mayor, Ms. Johnson. Perhaps we can reschedule if there's anything else we need to discuss?"

"I don't mind waiting," I said, not getting up, even though he was moving toward the door. *This wasn't how it was supposed to go. He was supposed to ask me to wait so I could inventory his books while he talked to Kerry.*

"I don't know how long this will take," he said. "She said five minutes, but the mayor does like the sound of her own voice." He smiled to show he didn't mean to sound snide.

Reluctantly I got to my feet. This whole charade was going to be a bust if I couldn't get the book titles. WWKMD? My foot nudged my purse and gave me an idea. Surreptitiously pushing it under the love seat with my toe, I beelined for the door, hoping Clay wouldn't notice my purse. Once we were in the hall, I shook his hand, thanked him for his time, and almost dragged him toward the elevators so he wouldn't lock the office door. When the elevator arrived with a ding, headed up, I saw him onto it with a cheerful wave and said, "I'll catch it on the way down."

When I was sure the doors were shut and the

'vator was rising, I said, "My purse!" for the benefit of anyone who was watching (not that I saw anyone) and hurried back to Clay's door. Ducking into the office, I was conscious of my heart thudding against my ribs. I closed the door. Funny how being in here alone was sending my blood pressure skyrocketing, when I'd been in this same office only moments before with no effect. I pulled my cell phone from my purse and scurried around the desk to open the glass doors fronting the book cabinets. They squeaked. I threw an involuntary look over my shoulder. *Silly.* No one could have heard it through the closed door.

I immediately began photographing the rows of books on Clay's shelves. Maud had warned me that we had to know the exact edition for each book, since the page numbering changed from edition to edition sometimes, so I tried to photograph the spines close up, which meant I could get only six or eight books in each picture. After each photo, I glanced at the door. By the time I reached the bottom row, sweat was trickling down my sides and I was practically hyperventilating. I was *so* not cut out to be a spy, or a PI like Kinsey Millhone, or anyone else whose job entailed sneaking around places where getting caught would result in embarrassment, humiliation, and a possible prison sentence.

The phone on Clay's desk rang. I jumped. I stared at it, hypnotized, until it quit after four rings. The heck with this. I snapped a single photo of the last shelf of books and turned to go. As I did, I knocked against the desk and one of the framed photos fell. I righted it. It was a casual shot of Fee and Clay, arms around each other's waists, on the deck of a cruise ship sailing in warmer climes, if Fee's teeny bikini was anything to go by. She looked darn good. I wished I could afford a cruise.

A footstep sounded in the hall. I lunged away from the desk and was halfway across the room before I realized the steps were passing the office. Letting out a long breath, I grabbed my purse. I was getting out of here. A thought stopped me. What if Shumer didn't keep the codebook on public display? What if it was in his desk? My watch told me only three and a half minutes had gone by since I'd walked him to the elevator, even though it felt like an eternity. Kerry had promised to keep him for at least five minutes. With a stifled "Aaagh," I returned to the desk and jerked open the middle drawer. No books. Ditto for the drawers down the left side. I paused to listen but heard no one approaching.

Conscious of time ticking away, I yanked open the top right drawer. It held a paperback edition of *Ender's Game* and a box of condoms. Eew. They made me want to spray the sofa I'd been sitting on with Lysol. Making mental note of the book, I closed the drawer. The second drawer stuck when I pulled at it, then slid open quickly enough to knock me off-balance when I tugged again. My mouth dropped open slightly when I saw its contents. A gun, black and menacing, nestled against a bottle of aspirin, a toothbrush and mini toothpaste, a packet of gum, and a spare shirt, still in its wrapper. I stared at the gun for a moment, wondering why the heck Clay kept a weapon in his office, then slammed the door closed as if the gun were a tarantula liable to spring at me. The snap of the drawer against the desk frame was loud enough to be heard in the hall, I was sure. I needed to vamoose. I gave a perfunctory tug on the lowest drawer—locked—before rising.

The doorknob turned.

Oh no. What would I say? How could I explain—? As unnerving thoughts swirled like disoriented bats, I almost hurdled the desk to get back to the vicinity of the love seat and my purse.

The door opened inward about a foot, then stopped. I heard voices but couldn't make out the words over the panicked buzzing in my ears.

I grabbed my purse by the strap and it tilted, dumping out a lipstick. It rolled under the love seat. Screw it.

I took a stride toward the door as it opened wider, admitting someone totally unexpected.

Chapter 16

"What the hell are you—?" Brooke's father-in-law, Troy Widefield Sr., got a grip on himself. "I apologize for my language, Ms. Johnson. I wasn't expecting to see you. Where's Clay?" His eyes under unruly white brows were watchful. The shoulders under an expensive charcoal-colored suit were squared and tense.

"Uh, I was just leaving," I said. "Clay got called up to the mayor's office. We were talking about the office offsite. I forgot my purse." I held it up as proof that my presence here was ordinary, routine, unsuspicious. My mouth was dry. "I'm sure Clay will be back any minute, if you have an appointment with him."

Sidling around Mr. Widefield, I reached the door. Escape was in view. I wanted to be gone before Clay returned.

"Just a minute, Ms. Johnson. Amy-Faye, right?"

Reluctantly turning back to face Widefield, I saw his expression was less certain than usual.

"You and my daughter-in-law, Brooke, have been friends for a long time."

He paused, as if expecting a response, so I said, "Yes."

He worked his jaw. "She's probably told you that she and my son want children."

I cocked my head noncommittally. *Where was he going with this?*

"You know that Troy Jr. is headed for a career in politics. His mother and I think it would be advantageous for him to get his feet firmly established on the political ladder before disrupting things with children. I know I can trust you to keep it under your hat until the official announcement, but he's throwing his hat in the ring for the state senate in the next election."

"Really?" I wondered if Brooke knew that, or even Troy Jr., and why Widefield was sharing it with me.

"Yes. In fact, you should be in charge of organizing the announcement event. How about I have his campaign manager get in touch with you about that?"

"I'd be happy to," I said, still not sure I understood his agenda, but always ready to take on more work.

"And if you and Brooke get to chatting about children, you could mention how much easier a campaign will be without an infant to worry about. Can't have the candidate's wife photographed changing diapers or breastfeeding the baby!" He forced a chuckle, but I could tell the idea of tending to the baby's biological needs in public disgusted him. I suspected he hadn't changed a single diaper for Troy Jr. or his sister. "You strike me as a sensible young woman—you're getting your business on a solid footing before settling down—so you should be able to help Brooke see the pluses to waiting a bit, just like you have."

"I wouldn't put my two cents' worth in without being asked," I said more hotly than was politic, but his cool assumption that he could buy my influence with Brooke for a job or two pissed me off royally. "That's a decision for her and Troy to make. It's none of my business." I didn't add *or yours*, but he got the point because his nostrils flared in his otherwise frozen face.

I heard the elevator doors ding open down the hall and added hurriedly, "I've got an appointment, Mr. Widefield, so if you'll excuse me . . . Oh, and I'll look forward to talking to Troy or his campaign manager about the announcement event." With a bright smile, I took off in the opposite direction from the elevators.

I felt like I had a target painted between my shoulder blades and I didn't relax until I rounded a corner. No one tried to stop me. I descended the stairs with shaky legs and paused for a moment in the lobby to steady myself as the adrenaline leached out of me. What business did Widefield have with Clay? This was the second time in a week I'd seen them together. Maybe they were buddies. I had a hard time picturing the almost seventy-year-old, moneyed, and powerful Widefield being pals with the fortyish and much less successful Clay Shumer. I exited the building, grateful for the blast of chilly air that greeted me and blew away some of the tension of the last half hour. It didn't matter what Widefield wanted with Clay. I wasn't going to worry about that or his un-characteristically clumsy—because spur-of-the-moment?—proposition to me. Right now, I needed to get the book photos to Maud so she could get busy on cracking the code.

I sent the photos to Maud from my car and got a return text telling me she'd get right on the code breaking. I texted her again to tell her about *Ender's Game* and she replied immediately to say she'd try that one first. "Well done, AF!" she added. I texted the other Readaholics to let them know the mission was accomplished and then headed to the office.

A note asking me to call Flavia Dunbarton waited for me on my desk. Returning her call, I got voice mail, left a message, and hung up. The call made me realize I needed to find a way to suss out what Fee Shumer and Doug had been doing at Ivy's house the day after she died. I'd gotten Clay's version of why he was there, and it sounded plausible. Despite that, I wasn't sure I believed him. I was trying to come up with a way to tackle Fee when Al popped his head in.

"That cop is here again," he said. He disappeared and Detective Lindell Hart's tall frame filled the doorway.

"Hi," I said, smiling, surprisingly happy to see him. "What's up?"

He gave me the kind of smile that told me he

was here on official business, and my smile faded
a bit. Had he learned something new about Ivy's
case?

In a tone caught between humor and gravity, he
said, "I'm here about a stolen beehive."

That took me by surprise. "The one at the Boy
Scout picnic?"

"Apparently." Rather than seat himself in one
of my client chairs, he crossed to the window and
propped himself against the deep sill, folding his
arms over his chest. "A farmer named Udo Yasutake called the station this morning to report
that one of his beehives was missing. He was quite
worried about the bees. Apparently, they don't
like changes in their routine. Mabel Appleman
took Mr. Yasutake's call. Her grandson is a Cub
Scout and he was at the picnic Sunday afternoon.
See where this is going? She told us about his getting stung. We drove over to the park and found
the missing hive. A call to the Boy Scout leader—
not one of your biggest fans—got us your name as
the one in charge of putting the event together.
Any idea how the hive ended up there?" He asked
it almost quizzically.

"Of course not," I said. "I certainly didn't put it
there, as you might well guess. The darn bees dis-
rupted the picnic and probably cost me future
business." I hesitated. "You might as well see this."
I hadn't planned on showing the police the threatening note, but since he was here . . . I pulled it out
of my purse, where I'd stuck it after taking it to
show Brooke, and walked it over to Hart.

He took it with a questioning look and read it

quickly. His lips tightened. "Where did you get this?"

I went through the whole story.

"Why didn't you bring it in?"

I shrugged. "I felt stupid. My friends thought I was making a big deal out of nothing. It felt . . . lame to bother the police with it."

He took my chin between his thumb and forefinger and tilted my face up. I blinked at him in surprise. "Well, why didn't you bother me with it?"

I had no answer. After a moment, he released my chin, pulled a plastic Baggie from his pocket, and tucked the note into it. "Probably a lost cause," he said, "since everyone you know has handled this, right?" At my nod, he continued, "But we'll see if we can raise some prints anyway. You said it was taped to your door—do you still have the piece of tape the writer used? It would hold prints better."

I shook my head sheepishly. "Threw it out."

"Any idea—any at all—about who would have sabotaged your function with the bees and left the note? Who's mad at you, Amy-Faye?"

Confession time. "The only thing I can think is that it's tied to Ivy's death. I've been poking around some, asking questions, and I think someone might be worried that I'll discover the truth."

Hart blew out a long, exasperated breath. "You sound like your friend Maud. There's no 'truth' to uncover. Ivy poisoned herself. End of story."

"What about the tea from her office?" I began hotly. "It—"

"Was tea. No oleander. It was a harmless herbal

concoction sold to millions by a retailer called Tea-vana. I got the report this morning."

I was quiet for a moment, absorbing the news. If the tea at her office was undoctored, did that mean that Ivy had, in fact, committed suicide? Wait . . . "What about the ledger page?"

A line appeared between Hart's brows. "What ledger page?"

I stared at him. "The one Ivy mailed to herself. The one written in code that I dropped off at the police station Friday night. I wanted to see you, but Officer Ridgway said you were in Grand Junction."

His frown deepened. "I didn't get it. Maybe Ridgway passed it to Chief Uggams. I'll track it down when I get back to the station. How, exactly, do you think this 'ledger page' relates to Donner's death?"

He listened to my involved story and the Read-aholics' combined thoughts on the page with a neutral expression tending toward disbelieving by the time I was done. Reading his face, I finished on a defensive note, using Maud's logic. "It doesn't make sense for something so strange not to be connected to Ivy's death."

"Amy-Faye." He paused as if to temper his words. "Amy-Faye. You intercept a letter at Ivy's house that you *think* she mailed to herself. There's been no handwriting analysis, so we don't even know that much. The letter turns out to contain a page your conspiracy-fiend friend Maud says is coded. You leap to the conclusion that it's related to Ivy's death because the two things happened within a day of each other. Faulty logic. If I walk into the Salty Burro and two minutes later it bursts into flame, it doesn't mean that I had anything to do with the fire. Just because two events occur within close proximity doesn't mean there's a causal relationship."

I would have interrupted, but he held up an "I'm not done" finger. "Even if Ivy did mail herself the page, it doesn't mean there's anything mysterious about it. Maybe it's something she requested that required her to send a self-addressed, stamped envelope to receive it."

I'd never thought of that. "But—"

"Maybe she plays chess, or some other game, long-distance with a friend and the 'code' is chess notations."

"It's not. I'd recognize chess notations; my sister's a grand master."

He looked interested at that. "Really?"

"Uh-huh."

"Okay, so it's something else. My point is, you and your friends have built this elaborate 'murder in small-town America' plot out of—if not thin air, then something remarkably similar. You have no proof. You've watched too many episodes of *Murder, She Wrote*. This is not Cabot Cove."

He had me questioning everything I'd accepted as fact until I remembered my trump card. I played it triumphantly. "The handwriting on the ledger page is Clay Shumer's. Kerry recognized it."

That gave him pause. After a long moment, he said, "Look, I'll dig up the page when I get back to the station and have a look at it. Then we'll talk again. Until then, leave this alone. If you're right and the threat is linked to Ivy's death, you don't want to go poking around anymore. Chances are it's related to something else entirely—"

"How many people do you think are that mad at me?" I asked with some indignation.

He grinned and I felt a flutter in my abdomen. "No telling. It's most likely a prank, but I'm taking it seriously. Keep a low profile until you hear back from me, hm?"

It wasn't until after he was gone that I realized I hadn't told him about Flavia Dunbarton and her conversation with Ivy about a big, scandalous, criminal story. Simple oversight? Or my reluctance to point him in Flavia's direction against the reporter's will? I would wait and see what Hart had to say after he examined the ledger page, and then decide whether or not to mention Flavia.

Right now I had a five thirty appointment with Madison Taylor at the country club where the reception was being held. Resolving to be congenial and professional, I gathered up my files and purse and headed out, telling Al to hold down the fort.

"The fort's going nowhere while I'm in charge, boss," he said, grinning.

Chapter 17

The Rocky Peaks Golf and Country Club, known more familiarly as "the Club," was five miles west of Heaven, several hundred feet in elevation lower than the town. It featured a links-style golf course that had significant elevation gains and losses over the course of its eighteen holes and that cost more to play than my monthly utility bill. This being Monday, the course was closed for maintenance. The pool was still covered at this time of year—it didn't open until Memorial Day—but there were people thwacking balls on the tennis courts, despite the chilly temps. The main club building, dating from the late 1800s, was built of enormous logs and furnished in lodge style, as were too many of the homes and vacation cabins in the area. Why on earth did living in the mountains mean all the decor had to feature moose, bears, and forest colors?

A broad veranda wrapped around the lodge on all four sides, and I crossed it to enter the lobby. A cavernous room with a stone fireplace big enough to roast a whole bison provided a focal point on one beamed wall, the logs blackened by smoke, and a bar, all copper and polished wood, took up the opposite wall. Danny, the bartender, waved to me and I waved back. Four huge chandeliers made of intertwined deer antlers lit the room. I didn't spot Madison immediately and was headed for the restaurant to begin a conversation with the manager about the reception details when I heard Madison's voice behind me.

"Oh, my."

I turned to see her staring up at the antler chandeliers.

"How many deer did they have to kill to make those?" She sounded distressed.

"They don't kill them," I said. "Deer shed their antlers each year. You can find them in the woods . . . kind of like driftwood."

"Oh." She laughed at herself. "That makes me feel better. Although that guy"—she pointed to a snarling grizzly head mounted over the door we'd come in—"is enough to take the edge off any celebration. Do you suppose he was from around here?"

"Half a century ago," I said. That bear had cost the hunter his leg, so the story went, in the mid-1960s. We still had bears in the area, plenty of 'em, but I didn't want to make Madison nervous. If she was going to live here with Doug—a big "if"—she'd run into one sometime.

She smiled and tucked her blond hair behind her ear. "Glad it wasn't yesterday. Anyway, hi, Amy-Faye. Doug says you and he got the guest list all sorted, so I guess we can move on to the fun stuff. I've got to go back to New York at the end of the week, so we need to get it all figured out today."

I led her across the lobby to the restaurant and introduced her to the manager, Wallace Pinnecoose, a quiet, highly competent man with the calm demeanor of someone who'd dealt with uncounted bridezillas, food poisonings, kitchen fires, and other emergencies too numerous (or well covered up) to mention over the course of his forty years in the restaurant industry. Within minutes, he and Madison were deep in conversation over the menu, table linens, and other details, with me interpolating a suggestion from time to time.

"If you want a reception line, it works best in the lobby," I said.

"Sounds good. Oh, and I don't want anyone flinging birdseed or rice at us. None of those fertility rituals." She laughed. "It's not like Doug and I want kids anytime soon, or even ever, necessarily."

I bit my lip. I knew Doug wanted kids, at least three of them. We'd discussed it numerous times while we were dating. Madison was young, I told myself; she'd grow to want kids, maybe after she made partner and felt more secure in her career. *None of my business, none of my business . . .*

Wallace intervened with a question about the passed hors d'oeuvres and we got back to the business at hand. Ninety minutes later, we had all the details hashed out, and Wallace escorted us to the bar, where he offered us a drink on the house and then excused himself. That was his habit whenever I brought a client out here to set up an event. I didn't particularly feel like having a drink with Madison, but she ordered a cosmopolitan, so I asked for an Angel Ale, one of my brother Derek's brews that the Club kept on hand.

"We're selling a lot of these," Danny said, sliding the bottle and a frosty glass onto the bar in front of me. "I'm looking forward to the brewpub opening." He presented Madison's cosmo with a flourish and a smile. She smiled back, not immune to his black Irish good looks and charm. Danny'd been in Heaven for three or four years, now, tending bar at the Club, and I don't think anyone knew where he'd come from. His skill with a shaker and his popularity with customers, male and female, gave him job security at the Club. He had a way with women and could banter like nobody's business, but he was careful not to overstep the line or piss off a woman's husband or date. He could just as easily talk hunting, golfing, or the Avalanche with the men without letting the conversation bore the women they were with. Quite a skill set. He occasionally moonlighted as a bartender for my events when he wasn't working at the Club.

"What brewpub?" Madison asked, sipping her drink.

I told her about my brother and his new business venture. "Oh, fabulous," she said. "Of course Doug and I will be there, unless we're in New York that weekend." She pulled out her phone and put the pub opening on her calendar.

I suppose I should have been grateful, for Derek's sake, but I found myself growling inwardly at the way she was already taking over their social calendar, making decisions without consulting Doug. *None of my business, none of my business . . .*

"So, A-Faye," she said. "Do you mind if I call you A-Faye? It's how Doug refers to you and it's just so *cute*. Tell me—"

"I prefer Amy-Faye, actually," I said. *Only my friends call me A-Faye.*

"Oh, well, sure." She accepted my correction with a smile. "I totally get it. I hate when anyone except my dad calls me Maddy. So tell me about Doug when he was in high school. I know he can't have been as perfect as he and his mom make out. I mean, it's high school and he was a jock." She smiled conspiratorially and leaned in so her hair swung forward in a golden swath. "Surely there's a good story or two? You must know them all since you were so close."

I worked at the bottle label with my thumbnail, trying to think of a response that wouldn't make me look like a total jerk. I didn't feel like sharing any of my memories of Doug with his bride-to-be, no matter how pleasant and engaging she might be. I didn't want to be her friend. Not yet, anyway. Maybe by the time they were celebrating their thirtieth anniversary. I pulled up a couple of lame recollections of pranks Doug had played on folks, and a story about the time he and a friend had sent a portapotty from a house construction site tobogganing downhill to its final resting place in the Club's swimming pool.

"Was anyone in it?" Madison asked, wide-eyed.

"The pool or the portapotty? Neither, actually. It was midnight."

"Goodness, that just doesn't sound like my Doug," she said.

That's because he was my Doug back then.

"Why, if something had gone wrong, he could have been sued. What if someone had gotten hurt? I'm sure it cost a lot to clean out the pool."

"Mr. Elvaston and Charlie's dad made Doug and Charlie do all the cleaning," I said with a reminiscent smile. "Took them two whole weeks of after schools and weekends." I'd been pretty sure Doug was going to smell like chlorine forever. The memory made me smile.

"You still care about him, don't you?" Madison asked, studying my face.

"Of course." I tried a carefree laugh. That didn't come off, so I chugged some beer and choked. Through my coughing, I said, "We've been friends forever."

"So you don't mind that he's marrying me? I know you guys have history, and if it's too painful, well, we'll completely understand if you want to back out of organizing the wedding. I'm sure there must be someone else we could hire, especially now that you've got it on track."

The "we, we, we" really got to me.

She gave me a kind and understanding look, full of sympathy—real or feigned?—and I squared my shoulders. I'd be damned if I was going to melt into a maudlin puddle of unrequited love in front of her.

"Madison, don't be ridiculous. It was over years

ago. *Years.* I'm sure there were men in your life before Doug, but you're not pining for them. You're probably relieved, like I am, that you didn't make the mistake of marrying one of those men when you were too young to know what real, lasting love was. Is. I feel really lucky that Doug and I are still friends and I'm glad he's found you. As a matter of fact, I'm seeing someone myself." I couldn't remember the last time I'd strung together so many lies at once. I emptied my beer.

"Really?" Madison perked up. "I didn't know. Who is he? I'll put him down as your 'plus one.'" She pulled out her phone, ready to make a note of my new boyfriend's name, and looked at me expectantly.

"His name's Lindell," I heard myself say. "Lindell Hart."

Chapter 18

In the van twenty minutes later, after escaping from Madison, I banged my head on the steering wheel. *Stupid, stupid, stupid.* Why had I let her goad me into telling her I was dating Lindell Hart? One lunch didn't exactly add up to a hot romance. Twilight had closed in while we strategized for the reception, and the evening's chill seeped through my sweater. I started the van and cranked up the heater. Maybe I could tell Madison that Hart couldn't come to the wedding because it was against his religion. No, the service was nondenominational, so that wouldn't work. I could tell her he was on duty that day. Or . . . the thought came to me as I made the turn onto Paradise Boulevard: I could actually ask him to go with me. The more I thought about it, the more I liked the idea. I wouldn't have to tell him we were supposedly "dating." I'd just casually mention the wedding and suggest it might be a great opportunity for him to get to know folks. The more I thought about it, the better I liked the idea. It would be far,

far better than showing up at Doug's wedding all by my lonesome.

Flashing lights caught my attention. They strobed from partway down a side street. What was going on? I slowed and craned my neck as I passed the turning. A fire truck was parked halfway down the block and firefighters were coiling up a big hose. Water puddled on the street. The truck blocked my view of the buildings and I rolled down my window to ask one of the gawkers what had happened. The acrid stench of smoke drifted in.

"It's the police station, Amy-Faye," the man, a friend of my father's, said. "I don' think it was anythin' big, though. Didn't take 'em but a couple minutes to put it out." He sounded a shade disappointed that there hadn't been a major conflagration.

"Was anyone hurt?"

"Nah. Closed up this time of night."

I'd forgotten that the station wasn't staffed at night. There was an officer or two on duty, I thought, but they were in patrol cars, not the station, and emergency calls were routed from somewhere else. Mesa, maybe. "Well, thank goodness for that," I said. The man waved, collected his wife from the ring of looky-loos, and headed up the sidewalk. I continued on my way home, trying to fight off the uneasy feeling that seemed to have worked its way into me with the smoke.

My phone rang as I got out of the van, and I looked at the display. Maud. My uneasy feeling intensified.

"Did you hear about the fire at the police station?" she asked when I picked up.

"I drove past it."

"Well, I heard about it on the scanner and made some calls. Care to guess what caught fire?"

"No."

"The evidence room," she said. "And I'll bet you my new Toshiba that the ledger page burned up. It's toast. Tell me you think that's a coincidence."

"Was it arson?"

"Looks like faulty wiring, although obviously they haven't done a full investigation yet."

"Faulty wiring sounds like a coincidence."

"Oh, Amy-Faye." Maud's weary sigh implied I was too naive for words. "There's no such thing as coincidence. Wait and see." She hung up.

Disproving Maud's theory that there are no coincidences, I found myself in line behind Detective Lindell Hart when I stopped in to the Divine Herb for coffee Tuesday morning. His curly brown hair was damp at the hairline and an image of him in the shower popped into my head, flustering me.

"Heard you had some excitement at the station last night," I said after we exchanged greetings. "In fact, I drove past as the firefighters were finishing up. Will you be able to work there?"

"It reeks, but yeah. Only a couple of rooms were affected, the evidence room and one office. My office and the chief's, as well as our waiting area, are fine. Smoky, but fine." He peeled the lid off his cup and blew on the coffee while waiting for me to pay for mine. I dug out my wallet, and when I did, something fell to the floor. Hart bent and came up with the Baggie of tea.

"Your stash?" he joked, holding it out to me.

I spilled coffee on my hand. "Ivy's," I said. "Ivy's tea. She brought it to my house for the book club, the night before she died. She must have left it by accident. Brooke found it night before last—it had gotten shoved behind my flour canister—and I was planning to give it to you. I put it in my purse this morning and was going to swing by your office later."

Hart gave me a look that seemed to question my story. Taking an evidence Baggie from his pocket, he put the tea Baggie into it. "Might as well test this, too," he said, voice neutral. "Just to be thorough."

Was I imagining it, or did the look he gave me say he was having the tests run because he doubted my story?

"She said she felt sick when she left my house," I remembered aloud.

Hart nodded. "You said that. Like I said, we'll test this. I'll put a rush on the test. This is turning into the case that never dies. Just when I think I've put it to bed forever, something new comes up." He patted the pocket where he'd stowed the evidence bag. "There's no other piece of evidence you've 'forgotten' to tell me about, is there?"

I didn't like his emphasis on "forgotten." "I don't suppose you had a chance to track down that ledger page yet, did you?" I asked pointedly. I accepted my change, and Hart and I moved to the condiments counter, where I added cream to my coffee.

"Actually, I found it at the bottom of the chief's

in-box, where Ridgway said he stuck it after you turned it in. Sloppy. I followed procedure and logged it into the evidence room before I left yesterday. I didn't really have a chance to study it—I was going to do that today." He gave me a rueful look.

"So it's gone," I said neutrally, my ears ringing with Maud's accusations.

"In all likelihood. We haven't inventoried everything yet, but it probably went up in smoke. I'm sorry. Do you have a copy, by any chance?"

"As a matter—" Something stopped me from confessing that we'd copied the page before turning it in. I wasn't absolutely convinced that the fire was an act of sabotage aimed at destroying the ledger page, but the coincidence—if that's what it was—was spooky enough to make me hesitate. "Why would we have a copy?" I asked instead.

He shrugged. "Long shot."

My brain was racing. Hours after I mentioned the ledger page to Hart, a mysterious fire at the police station burned it up. Would something similar happen to the tea I'd just given him? I stared at his profile as we made our way to the door through the caffeine addicts waiting for their fixes. What did I really know about him? He was new in town—from Atlanta. He was good-looking and seemed kind and competent—all things I found attractive. He had a sister and a brother. *He'd had a brother-in-law who was a firefighter, so maybe he knew all about how to set fires and make them look like accidents*. The thought popped into my brain, a product of my free-associating. He would have no reason to destroy the page, though, unless . . . unless he was somehow involved in Ivy's death.

I shook my head to dislodge the unwelcome thought. That was utterly ridiculous. He'd been in town only about ten minutes; he'd have no reason to kill Ivy or want to cover up for whoever did. We emerged onto the sidewalk. The day was sunny and crisp, with a promise of more seasonal temps later in the day.

"What caused the fire? Do they know?" I asked.

"Something electrical, I heard. We'll probably know more later today." He didn't sound worried about it.

I'd been going to mention the wedding to him, but now I hesitated. Oh, what the heck. Attending the ceremony with a possible arsonist/murderer was better than going alone. "Um," I started. "Um, I've been invited to a wedding—in fact, I'm organizing it—and I was wondering if you'd like to go with me. It's Saturday after next and I thought it might be a great opportunity for you to meet more people our age, you know, get to know more people here in town. I completely understand if weddings aren't your thing, though, and my feelings won't be hurt if—"

"Weddings are definitely my thing." Hart's eyes smiled down into mine and I felt a heat building that had nothing to do with arson. "I own a tux, can stumble through a fox-trot if I have to, and have caught more garters than anyone I know."

"Wow," I said, as if awed. "What a catalog of talents. You won't need the tux, though; it's a morning wedding."

"Too bad. I look devastating in a tux." He grinned.

I was sure he did. A little disconcerted by my reaction to him, I held up my coffee in a farewell gesture. "We can work out the deets later. I've got to get to work. We small-business owners have to scramble to make a living."

"Unlike those of us on the city payroll."

"You said it—I didn't." I scooted around the corner toward my office before he could get the last word. I passed a gaggle of women descending the stairs from the yoga studio, glowing from the exercise and chatting. Fee Shumer was among them, wearing a lavender and yellow yoga top and form-fitting capris. The top was loose enough to conceal any sign of pregnancy, if there was one. I greeted a couple of the other women, feeling guilty about not having been to a class in more than a week, and continued around to my office.

I came in through the French doors and stopped. Al was kneeling on the floor, khaki-clad butt facing me, painting what looked like a pink hippopotamus onto poster board. He looked at me over his shoulder. "You look cheery today, boss," he said. "Happy. Jolly."

"Lighthearted," I said automatically. "What in the world—?"

"It's for Alyssa Fenley's party tonight. She's the hippo-obsessed about-to-be-eight-year-old who wants to play 'pin the tail on the hippo.' I put in an order with JoyGraffics, but they did a rhino instead of a hippo." He pointed with the paintbrush at a piece of poster board leaning up against the wall. A two-horned rhino in sunglasses and a tutu twerked on the board. "They don't have time to redo it today—don't worry; they're giving us full credit plus a discount on our next order—so I'm doing my best."

"It looks great. I didn't know you had artistic talents."

"I've got all sorts of talents, boss." He laughed, dipped his brush into a vase full of water, and began to paint extravagant eyelashes on the hippo. "Remember I've got to leave by noon today. Class."

I left him to carry on and was almost to my office when he called after me, "Oh, your brother called."

I remembered guiltily that I'd told Mom I'd phone Derek and I'd forgotten. Plunking my purse onto the table, I dialed Derek's number. There were five of us kids in the family, but he was the only boy. In high school, I think he'd deliberately gone out for every sport, taken auto shop, and hung with a bunch of guys who smelled like locker rooms and diesel exhaust to make sure no girl stink—nail polish, hair products, basic soap and water—clung to him. Next in line after me, he was four years younger, but we'd always been close.

"Hey, brudder," I greeted him when he answered. "How's the brew biz?"

"Frustrating." He bit out the word. "Gordon has been surlier than a wolverine the last few days. I don't know what's up with him. The temperature gauge on my vat went haywire and I lost fifteen hundred gallons of a new brew. And the building inspector says the handicapped stall in the women's room isn't up to code. It's gonna be a cool two thou to redo it. I don't know, sis. Sometimes I feel like this venture is cursed."

"I'm sorry," I said, wishing there were something more concrete I could do to help, but my bathroom-remodeling skills were nonexistent, and what I knew about brewing beer could be inscribed on my pinkie nail. "Want me to have a talk with Gordon?"

That was a joke—Gordon and I did not see eye to eye. He'd asked me out a couple of times after Derek introduced us, but since he was twenty years older than me, had already seduced half the women in Heaven (according to the rumor mill), and was only separated from his second wife, I said no. We were polite to each other for Derek's sake, but that's as far as it went.

"Nobody can talk to Gordon these days," Derek said morosely. "I think his first wife's sicced a lawyer on him—something about nonpayment of alimony—and I don't think his recent trips to Vegas have been lucrative."

"How 'bout I pick you up and we go for ice cream? That'll make you feel better." Ice cream was our panacea for all woes. It had started in high school when he was a pitcher on the baseball team. I consoled him with ice cream whenever he lost a game. It had taken a whole gallon to help him get over the disappointment of not getting the baseball scholarship to CSU that he wanted. He returned the favor by taking me out for ice cream when I didn't get the part in the play, or when I tubed a test, and whenever Doug and I broke up.

"It's nine in the morning."

"So?"

"You're on." He sounded a shade more cheerful, and I was glad I'd called.

We had to go to the City Market to buy pints since none of the ice-cream parlors were open yet, and we ate them up by Lost Alice Lake, watching a second grade field trip group get a lesson in the area's geology. By the time I got back to the office, it was after ten and I was behind. It had been worth it, though; Derek looked considerably more relaxed when I dropped him back at Elysium Brewing than when I picked him up.

I worked like a demon until noon, fighting the urge to call Maud and ask if she'd made any progress on the code. She'd been somewhat daunted by the number of books Clay kept in his office and said it might be a couple of weeks before she found the right one. She'd call when she had anything to report. I gnawed on a hangnail. I didn't want to sit around and do nothing about Ivy's murder while Maud tried to crack the code. I still didn't know why Doug and Fee Shumer had visited Ivy's house the day after she died. It might be useful to know what they'd been doing there.

The only place I ever saw Fee was at yoga. We never said anything more than "good morning" to each other, but maybe I should plan on attending class tomorrow morning. I put it in my calendar with a note to bring my yoga gear. It would be easier to bump into Doug, but harder, in some ways, to grill him about what he was doing at

Ivy's. I didn't want him to think I thought he had anything to do with murdering her. I knew he hadn't. No way. Still, he might know something. I thought about how to approach him, how to engineer a meeting and ask the questions I needed to ask without pissing him off or making him clam up. An idea hit. I phoned and asked him to meet me at Bloomin' Wonderful.

"A-Faye, you know I'm not a flowers guy," he groaned. "I'll tell Madison you need—"

"No!" I wished I'd thought to tell him I needed his opinion on groom cakes or something. Too late now. "Wouldn't it be nice to . . . uh, have a special bouquet or plant delivered to Madison the night before the wedding with a note about how your love will continue to grow?" I covered the phone and gagged. "And one for your mom and Madison's mother? Just from you?" I was improvising, and I wasn't sure he would go for it. I held my breath.

"That is a nice idea," he said, "but you could pick out—"

"It should be personal."

After another long hesitation, he said, "Okay. But I've only got twenty-five minutes, so let's get going."

"Meet you there in five," I said.

Chapter 19

He beat me there and was waiting outside Lola's greenhouse when I pulled up. Sun glinted off the greenhouse glass, making the whole building seem to sparkle. With all the green inside, it looked like part of the set for the Emerald City. I didn't see Lola. Doug gave me an easy grin. "Hey, A-Faye. I didn't mean to carp at you. This is a good idea. And it's good to get out of the office." He turned his face up to the sun and unbuttoned his suit jacket.

I led the way inside and he followed me. It smelled lush and earthy and I breathed deeply of the humid air. Rows of plants—some in windowsill-sized containers on tables and others in huge planters—stretched before us. The sixty-six shades of green, plus the pops of color from blossoms, made me happy. No wonder Lola was such a calm person. Two sparrows flitted back and forth near the glass ceiling. It didn't take us long to pick out a rosebush to have delivered to Mrs. Taylor, his mother-in-law-to-be, at her house outside Oshkosh. "I'll bet she's got two dozen different kinds of roses in her garden," Doug said.

"Well, now she can have twenty-five," I said, crossing through her name. It took him a while to choose something for his mother, and longer still to find a plant he thought Madison would like.

"She's not really a plant person," he eventually said. "She says they're too much responsibility, what with needing to water them all the time and fertilize them and prune off dead leaves and what-have-you. She travels too much and they always die, which depresses her."

"Well, then, let's ask Lola to put together a bouquet."

He glanced at his watch and I knew he was going to take off soon, so I dragged him over to Lola, who had come in with Misty and was potting seedlings at a workbench in the back, and told her what we wanted. "Orange flowers," Doug said. "Madison likes orange. Orange and pink. She'll be staying at the Columbine the night before the wedding, so can you deliver them there?"

"Of course." Lola smiled. "I can include some tiger lilies and gerbera daisies, and perhaps carnations . . . Would you like to fill out a card to go with them?"

As we followed her out of the greenhouse to her office, I spotted three large plants in tubs by the door. I hadn't noticed them on the way in. Fuchsia blooms were gaudy against dark green leaves. "Hey, Lola, aren't those—"

She nodded grimly. "Oleander. This variety's called Calypso. I've decided not to carry any oleander anymore. A nursery from Mesa is sending a truck to pick them up."

Doug and I paused, staring at the plants, while Lola went on. "Poor Ivy," he said.

It was now or never. "So," I said, "I guess you didn't hear about her death right away, since you were at her house the day after she died." I tried to make it sound like a casual comment, but of course it came across about as casual as cement boots on a mob witness.

He gave me a long look, his face closing down. "How did you know that? Were you following me? Madison told me you were upset about us getting married, but I didn't believe . . . after all this time . . . How could you invade my privacy by following me? How could you sink so low?"

I was horrified. "No! No way. Of course I wasn't following you. It's nothing to me that you're getting married or who you're marrying, even if she can't even commit to an African violet—" I cut myself off before I babbled my way into deeper trouble. "No. A reporter was watching the house. She noticed you go in. I thought it was strange— that's all—because you told me you weren't really in touch with Ivy anymore. Of course I wasn't following you—how could you think that? I've got a life, Doug, and I'm sorry, but it doesn't revolve around you. Having Madison worship you has given you delusions of importance."

I rather liked that line. I waited, tense, hoping he would buy my uninterest. It was humiliating enough that half the town thought I was still pining for Doug; it would be slit-my-wrists time if he believed it, too.

He laughed ruefully. "Madison worships her career. I'm sorry, A-Faye. I'm an idiot. God! Put it down to prewedding jitters or something. Work stress, maybe. I was just surprised when you mentioned me being at Ivy's. She was a client. A recent client. We had an appointment Wednesday morning. And that's all I can tell you. Attorney-client privilege."

"Lawyers make house calls?"

He put on his poker face and I knew he wasn't going to tell me anything more. This investigating business was frustrating when people wouldn't cooperate. Spotting Lola coming toward us, I said, "Write something lovey-dovey on the card and get back to work before your wicked Boston boss docks your pay."

He grinned, scribbled something on the card and handed it to Lola, kissed my cheek, and said, "Mad and I are looking forward to choosing a band Thursday. See you then." He headed to his car. I resisted the urge to jerk the card from Lola's hand and read it.

"What was that all about?" Lola asked as we both watched Doug drive off.

I told her.

"Hm. So Clay went to Ivy's to retrieve some office papers, and Doug went because he didn't know she was dead and thought they had a meeting? Why in the world would Ivy need a lawyer?" Lola's tone gently questioned Doug's story.

"Good question. To make her will? That would shoot down the suicide theory, wouldn't it? I mean, if you're making a will because you're going to kill yourself, there's no point in killing yourself before you get around to the paperwork. How many unmarried, childless thirty-year-olds bother with wills? I don't have one. Do you?"

Lola nodded. "Oh, yes. I've got the business after all, and my grandmother and Axie to provide for."

Misty wound around my ankles and I started, laughed, and then bent to pat her. "Silly kitten. Well, Ivy didn't own a business, so she wouldn't need a lawyer for that. Maybe she was planning to sue someone." That didn't sound like Ivy, but I couldn't think of any other reason someone would need a lawyer, not unless they were on trial.

"Does Doug do that kind of legal work?"

"Not really. Who's that guy with the commercials, the ambulance chaser? Michael Werke. 'I'll make the legal system Werke for you!' He's the guy to call for suing people, I've heard."

We gave up trying to figure out what Doug had been doing for Ivy. Unless he told us, we were unlikely to ever know. I said good-bye to Lola, who headed around the side of the greenhouse. Taking a last look at the oleander plants, I picked up a shiny leaf that had dropped to the ground. That got me thinking. Anyone could have walked in here, or into any nursery in the area, and picked off a leaf or two, if they wanted to poison someone. You wouldn't even have to incriminate yourself by buying a whole plant. I inspected the three bushes, looking for evidence that Ivy's killer had stripped off a leaf. One of the plants had a raw spot where a leaf had been attached to a branch, and I fingered it. Although it looked as if a leaf had been forcibly removed, I had no way of knowing if someone had picked it or if it had been knocked off when Lola moved the plants, or maybe by the hose when she was watering. Sighing, I let the leaf slip from my fingers and returned to my van.

My cell phone rang as I closed the door. Flavia Dunbarton, the reporter. I answered, trying to decide how much I was going to tell her. I didn't completely trust her, but she had sources I didn't, so maybe if I shared what I'd learned with her, she'd do the same. Tit for tat.

We exchanged hellos and I filled her in on what I'd learned from Clay and Doug.

"Just barely plausible," she said of Clay's reason for entering Ivy's house. "If I were a betting gal, though, I'd guess he was really retrieving personal items he didn't want anyone to find—a toothbrush, robe, or something more recognizable. He didn't want the police finding his stuff at her house and wondering about the relationship. Or worse, showing up at his house—with his wifey listening in—to ask about it."

Flavia was good. I was struck by the sneaky way her mind worked. "You could be right. Maybe you can figure this one out." I told her about Ivy being Doug's client and about their meeting. "He didn't know she was dead," I finished.

Flavia took a bit longer analyzing Doug's presence. "You know what I think?" she finally asked.

"I think she could've been mixed up with the crime she wanted to tell me about, as an accessory of some kind, or maybe even a principal. She talked to the lawyer about getting immunity."

I was shocked. "Ivy? No way. She wasn't a criminal."

Flavia's silence dismissed my objection as clearly as a skeptical shrug would have. "You knew her. I didn't. But it makes sense. Only rich people and criminals need lawyers. And Ivy was no billionaire."

My mind was still chewing on what she'd said. "Maybe she wasn't involved . . . maybe she was worried about telling you, about being sued for slander or libel or whatever it is, and wanted a legal opinion."

"Oh, totally possible," Flavia said. "Why didn't I think of that? The *Gabbler*'s lawyers are always harping on fact checking and our exposure to possible lawsuits."

"Have you found out anything?" I asked.

"I've been poking around, sounding out some of my sources, seeing what rumors might be out there. I've heard there's a building inspector under investigation for taking bribes and that there's some money unaccounted for in the county Republican Party's coffers, but I can't imagine how Ivy would have a lead on any of that."

Her voice rose questioningly at the end, and I answered the implied question. "Me, either."

She hung up, after saying she'd call in a day or two. Putting the puzzle out of my mind for the moment, I pulled out lengthy lists of tasks to tackle for three different events and headed for my favorite caterer's, made arrangements with a party-supply rental place for folding chairs, and coordinated with a Baptist minister on the way back into Heaven. The town's new name and booming wedding industry had attracted a wide variety of clerics. When we were Walter's Ford, the only places of worship in town were St. Joseph's Roman Catholic and St. Luke's Lutheran, where we'd gone since I was a girl. Now we had our pick of Baptist, Episcopalian, Methodist, Presbyterian, Unitarian, Jewish, and Church of Christ services. I was pretty sure I knew every priest, rector, rabbi, and minister in town. I'd planned weddings with all of them and knew which ones would marry a couple on short notice and which demanded the opportunity to counsel the engaged couple before performing a ceremony. Sadly, there were a lot more of the former than the latter.

Chapter 20

I purposely arrived early for yoga Wednesday morning, wanting to be sure of getting a spot next to Fee Shumer. The room was large, floored with boards that needed refinishing. Mirrors lined the front wall, and mats and yoga blocks were neatly stacked against the back wall, which still showed grease smudges from where the previous renter, the bike repairer, had leaned bicycles against the wall. It smelled pleasingly of sandalwood from the candles Yael had burning on the windowsills. Fee was on the far side of the room from the door, but I determinedly wiggled my way through the assembled women, ignoring one who scooted her mat over to make room for mine. When I was within talking range of Fee, I gave her a bright "Good morning" and unrolled my turquoise mat. Fee nodded and turned her attention to Yael, the instructor. As we sat for some breathing exercises, I studied Fee covertly. Her blond hair was drawn back into a low ponytail, and a stretchy headband ensured no wispies escaped. She was makeup-less but still managed to look dewy and beautiful, with a flawless complexion that showed no hint of sun damage or the dryness that afflicted so many of us in this arid climate. She looked ten years younger than the thirty-five or six she must have been. I considered asking her what products she used but then turned my attention to the asanas.

I quickly realized that starting a conversation about Fee's presence at Ivy's house while doing warrior poses was not going to work. I'd have to catch her as soon as we finished, I decided, putting my foot down to balance myself. Dang. Even a few days away from class had affected my flexibility and balance. I concentrated on not landing on my nose and managed to block Fee's escape from the room by rolling up my mat in her direction when we finished. As with Doug, there was no graceful way to start this conversation. I took a deep breath, smiled brightly, and said, "Congratulations, Fee!"

She looked down her pointy nose at me as I bundled up my mat. "Come again?"

"The baby," I said, nodding toward her midsection. "Congrats."

The young woman beside us overheard me and squealed, doing a jazz hands kind of waggle. "You're pregnant, Fee? I didn't know! Oh, I'm so happy for you. When's the baby due?" When she went to hug Fee, I got a whiff of marijuana. OJ and MJ to start the day. I suppressed a smile, thinking it was a vice, like cigarette smoking, that you couldn't hide from anyone with a nose.

Fee looked daggers at me. "We haven't told anyone yet."

"Oh, I'm so sorry," I said. "I heard—"

"From who?"

I didn't want her mad at Brooke. Without thinking about it, I said, "Ivy."

"Ivy? Ivy Donner?" Fee's eyes narrowed, making her look strangely feline. "Ivy Donner told you I was pregnant? How the *hell* did she know?"

The other well-wisher backed away. Too bad I couldn't do the same.

"I shouldn't have mentioned it," I said. "I didn't know it was a secret."

Fee slung her mat carrying case over her shoulder. Her boobs seemed bigger than usual. The pregnancy. "Ivy Donner was a—" She cut herself off so abruptly her teeth clicked together. "Never mind. I hardly knew her."

"Really? Then what were you doing at her house the day after she died?"

She didn't ask me how I knew. "Inviting her to the baby shower, of course." She tossed the lie out with a sardonic smile, expecting me to recognize it as a lie. "I guess I shouldn't be waiting on her RSVP now, hm?"

"So you didn't know she was dead when you went to the house?" My hands trembled at her cavalier attitude toward Ivy's death, and I clenched them into fists.

"It would be stupid to invite someone I knew was dead, wouldn't it?" She leaned in close enough for me to smell the minty toothpaste on her breath and the vanilla of her body lotion. "Just like it would be stupid for someone to be poking her nose into things that were flat-out none of her business."

"Amy-Faye, we missed you." Yael, sensitive to the friction between us, had glided over to defuse the tension. She put a calming hand on my arm. "You seemed a little stiff today. You should come to the Bikram class this afternoon, as well."

Taking advantage of the interruption, Fee murmured good-bye to Yael and walked away. I watched her leave, answering Yael at random as I replayed Fee's final words. They had sounded an awful lot like "Mind your own beeswax." I tried to picture Fee loading a beehive into the back of her SUV and carting it to the park but couldn't do it.

Trotting downstairs to my office two minutes later and planning to change there, I spied Detective Hart as I rounded the corner.

"Casual Wednesday?" he asked, taking in the pale green scoop-neck top layered over a royal blue workout bra and matching yoga capris, and my bare feet. His gaze was appreciative and I smiled.

"Yoga. What brings you here so early?"

I fitted the key in the lock and pushed open the door, inviting Hart inside. He stayed where he was. "I need you to come down to the station."

"What?"

"We need your fingerprints."

"What?" I said again, feeling like one of my dad's stuck albums.

"For elimination purposes."

I drew in a breath. "The tea. You found something in the Baggie."

He didn't confirm or deny my guess. "Change, and come over as soon as you can, okay?"

Somewhat relieved that he didn't plan to escort me to the police station like a prisoner under guard, I nodded. "Okay. Can I stop for coffee on the way?"

"Sure. Bring me one, too. Black."

With a smile that made me feel less like a suspect, Hart flipped a hand in farewell and left me alone.

The first thing I noticed when I pushed into the police station was the smell. Soggy fire. It brought back memories of camping out when I was a girl, dousing the campfire with water from whatever lake we'd pitched our tent next to. This fire had a chemical overtone to it, though, probably from the plastics and what have you that had burned, so my initial buzz of pleasant memory gave way to distaste.

"How can you stand being in here?" I asked Mabel when she greeted me from the counter.

"After a while, you just don't smell it, hon," she said. "A little Vicks under the nose works wonders, too, just like they use at murder scenes."

Now that she mentioned it, I noticed a smear of goo under her nose.

"Thanks for coming in." Hart spoke from the hallway leading to the offices. "This won't take five minutes."

He led me into a small room and produced a fingerprint card and a pad of what looked like red ink. "Where's the black smudgy stuff they use on TV?" I asked.

"Hey, we're cutting-edge here in Heaven," he said. "Just let your hand relax in mine. Let me do everything."

"Lie back and enjoy it?" I grinned.

His mouth quirked at the corner. "Why, Ms. Johnson. If I'm not mistaken, that was a double entendre. How am I supposed to take that?"

I hadn't expected him to call me on it, and it knocked me off-balance. "As a joke? A snappy, if ill-timed quip from an English major who can't help herself when it comes to wordplay? You should laugh." I demonstrated: "Ha-ha."

"Damn. Not what I was hoping for."

The room suddenly felt very small. I didn't have the nerve to ask what he was hoping for. Not yet.

He grasped my right hand in his and pressed my fingers onto the ink pad. His hand was half again as big as mine, his fingers an inch longer. I watched his hand, fascinated, as he rolled each of my fingers, one by one, over the space allotted to them on the card. Fine hairs sprinkled the back of a hand ridged with strong bones. His fingers were long and oddly graceful, ending with nails that were neatly clipped and filed, but not polished, thank goodness. It may be totally unfair of me, since I occasionally get my nails done and think other women's painted nails are pretty, but polished nails on a man make me suspicious. I mean, a man who works for a living shouldn't have time to sit in a nail salon while someone rubs lotion into his cuticles, and the thought of a man standing over his kitchen counter, a little bottle of clear polish in hand, stroking the teeny brush across his thumbnail . . . well, let's just say it doesn't add up to the definition of "manly" for me.

I gave Hart my other hand, liking the way he gripped it firmly but gently. He stood to my left, his body warm and solid, a mere half inch from me. If I shifted a smidge, I'd be pressed against his side. I resisted the temptation.

"All done." He handed me a towelette to wipe what turned out to be almost invisible ink off my fingers.

"So," I said, before he could usher me out. "Tell me. There was oleander in that Baggie, along with the tea?"

He hesitated before giving a brief nod. "It raises questions. Ivy might still have killed herself, but it strikes me as a bit out of the ordinary for her to poison both the tea she kept at home and what looks like a mobile stash she kept with her. From where I stand, it looks like she filled the Baggie from her canister at home, not knowing it was poisoned. Why dose herself at your house? Unless," he continued as if talking to himself, "it was really a cry for help, and she thought she'd be sick enough that you'd get help?"

"No." I shook my head decisively. "If that were the case, she'd have made a bigger fuss out of feeling ill than she did. I told her she looked peaky and she shrugged it off, said her tummy was unsettled. If she was looking for attention, wouldn't she have played it up more?"

Keeping a noncommittal expression on his face, Hart moved toward the door. "At any rate, it's enough of an anomaly that I'm going to investigate further."

"Wait." I put a hand on his arm. He looked down at me with a question in his eyes. "There's something else you should know, if you really believe she was killed."

I told him about Flavia Dunbarton. It took me a good ten minutes to go through it all, and we stood by the door the whole time. I hadn't wanted to sic the police on Flavia, but if Hart was treating Ivy's case like a murder investigation—finally!—then he needed to know everything that might conceivably help. And Flavia's photos and her tale about Ivy coming to her with a big story definitely fell into that category. I wrapped up by telling him about my "interviews" with Clay, Doug, and Fee. "Doug didn't know Ivy was dead, and I'm not sure about Fee," I finished.

Hart's jaw worked from side to side. "You should have told me all this when the reporter first approached you."

His minatory tone rubbed me the wrong way. "She didn't want the police involved. And you would have dismissed it, just like you've discounted everything that wasn't evidence your lab could test, like the break-in and the fact that all of Ivy's friends told you she wasn't the suicidal type." I glared at him. "Oh, and the other piece of testable evidence I gave you just 'happened' to get burned up."

Hart frowned. "What's that supposed to mean?"

"You're the detective—you figure it out." I swept past him into the hall. I turned the wrong way and found myself outside a room with a closed door that had a jagged hole the size of a beach ball eaten through it. Flame tracks scarred the wood, reaching up and out, and the smell of charred things was overpowering here. The evidence room. Through the hole, I glimpsed a mass of melted, icky black goo and ash mounded in unidentifiable heaps. I backed up a step, feeling a bit like I'd peered into someone's grave.

Hart caught my arm. "You think this fire was deliberate? That I—or someone here—deliberately burned that ledger page?"

I shrugged his hand off and swept a lock of hair out of my eyes. "Do the math." Seeing the troubled look on his face, I softened. "I don't know. The timing seems"—I used Maud's least favorite word—"coincidental."

He didn't comment. "I'll need the reporter's contact info."

"I'm going to call her as soon as I leave here and give her a heads-up," I warned him, heading back toward the waiting area.

"That's fine."

I wished we could go back to double entendres.

Chief Uggams stepped out of his office and greeted me. "I thought I heard your voice, Amy-Faye. What are you doing here again? If you keep showing up like this, I'll have to put you on the payroll." He chuckled. "Hey, tell your dad I'm planning to come for poker night tomorrow evening. I'm feelin' lucky, so he and the boys better watch out." Apparently sensing the tension between me and Hart, he gave us a penetrating look. "What's going on?"

"I'll brief you, Chief," Hart said, gesturing for me to go on. "Ms. Johnson came in for fingerprinting."

"That's right." The chief looked at me from under heavy brows. His down-angled head made the pouches under his eyes pooch out even further. "Tell me again how you ended up with a Baggie of poisoned tea, young lady?"

I started to reply, but Hart stopped me. "I'm satisfied Ms. Johnson is not a suspect."

Wow, warm fuzzy.

"Of course she's not," Uggams said testily. "Why, I've known Amy-Faye since she was a toddler and her dad since we were part of the 3A state champion football team, back in—hell, a long damn time ago. The Walter's Ford Demons were a feared squad in those days, not like today where they couldn't beat a decent middle school team. Amy-Faye's got her faults, but killing people's not one of them."

Another ringing endorsement. I lifted a hand in farewell and pushed through the door into Mabel's domain.

As the door swung shut behind me, I heard Hart ask, "Have you got the report on the fire yet?"

Chapter 21

I called Flavia Dunbarton on the half mile back to my office and listened to her squawk when I confessed I'd given her name to the police. She accepted my position enough to hang up politely by the time I arrived back at my office to find Maud Bell reigning in my waiting room, erect posture making it easy to read her T-shirt's slogan: "I'm not paranoid. You're just misinformed." Her legs were crossed at the ankle and her booted foot jiggled. She was flipping the pages of a *Discover* magazine so quickly I knew she couldn't be taking in any of it. She leaped up when I came in, letting the magazine fall to the ground. "Amy-Faye! Finally! I've been waiting for hours."

"She's been here twelve minutes," Al said with a pointed glance at his watch. "I told her I'd let you know she came by, but she insisted on waiting. I told her I could call you, but she wouldn't let me. All she's been doing is distracting me with her pacing and foot tapping."

"Come into my office," I invited Maud.

"No. We've got to talk."

I noticed she was clutching her purse like it contained the cure for baldness, and raised my brows. "We can't talk here?"

"No. Somewhere private." She slid a sidelong glance at Al, which he intercepted.

His look of affront sat oddly on his young face. "Believe you me, I've got better things to do than eavesdrop on you. I've got statistics homework to finish before my six o'clock class, and a bat mitzvah to set up, and lots more besides. I don't know what makes you think you're so fascinating anyway, or that anyone would want to hear what you have to say. Just because you're old doesn't mean you're interesting."

I winced and decided it was time to have another talk with Al about thinking before he spoke.

Rather than take offense, Maud laughed. "Right you are, young man. But we're still going out." She grabbed my arm and steered me to the door. "No offense, Al. It's not about you. You never know who's listening."

"I get you." He nodded sagely and gestured to the computer. "The NSA."

I rolled my eyes. "Great. Now you've infected Al."

"I've enlightened him, you mean." She nodded to Al as we left.

"Where are we going?"

"The lake. No one can sneak up on us out there." She stopped beside her pickup, which was parked at an expired meter, beeped it open, and went around to the driver's side.

"You're lucky you didn't get a ticket," I said, pointing to the approaching meter maid.

"I was out of coins, and you don't really expect me to use my credit card, do you? The town council only installed the meters that take credit cards so they can keep tabs on our movements." She pulled out without checking traffic and a screech of brakes sounded from behind us.

I shut my eyes and pretty much kept them that way until we jolted to a stop at the lake. Driving with Maud was like getting on an amusement park ride: three parts terror and one part gratitude when it ended.

"Okay," I said when we got out of the car and headed toward the gazebo. "What's the big secret?"

Maud didn't answer until we had reached the white-painted gazebo with its pretty gingerbread work. She turned 360 degrees and apparently decided no one was surveilling us—the nearest potential spies were a four-year-old and his dog climbing on a fallen tree trunk a hundred yards away. The kid's mother was some yards beyond them, reading a book.

"I broke the code."

"You did? That's great! Was it *Ender's Game*?"

She shook her head. "No, the Merriam-Webster dictionary. It's a good thing, too, or it would have taken much longer to decode it. Half those books in Clay's office were textbooks, and some of them were out of print, so I'd've had to find them online at specialty bookstores, and it might have taken months to test them all against the ledger page numbers."

"We should call the others." I pulled out my cell phone, but she batted it out of my hand. That was a bit extreme, even for Maud, and I gave her a "what the heck?" look as I picked it up.

"Sorry. But you don't know how big this is."

"Tell me." I settled on one of the steps leading into the octagonal gazebo and leaned back on my elbows.

Maud remained standing. "It's gambling."

I made a "go on" gesture when she paused.

"It looks like Clay Shumer was—is—running a bookie operation. Each line of the ledger is a bet. It records who placed the bet, for how much, and on what. There are bets on everything from horse and dog racing to sports events to election results. He used a shorthand even within the code, so I couldn't figure out what some of the bets were for, but I don't think it matters. The big thing here is that he's running a criminal operation worth millions probably. If Ivy was going to expose it— him—by talking to that reporter, then I'd say he had a damned good motive for killing her."

A chill brushed me and I crossed my arms over my chest. I don't know what I'd expected the ledger page to reveal, but it wasn't this. Clay Shumer as a criminal mastermind and murderer. I didn't much like the man, but I wouldn't have guessed he was capable of this.

"I wonder why he didn't keep this on his laptop—wouldn't that be easier?"

Maud gave me the "how can you be so clueless?" look. She should patent it. "Easier—yes. Smarter—no. I don't care what kind of security you have—someone can hack your computer without even being in the same state. Heck, the same country. And it doesn't have to be an NSA-caliber someone, either. And let's face it—most folks don't have great security. They write down their passwords, never change them, leave their screens up when they go to the bathroom or out to lunch, go to wonky Internet sites for porn or games and pick up spyware. The ledger, especially with this code, is much more secure. The only way it gets compromised is the way it did—someone close to Clay stole it."

I held up my hands in surrender, guilty of all her charges except the porn thing. "So why are we out here? Why aren't we at the police station, handing over the ledger page so they can arrest Clay?"

"Because Clay's not the only one involved." Looking over her shoulder to make sure no one had approached while we talked, Maud pulled a piece of paper from her purse. "Here's the decoded page." She squatted and held it so we could both look at it.

I scanned it, noting that it must have been from several months back since there were a lot of football bets recorded. I wondered if Ivy had copied this page months ago and hung on to it, or if she'd copied it at random when she decided she wanted proof of Clay's activities, or for some other reason. I scanned the lines horizontally, but Maud used her fingers to focus me on the names of the bettors, rather than the events and amounts. "School superintendent, state senator, gazillionaire ski resort owner, Gordon Marsh—isn't he Derek's pub partner?—and look at the last name."

My gaze followed her pointing finger. As I read the line, my eyes widened. *Oh no.* I looked at Maud and she nodded grimly.

"Yep. It says 'Widefield.' Only problem is, with the corner torn off like that so the first name is missing, we don't know if it's Brooke's husband or her father-in-law. Or even Brooke."

"No way!"

Maud cocked her head and shrugged. "You're probably right. For one thing, I can't see Brooke betting fifteen thou on a NASCAR race. I'd be surprised if she even knows who Jimmie Johnson is."

"Do we tell her?" I thought it through aloud. "If we tell her, she'll be upset. On the other hand, she might know who it is."

"Or she might not, and confront Troy Jr. or Sr. and spark a family row . . . or worse."

"Worse?"

Maud met my gaze levelly. "Clay might have been running this gambling ring, but he's not the only one with something to lose if it blows up. This is all illegal." She shook the page. "How many people on this list stand to lose their jobs, their reputations, or possibly their families if it becomes public? I'm not voting for a state senator who bets fifty K on who the next *Sports Illustrated* swimsuit edition cover model will be."

She was implying that one of the gamblers might have killed Ivy, but I spotted a flaw in her logic.

"Maybe, but how would they even have known Ivy had the ledger page?"

Without a blink of hesitation, she said. "I can think of two ways. One"—she held up her bony forefinger—"Ivy told them. Two"—her middle finger went up—"Clay discovered she'd copied the page and told his clients that they might be compromised."

Compromised. It sounded like jargon from a spy novel. If Maud started talking about "wet work" or "termination with extreme prejudice," I was going to have to insist the Readaholics cut thrillers from our reading list. I let it go for now. "Why in the world would Ivy tell them?"

I read her thoughts in the look she gave me.

"No way," I said again. "Ivy is not—wasn't—a blackmailer!"

"I don't think so, either," Maud said, "but we've got to consider the possibility."

I shook my head so hard my hair flew around my face. "No. It's not a possibility."

Maud gave me a smile that was half-admiring and half-pitying. "You're too loyal, Amy-Faye."

"I'm not," I said, "not if you mean it makes me blind to my friends' faults. I know Ivy wasn't perfect—heck, she was dating a married man—but she wasn't a crook. Ham got all the crook genes in that family. I think she was doing just what she told Flavia: gathering evidence to support the story she was going to give her."

"One that would land her lover in prison."

I nodded unhappily. "I didn't say she was perfect. It had to be about revenge, didn't it? Getting revenge on Clay for breaking up with her?" I wanted Maud to tell me I was wrong, but she didn't. "I think Clay knew. I overheard him tell Troy Widefield Sr. that his assistant had been copying something."

"So Troy Senior and Clay both knew that Ivy was up to something, even if they didn't know what."

I nodded unhappily.

After a long pause, she said, "Do we show this to the others?"

I grimaced. The Readaholics were all involved in this, but I didn't think it was fair to the people whose names were on that page to expose them to more people than strictly necessary. I hated cutting Lola and Kerry and Brooke out of the investigation, but I couldn't think it right to show the page to all of them. I struggled to find a compromise. "Maybe we tell them about the gambling, but we don't show them the page or share the names?"

"That's all right by me," Maud said.

"We do have to share it with the police, though."

"Are you out of your mind? This is only one page out of potentially hundreds." Maud shook the page and then looked around to see if anyone had noticed.

The kid and his dog were gone, and I was pretty sure the blue jay jeering from a nearby pine was not interested.

"We don't know who else's names are in that ledger," Maud continued in a lower voice. "Don't forget that everything in the evidence room mysteriously went up in flames after you turned in the actual ledger page. I'm betting"—she caught the irony and let out a "Hah!"—"that one or more of Heaven's finest has a gambling problem. And don't you dare say 'No way,'" she added as I opened my mouth.

I shut it.

"Consider what happened to Ivy. I don't want someone poisoning my coffee, thank you very much. Or yours, either," she added as an after-thought.

After a moment's thought, I tried again. "Okay. Let's pretend it's remotely possible that someone from the police department deliberately destroyed the ledger page. Couldn't we make multiple cop-ies of the list, give the police one, and let them know we have others that will come to light in the event anything happens to us?" I felt unutterably silly saying those words. I mean, really? It was the stuff of bad spy novels: the hero handing his faith-ful sidekick or lawyer a packet to be opened or sent to the nearest media outlet if he died. Fifty percent of the time, the faithful sidekick or lawyer betrayed him anyway; heroes frequently have poor judgment when it comes to sidekicks.

Without waiting for Maud to acquiesce, I folded the page and tucked it in my purse. "I'm assum-ing you have electronic copies of this?"

She nodded.

"Okay. Then I'll give this to Detective Hart—he hasn't been here long enough to get mixed up with a gambling ring, I hope—and tell him we have copies of it. Okay?" I could see genuine worry in her eyes, so I added, "If I could think of any other way to investigate this and find out who killed Ivy, I would, but we can't interview everyone on this list, and as you pointed out, it's probably only the tip of the iceberg. The police can take this to Clay and force him to turn over the whole ledger. Then they can sort it all out."

Maud nodded reluctantly. "Marginally the best of several bad options. Be careful."

"You, too."

We looked at each other for a long moment and then made our way slowly back to Maud's truck. A squirrel chittered behind us, sounding like he was laughing.

Chapter 22

I had work to do, so I didn't trot over to the police department right away. At least, that's what I told myself as I sat at my desk making calls and marking items off my to-do list. I suspected I was merely postponing another awkward confession to Hart. He'd be mad I hadn't told him about having a copy of the ledger page. *Later. Worry later. Focus now.* I pulled a legal pad close and began to sketch the gazebo. Then I doodled a blond bride. Beside her, I drew a long, stalky potted plant, giving it a bow tie and cummerbund. Beneath it, I wrote, "Do you take this potted plant to love and to cherish, to repot and fertilize, to water regularly and to deadhead, as long as you both shall live?" Cocking my head, I studied the cartoon, adding some curlicues to represent flowers at the altar. I quite liked it. Using a black pen, I darkened one of the bride's thumbs.

Tucking it in a drawer, I made myself get back to work. I'd recently landed a job organizing Heaven's first-ever triathlon, which wasn't until next summer, and I was reaching out to contacts with some experience in that arena, figuring out what all went into organizing a major race. I wasn't in charge of laying out the course or anything like that, but I needed to get a Web site set up for the event with registration details, contact all the area lodging facilities, talk to my fave publicity guy about getting the word out, and dozens of other tasks. It took most of the afternoon to begin to realize how much I didn't know about an event of this type, and my brain was on overload when Al poked his head in at almost four.

"Mayor on the phone. I'm off to class."

I waved good-bye to him as I picked up the phone. "Hi, Kerry."

"You are not going to believe what just happened," she said in a low voice. "The police were here."

"Here?"

"City hall. My office."

"They finally caught up with you, huh? What is it—unpaid parking tickets? Jaywalking? Payback for cutting the police department budget?" I was typing an e-mail to a Web designer as I talked, amused at the notion of the police citing Heaven's mayor for something. It couldn't be anything too serious, because Kerry was a straight arrow.

"They pulled Clay out of a meeting and took him to the station for questioning!"

"What?" I stopped typing.

"We were having the weekly staff meeting in

my office and my secretary interrupted to say the police needed to talk to Clay. That new detective, the one from down south—"

"Atlanta. Detective Hart."

"Sounds like you've been getting to know him," Kerry said suggestively, momentarily distracted from her story. "He's attractive in a lanky sort of way."

"Clay?" I reminded her.

"Right. They asked Clay very politely if he'd come with them down to the station to answer a few questions. Clay got up, acting like it was no big deal, an inconvenience, and went with them without making a fuss. I could tell he wasn't happy about it, though. Tense. They didn't handcuff him or read him his rights or anything. Should I call Fee?"

The question took me by surprise. "I wouldn't. She'll find out one way or another. It's not your responsibility just because he was in your office at the time." I thought rapidly. There was no point in my taking the ledger page to Hart this second because he'd undoubtedly be tied up with Clay. I'd call him, hoping to get voice mail, and leave a message saying I needed to talk to him about the case. Meanwhile, I should give Kerry a heads-up about what the town's chief financial officer was up to, but I didn't want to do it on the phone. Maud's caution had infected me. "Look, Kerry. There's something I need to tell you about that *project* we're working on, the Ivy project. Maud made a breakthrough today."

She started to say something, but I talked over

her. "We should talk about it *in person*. When are you done for the day?"

"I'll be home in ten," Kerry said decisively. "Meet me there."

Kerry's daughter Amanda and her grandson were playing in the front yard when I arrived at Kerry's house twenty minutes later. Amanda and Henry lived in an apartment over Kerry's detached garage and had ever since Henry's father had ditched them. Amanda had been a college dropout of twenty at the time. Now she was back in school part-time and worked part-time. Kerry groused that Henry's other grandmother, who provided day care, was spoiling the toddler rotten. At the moment, he was shrieking with joy as he ran away from his mother and Amanda pretended she couldn't catch up. When the little boy headed toward the street, I stepped in front of him and Amanda lunged forward to scoop him up. "No, you don't," she told the two-year-old. "Hey, Amy-Faye. Mom's inside. Just go on in."

"Thanks. How're classes?"

"I hate math," she announced, "but I can't get my nursing degree without it."

I smiled sympathetically and made my way up the flagstone walkway to the double doors. Kerry lived in the large gabled house she'd inherited from her parents. She complained about being "house poor" and I knew a significant chunk of her Realtor's income went to maintaining the old place. She'd learned to do a lot of repairs herself, and she's the one I consulted whenever I had a house question. If I had some time on my hands this summer, I was going to ask her to help me refinish my front door.

"In here," Kerry called when I pushed open the door with a perfunctory knock.

I followed her voice to the larger of two living rooms, where I found her flat on her back in front of the brick fireplace. Old sheets covered the floor around her. She'd changed into jeans and a faded sweatshirt and had a smudge of soot on her cheek.

"Do you know what chimney sweeps charge?" she greeted me. On the words, she poked what looked like a giant-sized wire toilet brush up the chimney.

"Too much, I'm guessing." *Mary Poppins* was the source of everything I knew about chimney sweeps, and I was pretty sure Colorado sweeps didn't dance across rooftops.

"Got that right. If you were a bird, would you build a nest over an open flame where your eggs are more likely to end up hard-boiled than hatched? What's wrong with a lovely fir tree for a nest, or a nice, secure spot under the porch eaves?"

It seemed to be a rhetorical question.

"We built a fire two nights ago with that cold snap and you wouldn't believe the smoke. So tell me what Maud discovered. She decoded the ledger page, am I right?"

"Right. Is Roman home?" I didn't want her seventeen-year-old son listening in.

"Upstairs. Plugged into his iPod, allegedly do-ing homework, more probably Skyping with his buddies while playing Xbox. Trust me, he's not listening to us."

While she worked the brush into the chimney, I told her about Clay running a bookie operation.

"On city time?" She sat upright, looking outraged. If the brush had been a sword and Clay had been present, she'd have run him through.

"Presumably. Anyway, Maud and I think Ivy knew about it, or found out about it, and went to the reporter with the story."

Kerry chewed on that for a moment while a gentle rain of soot sifted from the hearth opening behind her. "Watch out for a woman scorned," she finally said.

"That's what Maud and I figured," I agreed. "She wanted revenge when he dumped her."

"You think he killed her?" She twisted and began to attack the chimney with a sharp upward plunging motion.

The wire brush against the bricks grated on my ears. I took a precautionary step back.

"It seems likely." A thought occurred to me. "Do you know what made the police want to talk to Clay today? I haven't told them about the ledger page yet."

"Uh-uh." Kerry's voice echoed strangely as she peered into the chimney. "That dratted nest is hanging by a twig. I can just about—"

A sound like pebbles rolling down a hill presaged an explosion of soot. It puffed out of the hearth opening, coating the sheets and hanging in the air so thickly I couldn't see Kerry. She coughed, and as the air cleared, I saw her, drenched in soot, her hair and brows thick with the stuff, her eyes the only spot of white in her blackened face.

"Are you okay?" I asked.

"Fine." She coughed again and wiped a hand across her face. It didn't help. She looked around at the room, at the film of black on the walls and furniture, and sighed. "You're going to need a shower when you get home," she said.

I looked down and saw that the soot clung to me as well, albeit much more lightly, like an even haze of dust. A finger swiped across my cheek came away black. At least I wasn't wearing my white suit. "Me?" I said with a grin. "You're going to need a fire hose to get that stuff off you."

"At least I got it." With her toe, she prodded a mass of twigs and leaves that lay on the hearth. "Roman!" she yelled at the top of her lungs, making me jump. "Come down here, and bring a bucket and a package of sponges." Satisfied by the incomprehensible (to me) mutterings that answered her demand, she turned back to me. "So case closed? Clay killed Ivy?"

I frowned slightly. "I guess so. It just feels kind of . . . anticlimactic."

"You wanted a confrontation with guns blazing and fisticuffs, à la *Falcon*?"

Her words stirred a memory. "Did you know Clay had a gun in his office?"

"No! The way our budget meetings go, I'm surprised he didn't pull it out and shoot anyone. I've been tempted myself, on occasion." Looking a bit self-conscious, as if worried her comment was too flip for the circumstances, she added, "I wonder why. Protection? If he's big-time into the bookie biz, he might have received threats."

"Or he used it to threaten people who didn't make good on their debts. I wonder if he had a— What do they call them? Enforcer?"

"You know," Kerry said, "the more I think about it, the more I'm sure Ivy must have known about his sideline all along. I mean, come on—she was his assistant; she answered his phone half the time. She had to have known something was going on besides city business."

"I don't know. He probably used a cell phone, something that couldn't be traced to him. How likely is it that he'd give the office number to his gambling clientele?" If Kerry was right, though, did that mean that Kirsten, Clay's new assistant, knew what was going on?

Clomping footsteps heralded the appearance of Roman, a big kid with a mop of black hair and a couple of acne spots. He stopped on the bottom tread and stared at us. "Shit, Mom, what happened? This is worse than that time I set the spray paint can on the stove, not realizing it was hot, and—"

"Don't use that kind of language, and no, it's not. Find the bucket—no, get the Shop-Vac first— and get started in here."

When Roman had disappeared into the garage, I said, "You know, I think I'll check with Detective Hart"—Kerry put on a knowing smile but I ignored her—"and see if he can tell me why they picked up Clay. They didn't arrest him—maybe he's 'helping the police with their inquiries,' or however they say it on cop shows."

"Right. And the Publishers Clearing House guy is pulling up to my door right now." Kerry shooed me out. "I need a shower—I'm starting to itch. Heaven knows what's in this soot. Let me know if you find out anything."

Chapter 23

I was halfway to my van, trying to figure out how to approach Hart with my questions, when my phone rang. The man himself, returning my earlier call. Serendipity. I smiled and answered.

"You said you have more information for me," he said without any preamble. He sounded pressed for time and cop-ish.

"I'll buy you a beer," I said, hoping what I had to tell him would go down better with a little alcohol.

"I'm still working. I'd appreciate it if you'd come to the station."

Uh-oh. That didn't bode well. "Um, okay. Now?"

"Now would be good." After a brief hesitation, he said in a lowered voice, "I'll take a rain check on that brew."

I told him I'd be there in half an hour—I needed a shower and soot-free clothes—and smiled as I hung up.

I fed the meter outside the police department and was walking toward the doors, head down to restore my wallet to my purse, when I bumped into someone exiting the station.

"Oh, sorry!" I said, looking up.

Clay Shumer shouldered past me without acknowledging my existence. His face was pale and set, his lips drawn into a thin line. I didn't think he was being rude; I was pretty sure he didn't even notice me. Fiona followed him out, her expression also set to "death mask." She noticed me with a flick of her gaze in my direction, but she was so focused on her thoughts, or on Clay, that she couldn't be bothered to say hello or even sneer at me. I was reaching for the station door when someone yelled, "Hey, Mr. Shumer! Over here."

I spun in time to see a photographer from the *Heaven Herald* aim a camera at Clay and Fee.

"You can't do that!" Fee screeched, lunging toward the photographer.

He sidestepped nimbly, taking photos nonstop, until Clay grabbed Fiona's arm and stuffed her into their car. He hadn't said a word since the photographer hailed him. Hunching and cupping his hand to obscure his face, he slid into the driver's seat and peeled away from the curb. The photographer, who had approached to take photos through the car window, sprang aside with a curse. Sobered by the encounter, I stepped into the station. The smoky odor had dissipated somewhat after a day with all the windows open, and the place now smelled like a charcoal grill whose ashes hadn't been emptied.

Mabel Appleman greeted me. Her perm looked a bit frizzy today, the gray curls poking up around the glasses she had tucked into them.

"Detective Hart's expecting me," I said. Lowering my voice, I added, "What's up with them?" I nodded in the direction of the departed Shumers.

Mabel glanced over her shoulder to ensure that no one was listening. "Well, I really can't talk to you about police business, but let's just say there's been big doings this afternoon. Big doings. I heard Detective Hart say you were right." She gave me a congratulatory look.

"About?"

"About Ivy Donner being murdered. And I didn't say this"—she laid a finger alongside her nose—"but you may have just bumped into the guilty party."

"Thanks for coming, Amy-Faye." Hart had come into the room without either of us noticing. He looked harried, his tie slightly askew, and a shade grim.

Mabel started guiltily and immediately turned her attention to a folder open on the counter.

"Happy to," I babbled, hoping I hadn't gotten Mabel in trouble by asking about the Shumers.

Hart led me back to his office, a small room with windows on two sides, and I looked around with interest. Paint, flooring, and furniture were all taxpayer-funded blah and utilitarian, but a full set of Sherlock Holmes novels and short stories were bookended by a plaster deerstalker cap and pipe, a set of golf clubs slouched in one corner, and a stuffed bulldog wearing a red jersey perched atop the printer.

"You went to the University of Georgia?" I asked.

"On a football scholarship," he said. "Sit, and tell me what you've got this time."

I sat, slightly chastened by his emphasis on "this time." Silently, I pulled out the decoded ledger page and passed it to him. As his gaze swept over it, I said, "That's from a copy of the page I gave you earlier. The one that got burned up. *Accidentally.*" Two could play that game, I thought. "Maud— Maud Bell—decoded it."

As his brows rose ever higher, the whole story spilled out in a rush: Maud determining the cipher was a book code, my visit to Clay's office, the list of books, Maud's decoding efforts, and our conviction that Clay was running a gambling business and might have killed Ivy to keep her from spilling the beans. I finished, flushed, and looked at him for a reaction.

Putting both palms down on his desk and taking a deep breath through his nose, he studied me for a long minute. "Damn it, Amy-Faye," he said finally, the words no less hurtful for being uttered in a low voice. "You are messing around with a potential murderer, putting yourself in the line of fire. I don't want to see you end up like Ivy Donner! Is this everything you have that pertains to the case?" He slapped his hand on the page. "And I mean *everything*?"

I blinked away tears at his harsh tone. Then it occurred to me that he seemed angrier about the possibility of me being in danger than about my withholding evidence, and I regained my composure. "Yes. Everything. I'm sorry."

"You should have given this to me immediately, and not run around like Miss Marple—"

"Can't I be Stephanie Plum or Kinsey Mill-hone?" I asked. "Miss Marple is in her eigh—"

My attempt to lighten the atmosphere failed when he cut me off with "This isn't fun and games. This is murder. Cop business. By all rights, I should arrest you for impeding an investigation."

"I haven't impeded," I said, getting mad myself. "I've given you evidence you didn't dig up on your own because you didn't believe Ivy had been murdered. And if you want to know why I didn't come running straight here with that"—I pointed to the page—"it's because that's only a partial list. We don't know who else's names are in Clay's little black ledger."

"So?"

I drew in a deep breath. "So, given that the original ledger page got destroyed, I can't help but wonder if one or more of Heaven's finest appear in that book."

To his credit, he didn't immediately discount the idea. Instead, he leaned back slightly and thought it through. "I'm honored that you trust me," he said finally.

I was still pissed off enough to come back with "Yeah, well, you haven't been here long enough to get in bed with the crooks."

That got a small smile, like he knew that wasn't the only reason I'd come to him. "Still, thank you for trusting me with this."

"What will you do now?" I ventured to ask.

"Hell if I know." He stared at the ledger page with distaste. "I'll get a search warrant for Shumer's home, office, and car to see if we can't dig up the ledger itself. And I'll hope like crazy that the judge who signs the warrant isn't one of Shumer's clients. Then I'll get Shumer back in here to see if he knew Ivy had copied a page, and if so, what he did about it. It doesn't look good for him."

"Why did you bring him in today?"

"We got a photo in the mail." Hart wrinkled his nose with distaste. "A grainy, long-distance shot of Shumer and Ivy. Kissing. And not the way you'd kiss a sibling or your best buddy."

"Oh. Who was it from?"

"I'd like to know that myself. We got Shumer's fingerprints, and an initial comparison shows his dabs all over Ivy's place—including on the tea canister."

"And the Baggie?"

He shook his head. "Nope—his prints aren't on it. Which makes me think Ivy filled the Baggie from the canister, like we thought. So whoever poisoned her had access to that canister."

The scenario he was painting made me feel sick to my stomach. I couldn't imagine what it would be like to have someone you loved poison you, sneak into your home and slip a toxic substance into something you ate or drank. A bullet through the head would almost be more merciful. I wondered if Ivy had died thinking that Clay, the man she loved, had caused her agony. "That's so sad," I murmured.

He came around the desk and helped me to my feet, holding on to my hand for a moment. "Murder is almost always sad. Sometimes grotesque or perplexing or enraging, soul eating or tragic or all of the above, but always sad. Sad for the person who was killed, sadder for the ones who loved him or her, and even sad, lots of times, for the murderer. More murders than not are in the heat of passion when a boyfriend or spouse loses it. Their grief, when they realize what they've done, is genuine."

"Do you think Ivy's murderer is sad?" I asked, my hand tightening unconsciously around his.

"This was planned, premeditated, and executed with cold precision. I'd guess not. Only time will tell." His hand returned my pressure and his eyes gazed into mine. For a moment, I thought he would pull me into his arms and kiss me. I caught my breath, but a sound from the hall reminded us where we were and he stepped back. Good thing. It was early days for kissing, even though for a moment I'd really, really wanted to. Reaction to the stress, to talking about murder, I decided, taking hold of the doorknob. A need to experience something life affirming. *Total BS.* He was hot and it'd been way too long since I'd kissed anyone. Feeling myself blush, I let myself out with a strangled "good-bye."

I walked away too quickly to hear what he said in reply, but I thought I caught the words "rain check."

Chapter 24

Thursday morning's *Heaven Herald* had a large photo of Clay Shumer on the front page above the fold with a caption that said Heaven's chief financial officer had been asked to assist the police with their investigation into the death of Ivy Donner, now categorized as a homicide. Fee was in the background, the tendons on her neck standing out in an unflattering way. I suspected neither of them would be happy with the article, which combined innuendo and vague quotes to make it sound like Clay was the main suspect in a homicide investigation. Which, of course, he was. A long, rambling quote from Ham Donner said he'd known all along that his sister wasn't the type to kill herself and said he'd been pushing the police to pursue the investigation. I made a disgusted sound, folded the paper, and went to work. No yoga today. I didn't know if Fee would show up for class, but I didn't need another confrontation to start my day. I was already semidreading the day, what with the appointment to listen to bands with Doug and Madison scheduled for this afternoon.

Work today started at the Club. I needed to talk to the pro about setting up the tournament for Madison and Doug's family and wedding guests. It never ceased to amaze me how often golf played a role in destination weddings. I guess it gave the men an alternative to mani-pedis and oohing and aahing over gifts. Women played, too, of course, but it was mostly men, in my experience. When I stepped into the pro shop, it was almost eight thirty, so the early morning golfers were well on their way around the championship course. A lone man was examining drivers set in racks beneath the plate-glass window that looked out to the ninth green and a row of golf carts. The pro shop carried the usual assortment of clubs, shoes, gloves, and golf apparel. I'd bought Doug cute club head covers here one Christmas when we were still dating. Looney Tunes characters: Bugs, Daffy, and Tweety Bird. I smiled sadly at the memory and headed toward Betty, who was giving someone a tee time over the phone.

Betty Bullock, the Club's pro, was a short, no-nonsense woman in her sixties who had competed on the LPGA Tour for six or seven years. Her skin, baked by too many rounds in the sun, had the texture of a golf bag, and it creased when she saw me and grinned. "Amy-Faye! Here for another lesson?"

This was a joke. Doug had encouraged me to learn to golf when we were dating and I'd signed up for a series of five lessons. To say I had no aptitude for the game was to grossly understate the case. I'm sure gophers have moved into some of the divots I dug into the course—that's how deep they were. And I'm pretty sure that by our third lesson, Betty was having to fortify herself with a shot of Cuervo Gold before meeting me on the driving range. I nodded with feigned eagerness.

"Yes, indeed! I've noticed that a lot of networking and business gets done on the golf course, and I need to be able to play a respectable round to get in on that. I need to develop a wider customer base. Does Tuesday afternoon work for you?"

Betty blanched but then caught my grin. "Had me going there for a moment. Now, what can I really do for you?"

We worked out the details for a best-ball tourney and she blocked out the tee times. "I've hired two vans to get them all here on time," I told her. "I'll let you know by Monday how many of the players will need to rent clubs." I made a note to ask Doug how many of his guests were traveling with their own clubs.

"Things go smoothly when you're in charge," Betty said.

Her compliment made me feel surprisingly good. "Thanks, Betty. Back atcha."

The clicking of plastic spikes heralded the approach of multiple golfers. I turned and found myself facing the Troy Widefields, Junior and Senior, and a man I didn't know. They were kitted out for golf and discussing the terms of their bets for the day. "Five bucks a hole," Brooke's husband said.

"With a hundred for the winner to make the round worthwhile," her father-in-law replied. "No mulligans."

The stranger assented with a nod.

They noticed me and Betty and greeted us. Troy Jr. looked away from me and made a big production out of picking out a scorecard. I guessed he wasn't over our tiff at his house.

"Is our fourth here, Betty?" Troy Sr. asked.

"Ready and waiting with the cart at the practice green."

I couldn't help wondering, as I said my good-byes to Betty, whether it was Junior's or Senior's name in Clay's ledger. Who was the big bettor? If it was Senior, well, he might be a bit embarrassed to have it come out that he placed bets with the city's CFO, but if it was Junior . . . I didn't think Brooke and her husband could afford to lose a fifteen-thousand-dollar bet. Also, if Troy Jr. was about to run for state senator, it wouldn't do his campaign any good if word got around that he had a gambling problem. The question was: Did he care enough about it to silence Ivy? My eyes slid to his father, handing Betty a credit card to pay their greens fees. Troy Sr. certainly cared enough about his son's future to take care of any problems that arose. Would he, though, resort to murder to solve those problems? Maybe I should just ask, seeing as they were both standing here in front of me.

"Did you see the article about Clay Shumer in the paper this morning?" I asked, directing the question impartially toward the four people standing at the counter. "Hard to believe, wasn't it?"

Troy Sr. looked down his nose at me. "Speculation. Shumer's a good man."

"You're not still on about that, are you?" Troy Jr. asked, a hint of exasperation in his voice. "Give it a rest already, will you?"

"Give what a rest?" Troy Sr. asked, looking from his son to me.

"Nothing," Troy Jr. muttered. Then, as if unable to keep mum, he added, "Amy-Faye is convinced that someone murdered Ivy Donner and is now out to get her."

Troy Sr., the stranger, and Betty all looked at me and I flushed. "Not exactly," I said, wishing I could punch Troy Jr. "You've got to admit I was right about Ivy being murdered. The police have reclassified her death as a homicide."

"Even so, why would someone be out to get *you*?" Troy Sr. asked with a slight frown.

"They're not," I said shortly, hoping that would end it. I was sorry I'd started this conversation.

"Because she found a ledger page at Ivy's, written in code allegedly, that she thinks is connected to Ivy's death."

I glared at Troy Jr. I'd known he was immature and spineless, but his betrayal of my confidence, of what I'd told him and Brooke privately, hurt and enraged me. Still, would he have mentioned the ledger page if he was afraid his name might be on it?

Troy Sr. made a dismissive gesture. "I suppose you decipher it with the secret decoder ring from a box of cereal?"

The three men laughed, Troy Jr. a bit shame-facedly, and Betty looked at me with sympathy.

"Have a nice round," I said, hoping they each put half a dozen balls into the several ponds on the course and lost a few more in the woods that bordered the narrow fairways. Maybe Troy Jr. would get bitten by a rabid gopher. I said another good-bye to Betty and headed toward the door.

My encounter with the Widefields put a damper on my mood. I was feeling bummed out as I reached the van and unlocked it. As I drove away, I glanced toward the course and saw a foursome bumping their way to the first tee box in two carts. Troy Jr. and the man I didn't know were in the lead, with Troy Sr. driving the second cart and Chief Uggams seated beside him. I watched until they rounded a bend and I couldn't see them any-more.

I was driving back to the office when, on impulse, I detoured to Brooke's house. Troy was on the golf course; we could talk privately. The more I thought about it, the more I thought I was wrong to hide what Maud and I had discovered on the ledger page from my best friend. She had a right to know. Now that the police had the decoded page, it was in severe danger of becoming public and I didn't want Brooke's first hint of trouble to be an article in the *Herald*. Besides, she might be able to tell me whether it was her husband or her father-in-law who enjoyed wagering a sum large enough to pay my annual mortgage on a NASCAR race.

I called ahead and discovered she wasn't home; she was pulling her shift at the animal rescue shelter she had helped found a few years back. I pulled up outside Heaven Animal Haven ten minutes later. HAH was located on five acres of land on the east side of Heaven. Bordered by a scraggly line of lodgepole pines and set three-quarters of a mile off the road, it wasn't the kind of place you'd run across by accident. A mobile home served as the office, while two buildings housing animal kennels and runs took up the rest of the clearing. HAH cared mostly for abandoned cats and dogs, but people sometimes brought in wild animals, which volunteers rehabbed, if possible, and released to the wild. The wild animals stayed on the far side of the compound, completely separate from the domestic pets and the people who came to adopt them. HAH didn't always have wild animals on hand, but since Brooke's car was parked outside the rehab complex, I deduced that there must be at least one critter in residence.

A painful screech startled me when I walked into the concrete-block building. I whirled and found myself facing a tiny screech owl in a flight enclosure. Unblinking golden eyes were set in the white dish of feathers that made up his face. He let out another ear-piercing shriek and turned his back on me.

"Brooke?"

"Back here."

I followed her voice to the nursery, where I found her seated on a chair, a tiny red fox kit in her lap, nursing from a bottle. The kit's sibling mewled from a blanket-lined box set atop the table.

"Oh, how darling," I cooed, completely forgetting why I'd come.

"Hersh brought them in yesterday. He found them when he was replacing fence posts in his orchard. He heard them crying and located them in an old tree stump. He got his youngest to keep watch for half a day, but when the mom didn't show up, he brought them here. She was probably hit by a car, or maybe coyotes got her. Here, you feed Copper."

She passed me the kit, wrapped in a hand towel, and stood to get another bottle and the other kit. "This is Penny. I don't know if she'll make it—she's awfully weak. I think the mom must have been gone for a day or so before Hersh rescued them."

Copper resembled a newborn kitten, except for his fuller tail and his pointy snout. His eyes were closed now as he suckled, but he'd opened them when Brooke passed him to me, so he must be a couple of weeks old. I ventured to stroke the top of his head with one gentle finger.

"Ah-ah," Brooke said, shaking her head. "We want to release them eventually. No bonding. No making them like people."

"I thought you weren't supposed to name them, either," I said.

She gave me a guilty look. "I have to call them something."

When the hungry foxes had had their fill of

milk or formula or whatever it was, we placed them gently in the box and Brooke slid it into a plastic-sided kennel. They had curled around each other, tails over their noses, and were fast asleep. Brooke made notes related to time and amount of milk they'd drunk, and led me into the hall.

"You should do this full-time," I blurted. "You could raise funds, get professional staff, get people trained. You'd be great at it, and you'd love it."

Brooke looked startled and pushed her heavy hair off her face. "I do love it, and it's important work."

"You could build a Web page and advertise the pets for adoption across the country. I've seen animal rescue places that do that. You could put a Web cam in with the foxes, or the owl or whatever animal you're rehabbing, and get donations from everywhere." I was getting excited by the idea, completely forgetting why I'd tracked Brooke down.

"I'll think about it and talk to Troy," she said.

That reminded me why I was here. As we trekked across the gravel parking lot from the rehab building to the adoption center, I said, "I saw the Troys at the golf course this morning."

"What were you doing out there?"

I told her.

She gave me a searching look. "Are you coping okay? With Doug's wedding?"

I answered as if I'd misunderstood her. "Oh, yeah. It's a simple one. No live animals or roller skaters in the wedding party, only a hundred fifty guests, reception at the Club. I could plan it in my sleep."

She blew a raspberry. "You know what I mean."

I shrugged. "I'm not thinking about it much." Realizing I'd drifted away from my purpose again, I said, "Maud decoded the ledger page. It's a list of names of people who placed bets with Clay Shumer. You saw the police took him in for questioning? I guess he was a bookie, running a pretty significant betting operation." *Not that I'd know what was small potatoes and what was big-time.* "Anyway, there are lots of names there and, of course, it's only one page, probably from a while back. Maud thinks anyone on there might have been afraid of Ivy making it public and killed her."

Brooke's eyes widened. "Really? What do the police say?"

I felt vindicated that Brooke immediately assumed the police should have the page. "They're interviewing people." We had reached the entrance to the adoption center, and muffled woofs came from inside. We pushed through the door and heard another volunteer telling a dog to hush up and eat. The place smelled like disinfectant and animals—not in an unpleasant way—but such that you knew immediately there were plenty of dogs and cats in residence. Of course, the bags of dog food and kitty litter stacked against one wall were a big clue, too.

"Donation from a pet store going out of business in Grand Junction." Brooke nodded at the bags. "Help me move them into the storeroom?"

"Sure. In a minute." I bit my lip. "One of the names on the ledger page was Widefield," I said.

Her smooth brow wrinkled. "Are you telling me that Troy—?"

"Or Troy Sr., or your brother-in-law, or Clarice, for that matter," I hastily added. "It was a big bet—fifteen thou on a NASCAR race." She went silent and I asked, "Do you know who—?"

"No." She bent to pick up a forty-pound bag of dog food, hiding her face. She lugged it to an open storeroom door and I picked up a similar bag and followed her. "It's not my Troy," she said, letting the bag fall with a rattle of dog kibble. She nudged it against the wall with the side of her foot.

"Okay." I accepted that for the moment, sensing that it would only alienate her if I pushed. "Troy Sr., then?"

Putting her hands on her hips, she faced me. "Why are you doing this, Amy-Faye? Why are you trying to make it look like someone in my family killed Ivy Donner? If she was blackmailing the people on that list, she deserved what she got."

I jerked back as if she'd hit me. Where had that come from? "Ivy wasn't a blackmailer. Clay could have told his clients Ivy had copied the page, warned them that she might make it public."

"I didn't mean that. Of course she didn't deserve to die." Brooke's voice was hoarse, and I suspected she was fighting tears. "Didn't the article this morning say Clay probably killed her?"

"Not in so many words, but I think the police consider him a solid suspect."

"Well, then. There's nothing left to investigate. The police—and you—should burn that list, forget it ever existed."

"Someone tried that."

She gave a tiny gasp, but then silence stretched between us. Dust motes floated in a sunbeam from the room's one small window set high on the wall. A rhythmic *skritching* sound puzzled me for a moment, but then I decided a mouse was enjoying the dog food before it was dished out to the shelter's canine residents.

"Brooke, what's wrong?"

She sniffed and headed out the door. "Nothing."

We transferred the bags in silence for twenty minutes, and then she fetched a broom to sweep up litter and dog food dust where the bags had been stacked. I didn't like seeing her like this— silent, withdrawn, and obviously worried about something—but I didn't know how to help. Music from an oldies station drifted in to cover the silence, and the splat of water on concrete told me the other volunteer was hosing down the dog runs.

When Brooke emptied the dustpan into a trash can, I said awkwardly, "I should be going. Al will think I drove off a cliff."

Brooke had been giving me her classic profile for the past twenty minutes, but now she faced me. The hollows under her cheeks seemed more pronounced than usual. "Let it go, Amy-Faye. Can you do that? For me? The police have their killer. Does the rest of it really matter?"

I studied her face, troubled. Brooke was my best friend. Ivy was dead and nothing was going to change that. In all probability, Clay Shumer had killed her. Did the details, the whys and wherefores, really matter? Not more than my friendship with Brooke, I decided.

"Okay," I said. "Okay."

Relief lightened her face and she hugged me. "Okay."

I left, not sure anything was really okay.

Chapter 25

I was abstracted on my way back to the office, thinking about the names on the ledger page and about how little each of us knows about our neighbors, and even our friends and family. Undercurrents roiled beneath smiling surfaces meant to convince others that everything was moving along smoothly, that there were no submerged logs or boulders in the stream of daily existence. The encounter with Brooke had me wondering exactly what was going on in her marriage. It wasn't my business, but I loved her and I was worried. In all honesty, I had to point a finger at myself. I mean, how many people realized how torn up I was about Doug getting married? *Bad example.* How many people knew I worried about growing my business so I could meet my mortgage every month and keep Al and me employed? Who knew I felt guilty about not making it to church more often and the fact that I didn't keep in touch better with my sister Natalie? We all had issues that we covered up or disguised almost as a matter of course; others—like whoever killed Ivy—were more proactive and deliberate about their cover-ups.

My thoughts distracted me, and I was halfway from the van to my office door when I noticed someone lurking at the end of the walkway where it emptied into the garden. There was something vaguely threatening about the figure backlit by the sun, something stiff and tense. It was early afternoon on a sunny day, but the walkway was shadowed by the house, and there were only a couple of small windows—bathrooms—in the brick façade. For a moment, I felt isolated, and a remnant of the fear I'd felt when I found the "mind your own beeswax" threat prickled through me. I stopped. The figure took a step toward me. I half turned, prepared to make a dash for the safety of the street, when a voice stopped me.

"Wait! Amy-Faye, it's me. Fee. Fiona Shumer."

I paused and she came toward me. She stopped a few feet away, clutching her purse tightly to her chest with both arms, and we studied each other. She looked like a different woman from the sleek blond yoga goddess who had taunted me yesterday. Red eyes testified to copious weeping, binge drinking, a sleepless night, or all of the above. Her hair and skin looked dull and her shoulders drooped. She'd apparently dressed all by guess, or in the total dark.

"Fee, are you okay?" I asked, taking a step toward her.

"You've got to help me," she said, her eyes pleading with me. The hands clutching her purse shook.

"Of course. Let's go into my office—"

"No!" She looked over her shoulder, as if expecting to see a werewolf sneak around the corner and come after us.

"Okay," I said in a calm voice. "Not my office. When did you last eat?"

She waved an impatient hand. "I don't know. Last night? Yesterday lunch? Before . . ."

Before the police picked up Clay for interrogation? No wonder she looked so bad. "You need food. You're eating for two, remember? You'll feel better with a little soup in you. Let's go to the Divine Herb."

Her dull gaze sharpened and she looked down at herself. "I can't. Not looking like this."

I thought. "Okay. You wait here, or better yet, in the garden." I pointed. "I'll get some lunch to go and then we can talk."

She nodded but didn't move. When I made a little shooing motion with my hands, she turned and walked like a zombie toward the garden outside my office. I watched her shamble away, then trotted toward the café. In about five minutes, I was back in the garden, two take-out containers of minestrone soup cradled against my chest and a couple of cookies in a bag dangling from my hand. Fee sat on the stone bench under the apple tree not yet in bloom, and I sat beside her. Silently, I handed over one of the soup containers, several cracker packets, and a spoon. We ate in silence.

With nourishment, Fee seemed to recover herself a little. Squeezing the empty take-out bowl between her hands, she exhaled heavily and said, "I have screwed things up beyond comprehension. I mean, look at us." She waved a hand between us. "I don't even like you, and I know you don't like me, and yet I'm here looking for help."

I didn't bother to contradict her about the liking thing. It was true.

When I didn't respond, she huffed a broken laugh and went on. "You're the only one who can help me straighten out this mess. Lord knows I can't go to the police. They've arrested Clay, and it's my fault."

I stiffened. Was she confessing to Ivy's murder?

She must have felt my reaction, because she looked at me, startled. "*That's* not my fault, although if she'd been standing in front of me when I found out she was sleeping with my husband, I might have strangled her. No, it's my fault the police think Clay did it. I should start at the beginning.

"A couple of months ago, I started to think Clay was fooling around on me. The wife is always the last to know, right? I should have picked up on the clues earlier, but I was too dumb . . . or too complacent. I mean, I'm not exactly a dog." She seemed to realize she wasn't looking her best and self-consciously smoothed her hair. "Well, not in the normal course of things, anyway."

"You're beautiful, Fee."

A grateful smile slipped out, but then she turned waspish. "Don't patronize me, please. Anyway, I hired a private investigator—a man from Grand Junction because I didn't want anyone in Heaven knowing that Clay was cheating on me—and it didn't take him more than two days to get photos of Clay and Ivy Donner. Screwing." Rage flushed her face and her fingers picked at the soup bowl, tearing away bits of foam that drifted like stiff snow to the grass. When she had herself under control again, she went on. "I stewed over it all day, waiting for him to get home from the office. We ate dinner like usual and opened a bottle of wine, and I waited for bedtime. When Clay went upstairs, he saw the photos. I had taped them up all over our bedroom. You should have seen his face. He literally turned green. I lost it then, asked him if they'd done it in our bed, asked him how long it had been going on, told him I would never, ever forgive him. Finally, I told him I was pregnant. I got the test results the same day the PI gave me his report." She smiled bitterly. "Clay was stunned by all of it. He asked me over and over again if I was sure, until I gave him the lab report. He started crying then."

I sat motionless, overwhelmed by her misery and by the evidence of the damage Ivy had done. The fact that I didn't much like Fee didn't keep me from feeling sorry for her. "That's awful," I murmured.

"'Awful' doesn't begin to describe it. We talked and shouted at each other all night. I'll spare you the gory details. In the end, we agreed that we would try again—for the baby. He said he'd break up with Ivy, that he'd manage it so he wasn't working with her anymore. I was hoping he'd fire her, but he got her promoted. We were making it day to day, until Ivy died."

"I don't understand."

"When she died, Clay lost it. Broke down. Said

he'd killed her. He meant he'd driven her to suicide by breaking up with her. I saw then what I'd never let myself understand. It wasn't just about the sex—he loved her. I . . . I wanted to punish him. When it seemed as if she had killed herself, well, his guilt was punishment enough. When it began to look like the police were investigating her death as a homicide, he was actually *happy*. It meant she hadn't poisoned herself over him. I couldn't stand it. He couldn't get off so easy. So I sent the police a picture. Of Ivy and Clay." She gave me a sidelong look.

I knew what she was talking about because of what Hart had told me. I nodded.

"I thought it would embarrass him, being grilled by the police. That's all I wanted. I didn't mean for him to get arrested or go on trial! I didn't know when I sent it about the gambling." She cut herself off.

"But you do now?"

"Yes. He told me all of it yesterday, after we got home from the police station. He told me he'd been running this side business"—she said it as casually as if he had a paper route—"for almost ten years. He told me that after he broke up with Ivy, he found a page from his ledger, the one he keeps all his transactions in, in the copy machine tray. Someone had made two copies by mistake. It scared the crap out of him. He confronted Ivy at her house. She'd worked with him for so long that she had figured it out, she told him. She'd only kept quiet because she loved him. Now that he'd ditched her, she was going to make him sorry."

"What did he do?"

"There was nothing he could do. He warned a few of his best clients that there might be an investigation."

"Troy Widefield?"

After a brief hesitation, Fee nodded. "Among others."

"Junior or Senior?"

"Senior, I think. I'm not sure. Clay just said 'Widefield.' He said he felt like he was living on top of a time bomb, waiting for it to go off. And then Ivy died."

I studied her face, which had a hint of color in it now. "I don't understand, Fee—what do you want from me?"

She gave me a look that said I was being dense. "I want you to find out who really killed her, of course. Everyone knows you've been asking questions about Ivy's death, that you never believed she killed herself. When I sent the photo, I didn't mean for Clay to get in this much trouble. It never crossed my mind that he'd actually be arrested or have to stand trial. I thought he'd just get a taste of humiliation. But because of the bookie stuff and that stupid ledger page Ivy stole, the police think he had a real motive. For obvious reasons, he can't confess to the betting thing, can't tell the police one of his clients must have killed Ivy to keep from being exposed, so you'll have to figure out which one of them did it. Have you found anything out already? Do you have any idea who it might have been?" Fee looked at me hopefully.

I asked slowly, "What makes you so sure it

wasn't Clay? He had motive and opportunity, and I don't imagine he'd find it hard to come by a few oleander leaves."

She swallowed hard. "You didn't see him when he heard she was dead. He loved her, truly loved her." Her voice was no more than a whisper. "There's no way he killed her."

The admission had cost her a lot, and she suddenly stood. She swayed and I put out a hand to steady her. She shook it off. "Look, I know you don't like me, Amy-Faye, but you were Ivy's friend—you must want to know what really happened to her."

The blatant attempt to manipulate me made me say, "I don't know if I can."

Her nostrils flared. "You can't hate me that much, to refuse to help keep an innocent man out of jail—"

I wasn't wholly convinced of Clay's innocence in any context, but I said, "It's not that, Fee. I sort of told someone I'd drop it. I don't know—"

"I'll pay you."

"I don't want money." A squirrel that had approached, hoping the take-out container crumbs were edible, fled up a tree at the sharpness of my tone.

"Then, what?"

I was torn. I'd told Brooke I'd drop it, but I found myself believing Fee when she said Clay didn't kill Ivy. If not, then the real murderer was walking the streets of Heaven, as pleased as punch that the police had arrested Clay. I could tell the police what Fee had told me, about Clay warning his clients, including Troy Widefield, but I didn't think they'd be able to get a search warrant or even question him based on my thirdhand information. Frustration built in me. "I'll think about it," I told Fee.

"Thank you." She paused, as if going to say more, and then walked away.

I looked up at the squirrel, frisking his tail on the branch above me. "You think I should do it, right? Look into it some more?"

He chittered.

"But what about Brooke?"

The squirrel scampered to the crook where the branch met the trunk and scratched his ear briskly. "You're right. The truth is more important. And we can't have a murderer running around loose in Heaven."

"Talking to yourself, boss?" Al's voice came from the office doorway behind me. I turned to see him lounging against the jamb, arms crossed over his sweater-vested chest. "They say that's a sign of senility. Or just plain crazy." He made looping motions beside his ear.

I didn't think it would improve matters to tell him I'd been talking to the squirrel, so I said I'd been thinking out loud and herded him in front of me into the office, asking for status updates on his events.

Chapter 26

I replayed my conversation with Fee several times throughout the afternoon and hadn't reached a decision by the time I needed to leave to meet Doug and Madison to choose a band. Ironically, I found myself actually looking forward to hooking up with the happy couple because it would enable me to put off making a decision for a few more hours. As far as I could see, if I decided to pursue the investigation, I'd have to talk to Troy Widefield Sr., since Fee was sure Clay had warned him about Ivy having the ledger page, and I knew Brooke would hear about it and feel like I'd lied to her. Frankly, the thought of confronting Senior intimidated me, too. If he'd killed Ivy and tried to sabotage my business and discourage me from investigating with the beehive incident, who knows what he might do if I showed up in his office and told him I knew about the gambling. I frowned. I had a lot of trouble envisioning the patrician Troy Widefield lugging a stolen beehive to the park, and an even harder time matching him up with the "mind your beeswax" language in the threatening letter. I tried to put it out of my mind and left to meet my clients.

The first band Doug and Madison and I were going to listen to was set up in the basement of the New Way Church, a nondenominational wannabe megachurch that would have a much better chance of reaching mega status if it were located in a town with more than ten thousand people. I arrived ten minutes early and heard the clash of cymbals before I even entered the building. Doug and Madison weren't here yet. I glanced into a worship space with enough pews for every man, woman, and child in the county, a bank of choir stalls, strategically placed speakers, and large TV screens overhead. *For instant replay on the sermon?* Despite the trappings of entertainment, it was a peaceful space and I lingered in the doorway, not thinking much about anything, until I heard Doug's voice behind me.

"Getting religion in your old age, A-Faye?"

I wasn't sure if I was more annoyed about the age jab or the implication that I wasn't religious. I might not be a regular churchgoer—I got to St. Luke's once or twice a month—but God and I talked almost daily. I disguised my irritation with a smile and turned. Before I could respond, he added, "Hey, Madison tells me you've got a new guy. We'll meet him at the wedding, right? He's a cop?"

Dang. I hadn't thought that Madison might mention our conversation to Doug. How to get out of this? I knew: keep lying. Would God strike me dead for lying in his holy place? I edged away from the sanctuary door. "That's right." I smiled. "Lindell Hart. He's excited about attending the wedding and said to pass along his congratulations." To forestall more questions about Hart and our imaginary relationship, I asked, "Where's Madison?"

A shadow passed over Doug's face. "Where is she always? Working. She has a brief she has to e-mail by COB New York time, and she's crashing on that. She told me to come ahead and choose a band, since the music is really my thing anyway."

That was true. It had been Doug who insisted on actually seeing their top two bands in person after I gave them CDs of several area bands to listen to. He was a music geek from way back. The thrum of an electric bass vibrated up from the floor below, and I said, "Let's get to it."

We descended the stairs and found the band in a large open room that was probably used for church suppers if the tables and chairs stacked on dollies were any indication. The band had set up on a small dais at the far end of the room and the drummer hailed us with a rim shot when we came in. I'd worked with them a couple of times before, and I introduced them to Doug. He and the lead singer immediately got into a discussion about the guitar he was playing. I rolled my eyes good-humoredly and pulled a couple of folding chairs off a dolly for us to sit in. Doug joined me in a moment.

"Give us one minute," the bandleader said, stepping over wires to talk to the keyboard player.

We sat side by side in our cold metal chairs, the only audience members waiting for a concert to begin. I'd done this numerous times with other brides and grooms, but today it felt awkward. Maybe because Madison wasn't there and I sensed Doug's anger or disappointment about her defection. Maybe because I was still unsettled from the spat, if you could call it that, with Brooke. *Maybe because Doug's getting married in a week and it makes me sad.* Mostly to break the silence, I asked, "Did you see the article in today's *Herald*?"

Doug furrowed his brow. "Yeah. I have to talk to the police tomorrow, when I've got more time."

I raised my brows at him. "About what?"

He hesitated. "I suppose it doesn't matter if I tell you since I have to tell the police anyway. Now that they're calling Ivy's death murder, I need to tell them she hired me a few days before she died to draw up a will."

"Really?" All my and Flavia's imaginings about Ivy talking to him about protecting herself from libel charges or prosecution vanished. It was nothing so interesting. She wanted a will, like millions of other people.

"When she called me, the Wednesday before she died, I thought maybe she was ill and that had prompted it."

"You did? Why?"

"I don't remember her exact wording, but I got the impression she thought she might die soon. She didn't actually say she had cancer or anything, but that's where I went. She wanted the will quickly and I gave her the draft on Friday—it was simple, mostly boilerplate, a couple bequests, a request for spreading her cremains. Now that the police are saying she was killed, I can see that she might have meant something else, which is why I've got to talk to the detective. Your new sweetie." Despite the somberness of the topic, he grinned.

Uh-oh. I sent up a quick prayer that my name would not come up when Doug talked to Hart. I had a sinking feeling that God's answer was *You got yourself into this, so you can get yourself out.*

"So she left everything to Ham," I said.

"No. She was leaving half to Heaven Animal Haven and half to her college."

"But Ham's already made arrangements to sell her house!"

"That's because she didn't sign the will. Without a will, a person's estate goes to their nearest living relatives, a spouse if married, then children, parents, or siblings."

I guessed that made sense. Before I could think about it, the band launched into its first number, a Def Leppard cover, obviously requested by Doug.

I leaned in to speak in his ear. "You're kidding, right? People want to hear 'YMCA' and 'Shout' at a wedding, maybe a little Frank Sinatra, Nat King Cole, and 'Fly Me to the Moon' for the older crowd."

Doug grinned and my heart skipped a beat. "Yeah, but they're good."

When the band brought the number to a close, Doug applauded and said, "You know any Nat King Cole?"

"Of course, man." The lead singer counted out a slow three-count and the band eased into "Unforgettable."

"C'mon." Doug grabbed my hand and pulled me up.

"Wha—"

"Got to practice my dancing. Don't want to embarrass my bride by trampling her feet."

Before I could object—which I was absolutely going to do—he pulled me against his chest and led me into a haphazard waltz. His hand clasped mine firmly and his other hand wrapped around my waist. The scent of his familiar aftershave brought back memories of slow dancing in the high school gym with crepe paper streamers and chaperones; of making out in his car, afraid to go too far and prevented from it by the stick shift and bucket seats; of the first time we made love, both of us virgins, in his college dorm room. I nestled closer and felt his arm tighten around my waist. After a few more bars of the smoky tune, both his hands went to my waist and my arms went around his neck and we moved in slow circles. When I closed my eyes, the church's linoleum flooring became the polished wood of the gym floor. All that was missing were the delinquents trying to dump vodka in the punch bowl, and the gaggle of girls talking animatedly on the sidelines, trying to pretend they didn't care they didn't have anyone to slow-dance with. Doug bent his head so his cheek rested against mine and I could feel his breath on my ear. If I turned my head a fraction our lips would meet.

"Just like old times, eh, A-Faye?" His voice was husky.

"Pretty much," I agreed weakly. The melty lassitude of desire made my limbs heavy. My body ached with warmth, and I was ultrasensitive at every point where we touched. A day's growth of beard rasped my cheek. His hair was crisp at his collar where my fingers laced. I was light-headed. I could tell by the way his breathing deepened and slowed that he was feeling the same tug of desire.

The song ended and the band clapped for us, laughing. I pulled away, face flaming. What was I thinking? He was getting married in just over a week. This trip down memory lane was dangerous and wrong.

"A-Faye—"

"I think they're good, don't you?" My voice was brittle. I was mad at him for playing these games with me, and mad at myself for getting sucked in.

"Yes." He clipped the word short, obviously not interested in discussing the band. The fluorescent lights gleamed off the wheat-colored streaks in his dark blond hair. His green eyes searched mine and I thought I read concern and confusion in them. "I'm sorry. I shouldn't have— I didn't mean— It started out as just a dance."

"No, you shouldn't have. *We* shouldn't have." Clarity broke over me, like a gallon of cold water dumped on my head. "I don't think I'm the one to plan your wedding, Doug. I appreciate that you and Madison were trying to push some business my way, but I'm backing out. I'm sure Madison can take over from here, or your mom. I'll pass along all my notes and details about the arrangements I've already made. No charge."

"Don't do this."

Doug looked stricken, and I knew it was about more than having his wedding planner flake out a week before the big day. His face said he knew our friendship would never be the same.

The band started in on a soft version of "You've Lost That Lovin' Feelin'," and I shot them a dirty look.

"I have to." I leaned forward and kissed the corner of his mouth. "I truly hope you and Madison will be very happy. I'm sure you will be."

His hand came up to my shoulder—to draw me closer or push me away?—but I stepped back and it fell to his side. Without waiting to see his reaction, I fled from the basement.

"—now it's gone, gone, gone, woh-oh, woh-oh," the lead singer crooned behind me. *Ass.*

I made it to the parking lot before I noticed I wasn't crying. I blinked my eyes a couple of times to be sure. Nope. Dry. I inhaled deeply and realized that although I was sad, my uppermost emotion was relief. I'd finally done the smart thing, the right thing, what I should have done the moment Madison told me she was marrying Doug. Pleased that I hadn't mentally stuck a "my" in front of "Doug," I got in the van and fiddled with the tuner. I didn't need sappy country songs right now. Finding a station that played pop music, I drove away singing along with "What Does the Fox Say?" perhaps the most inane song produced this decade. It fit my mood perfectly.

Chapter 27

I considered calling Lola, or dropping in on my folks, but I really just wanted to be alone and wallow. So I bought some brownie mix at the City Market on my way home and whipped up a batch of chocolatey goodness while watching *An Affair to Remember*. The aroma of baking brownies was the perfect complement to Cary Grant's suavity and banter. I ate a couple of warm brownies with a glass of cold milk and made it a double feature with *Sleepless in Seattle*. It wasn't as masochistic as it sounds. I let myself get weepy, and it felt cathartic. Before going to bed, I ground the rest of the brownie batch in the garbage disposal and washed them away to keep from finishing them off for breakfast.

Friday morning I awoke feeling refreshed. A little sad, but basically okay. My eyes were puffy, but concealer and a darker eye shadow than usual covered that up. I went to yoga and was not surprised to find that Fee was absent. The hour of stretching made me feel limber and relaxed, and I was feeling good enough to tackle any task that came down the pike by the time I changed and started working. The first thing I did was forward all my notes and e-mails about the wedding to Doug and Madison. The stuff that wasn't e-mailable I stuck in an envelope; I scribbled their names on it and popped it into the mail. When Al came in, I told him that we were no longer working the Taylor-Elvaston wedding.

"Thank God," he said with an expressive eye roll.

"What?"

"I always thought your taking on that wedding was stupider than sticking your finger in a light socket," he said, sitting at his desk and sifting through his files.

"You did? Why didn't you say so?"

"Right. Like it would have done any good."

Was this Al? My Al? The one who blurted every thought? "Who are you and what have you done with Al Frink?" I asked.

He gave me an affronted look. "It's not like I say everything that comes to mind, you know. I do have some tact."

Could have fooled me. I let it go. "Give me a rundown of your events for this weekend. Do you need my help with anything?"

When he told me he had everything under control, I found myself at loose ends. The wedding had been my big project, and now I had time on my hands. I spent half an hour sorting paper clips, changing printer cartridges, and deleting old e-mails, but then shoved back from my desk. Maybe my lack

290 / Laura DiSilverio

of occupation was a sign, a sign that I should get off my fanny and go talk to Troy Widefield Sr. The thought of Brooke's reaction, if she heard, stopped me. I didn't want to be precipitate. Yes, Fee had said Clay told Widefield that Ivy was going to out their gambling connection, but he surely wasn't the only one.

I started thinking about the timing. I'd been assuming that Troy Jr. had told his dad about me having the ledger page, but I hadn't told Brooke and Troy about it until after the bee incident. So either Senior hadn't been involved in relocating the beehive and leaving the threatening message, or someone else had told him about the ledger page. I got out an unused notebook. I needed a timeline. It all had to revolve around the ledger page, because nothing else made sense. The ledger page could send people to prison; it was worth killing for, moving beehives for, threatening for.

I wrote:

- Ivy calls Flavia, tells her she has a big story, criminal scandal, etc. (Tues before she dies)
- Ivy calls Doug, tells him she needs a will because she realizes she might be in danger? (Wed before she dies)
- Ivy copies ledger page (when?) and mails it to herself (to avoid being caught with it?)
- Clay finds duplicate copy in machine, confronts Ivy (find out when from Fee)
- Ivy tells Clay she's going to give the page to a reporter; he warns a few clients (including Widefield)

- Oleander put in Ivy's tea stash (when?)
- Ivy dies (Tuesday)
- Doug, Fee, and Clay go to her house, seen by Flavia (Wed)
- House is searched (late Tues/Wed/Thurs/early Fri)
- Ledger page arrives at Ivy's/I find (Fri)

I pondered that last item. Where had the ledger page been between when Ivy copied it and when the mail carrier delivered it to her house? Clearly, she hadn't popped it into the nearest mailbox. I visualized the envelope in my mind. It hadn't had a regular postage stamp stuck in the corner. It had been through one of those metering machines. I tried to put myself in Ivy's place. *I'm Ivy. I've decided to skewer my former lover by publicizing his illegal bookie biz. I contact a reporter. She tells me she needs proof. I know where Clay keeps his ledger, but I can't get caught copying it. The weekend! I go to the office on Saturday or Sunday—Sunday would be better—to get the proof. I jimmy Clay's bottom drawer—or maybe I know where he keeps the key—and copy a page from the ledger. I'm putting the ledger back when I hear a noise. Someone's coming!*

I paused in my reconstruction. Who would be there on a Sunday? A janitor? A security guard? Clay? No matter. *I only have a second. My purse is in the other room. I pop the page into an envelope and scribble my name on it. Then I drop the envelope in an out-box, greet the janitor or security guard, and stroll casually out of city hall.*

Hm. It could have happened that way. Then maybe

the envelope sits in an out-box for a day or two before it gets down to city hall's mailroom. Government efficiency being what it is, it's another day before it gets sorted, weighed, fed through the metering machine, and handed over to the U.S. Postal Service. It goes to some sorting center—Grand Junction?—and comes back to Heaven, getting delivered on Friday. I tapped my pencil on the pad, pleased with my reconstruction. I called Fee.

When she answered I asked her when Clay confronted Ivy about the copied ledger page. "Monday. The day before she died," Fee said. She sounded more with it than she had yesterday. "Are you looking into it? Have you found out anything?"

"Just doing some thinking," I said, and hung up before she could press me further.

I entered "Monday" onto my timeline and stared at it. It made sense. If Ivy copied the page on Sunday, Clay could have found it on Monday. She was taking a personal day, but he probably hotfooted it over to her place. If Clay and Ivy had it out at her house on Monday, that didn't leave much time for him to decide to kill her, come up with the oleander plan, collect a few leaves and introduce them into her tea canister by Tuesday. Actually, by Monday evening, I realized, because Ivy had poisoned tea with her when she came to the Readaholics meeting. The more I considered the timing, the more I realized how unlikely it was that Clay had killed Ivy. Fee was right.

The phone rang twice, but Al picked it up. I went back to my timeline, but Al appeared in the doorway.

"Hamilton Donner on the phone. Says it's about spreading ashes?" Al quirked an eyebrow at me.

"Oh." I'd almost forgotten about promising to spread Ivy's ashes with Ham. I picked up and greeted Ham.

"Hey, Amy-Faye, I was thinking about spreading Ivy's ashes today on my lunch hour, in about forty-five minutes. Does that work for you?"

It seemed borderline disrespectful to squeeze it in over a lunch break, but I didn't argue. I'd told him I'd go with him. I was happy to do this for Ivy. "Sure. Meet you at the tree house."

I hung up slowly. His voice had triggered a disturbing thought. I read through my timeline again, focusing on the Wednesday before her death when Ivy contacted Doug about a will. I drew a box around the word "will." Doug said she hadn't left Ham a penny, and yet here he was, selling her house, making plans for spending her money, and all because she had died before she had the opportunity to sign the will. I licked my lips with a suddenly dry tongue. Could Ham have known? Had Ivy told him about the will, or had he seen it somehow? He had a chip the size of Mount Rushmore on his shoulder about his family not believing in him, not investing in his projects . . . How would he have reacted to discovering that his sister was leaving her money not to him, but to a bunch of animals and a college?

Had I gotten so caught up in the Clay scenario, with its codes and criminality, that I overlooked the statistically more likely possibility, that Ivy had been killed for her money? By Ham. The two circumstances were connected, of course; Ivy wouldn't have made a will if she hadn't been worried about the repercussions of exposing Clay. I brought myself up short. This was Ham I was thinking about. Kind of a jerk, sure, but one I'd actually gone on a date with, someone I'd known for fifteen years. Did I really think he was capable of slipping oleander into his sister's tea canister? If she'd been whacked over the head or pushed off a convenient cliff, okay, maybe. But oleander? It didn't seem very Ham-ish. On the other hand, I'd thought a couple of times over the past few days that we knew less than we thought about even close friends and family members . . .

I shook my head. All in all, Ham wasn't a very likely candidate, despite the money, but I could take advantage of meeting him at the tree house to figure out if he'd known anything about the will. I felt a moment's pause about being alone with him but felt too silly to call Hart or anyone to go along as a bodyguard. Then I remembered Brooke and Lola saying they wanted to be in on spreading Ivy's ashes. Relieved to have a good reason to ask them to come, I called them, leaving a voice mail for Brooke and agreeing to stop by Bloomin' Wonderful to pick up Lola on the way.

I flipped my steno pad closed and tucked it into my purse. Telling Al I was taking an early lunch, I left the office and drove to Bloomin' Wonderful, where Lola supplied me with a bouquet of sprightly daisies to leave with Ivy's ashes but said she couldn't go after all.

"Wish I could come with you and pay my last

respects," she said, "but my delivery guy just called to say he'll be here any minute now." She looked distressed. "If he unloads quickly, I could get there before you're done, maybe."

"Don't worry about it," I said, putting a hand on her arm. "I'll tell Ivy these are from both of us."

Lola smiled sadly and waved as I drove off. I had to wait for a semi to make the turn into her driveway before I could get onto the main road. As a result, I was running a few minutes late when I got to Ivy's old address and parked in front of the house with its virulent pink flamingos. I wondered if they glowed in the dark. Ham's truck was already there, and he got out when I pulled up, holding a wooden urn in the crook of his arm. He wore jeans and a white shirt with his name over the pocket, and his hair was neatly slicked back with some gel.

"You said you're on your lunch break—where are you working?" I greeted him.

"Delivering product for vending machines," he said, leaning in to kiss my cheek.

I allowed it, given the occasion, and even refrained from wrinkling my nose at the odor of cigarettes that hung around him. I found myself thinking he ought to smell differently but couldn't figure out why. My brain niggled at it as we turned and made our way toward the woods.

"Brooke said she wanted to come," I said, hesitating at the tree line. "And Lola. We could wait for them."

"I've got to get back," Ham said impatiently. "My boss is a real whip cracker. Docks my pay if I'm thirty seconds late." He plunged ahead.

Somewhat reluctantly, I followed him into the woods.

"Damn, I haven't been here in ten years, I'll bet," Ham said. "Not since a couple years before my folks bought it in that car crash. We weren't getting along too well that last year or so. No one in my family ever had any faith in me." The weight of grievances long held dragged down the corners of his mouth.

I took his words to mean no one would give him money for his harebrained get-rich-quick schemes.

"I like those flamingos," he added. "They add something to the old place. They're cheery."

We continued down the overgrown path in silence, only the crunch of leaves under our feet marking our progress. When we came within sight of the old tree house, Ham quickened his step. "Damn, it's still here," he said.

He walked beneath it, studying it from all angles. "We did a good job, Pop and me. Who'da thought it'd still be here after all this time? You know, A-Faye, working on this with my pop, it's one of the best memories I have of him. We built it that summer we moved here. I was pissed about leaving Des Moines and all my friends, but my folks said Walter's Ford would be a fresh start. When we bought this house, my pop promised we'd build a tree house together. I didn't think we really would, but damn if he didn't tell the truth, for once." Ham placed a hand on a ladder rung, seeming to test it for solidity. "We did good."

"It's a great tree house, Ham. It's too bad there

aren't any kids in the neighborhood to use it anymore. Ivy and I had good times up there."

At the mention of Ivy's name, Ham looked at the urn he carried. "Well, I suppose we should get it done. From up there?" He jerked his chin up.

"Sure. You first." I did not want Ham Donner admiring my rear view all the way up the ladder.

"Hold this." He thrust the urn into my hands. It was warm from being held against his chest, and I found that distasteful. I held it at arm's length while he climbed, and then passed it up to him. When I reached the opening, he was looking in the cupboard like I had when I came here a couple days after Ivy died. The urn sat on the floor.

"Nothin' in here," he said, smacking the door closed with a backward flip of his hand. "My pals and I used to smoke the occasional doobie up here"—he mimed holding a toke to his lips with thumb and forefinger—"and I thought there might be a hit or two left. You and Ivy must have finished them off."

That's what I'd been expecting him to smell like, I realized—marijuana. But why? "Not me," I said. "Ivy maybe." She'd tried once or twice to get me to try marijuana, and I'd taken a single puff once to appease her, but it had tasted nasty, made me cough, and I'd been worried about what my folks would do if they ever found out, so I'd steadfastly refused to give it another try. Ivy had laughed at me, not unkindly, and had never lit up again in my presence. Actually, looking back, I thought she'd been a bit relieved, like my refusal made it okay for her not to do it, either.

"I don't toke anymore, anyway," Ham said. "Realized a couple years back that I needed a clear head if I was going to be a successful entrepreneur. A clear head and some dough. I just needed a little backing, a little cash, and now I've got it, so look out, world! Ham Donner is about to make a splash." He threw his arms wide and almost kicked over the urn.

It hit me. I knew why I expected Ham to smell like marijuana and why his announcement that he'd given it up rang hollow: I'd seen a Baggie of marijuana on his bedside table when I met him at his room to talk about Ivy's funeral. It'd been partially concealed by a lamp . . . The image came back to me, and I froze. A snack-sized Ziploc Baggie, half-full of what I'd immediately assumed was weed. What if . . . what if it was *tea*? Tea mixed with oleander? That would certainly explain why he didn't smell like marijuana—he was telling the truth about having given it up. I struggled to keep my face expressionless as I realized that my earlier thoughts might not have been far off the mark. There was no proof he'd seen the will, though. Or was there? Doug had mentioned that the will specified what she wanted done with her remains . . .

I picked up the urn, turning it in my hands, and said, as casually as possible, "What made you think of spreading Ivy's ashes from here, Ham? I mean, it's perfect."

There was silence. I looked up to find him staring at me, his piggy eyes narrowed and speculative. I realized I had grossly, grossly underestimated his intelligence, or at least his survival instincts. I knew if I asked Doug that he'd say Ivy had wanted her cremains spread from the tree house. I backed up a step involuntarily and immediately knew it was the exact wrong thing to do.

"Whaddaya mean, how'd I think of it? It just came to me, like it was the right thing to do. I knew my sister pretty well, you know. We were close." While he was talking, Ham came toward me. His heavy footsteps made the platform vibrate.

"I know you've got to get back to work," I said. "So we should do this." I thrust the urn at him and he took it automatically.

"You do the honors," he said, handing it back to me almost gently. His gaze never left my face.

I had to be wrong with what I was thinking. Ham wasn't the subtle type. Oleander? I doubted he'd ever heard of it. He wouldn't know it from parsley. My logic didn't quiet my fears.

With a trembling hand, I tried to lift the lid on the urn. It was sealed somehow and I pulled harder.

"You need to work out more," Ham said, encircling my upper arm with one big hand, like he was assessing my biceps. His fingers crunched down and fear gave me strength. The lid popped open. I sidestepped to put some distance between us, but Ham didn't let go of my arm.

My hand hovered over the ashes. In the "ashes to ashes" speech at funerals, the priest sprinkled something into the grave, but I'd always thought it was either dirt or generic ashes, not someone's remains. I was reluctant to scoop up the chunky-looking ashes in the urn and scatter them around the tree house. "Do I dump it out or what?" I asked uncertainly.

"You've figured everything else out," Ham said in a voice that left no doubts. "I'm sure you can figure this out."

Without warning, I flung a handful of ashes into his face and tore myself away.

Ham cursed and rubbed his eyes. I made for the ladder. My breaths came fast and I slipped putting my foot on the first rung. *Got to get away.* I was only two rungs down when strong arms grabbed me under the armpits and hauled me back into the tree house. My thighs scraped the boards and I yelped.

"Too smart for your own good," Ham observed. "Always were."

He released me, and hope flared momentarily. Then his hands closed around my neck and he began to squeeze. "She didn't have to die," he said. "If she'd only believed in me. That's all I wanted—someone in my goddamn family to have a little faith. But none of them did. When I saw her will and realized she was cutting me out, well—"

Ham's thumbs digging into my trachea hurt, and it was hard to breathe. "I won't tell," I gasped. "Please don't—" I couldn't suck in air, no matter how hard I tried. I tugged at his hands, scratched them, but his grip didn't loosen. I kicked wildly, my feet thudding against his shins, his ankles. My pumps flew off and my bare feet were ineffectual. He thrust me away, holding me at arm's length, and continued to squeeze my throat. My vision grayed at the edges.

All sorts of things went through my mind, but I was most conscious of being unbearably sad about the grief my parents would feel when they learned I was dead. Couldn't . . . do that . . . to them. With the last of my strength, I flung myself backward, toward the tree house wall only a foot behind me. Caught off guard, Ham stumbled after me, his hands still encircling my neck. I slammed into the wall and felt it give. Ham, unable to stop his forward momentum and still keep strangling me, thudded against me. Our combined weight was too much for the old wood. It cracked. I felt the wood start to bow, and then there was nothing but air behind me. I was falling. Ham's eyes widened with fear as he plummeted after me. Somewhere in midair, his hands let go and I sucked in a huge breath just as I smacked into the ground.

I landed on my back and it knocked the air out of me. Tears came to my eyes, but I had enough presence of mind to roll slightly to my left—all I could manage—to keep from having Ham land on top of me. The ground shuddered when he landed. I concentrated on dragging in a small breath, then a slightly deeper one. The duff, years' worth of matted pine needles and leaves, had cushioned the fall somewhat. I wasn't dead. No time to catalog my aches and pains. I tried to push myself to a sitting position. Pain zinged up my arm from my left wrist and knocked me down again. Ham stirred beside me and grunted, and I knew I was out of time.

Ignoring the pain in my broken wrist, I latched onto an aspen sapling with my right hand and pulled myself to a standing position. Had to get to the street. I took two tentative steps. My knee hurt, but it would hold me. Spotting a piece of wood as long as a baseball bat, I picked it up and jogged toward my car. It was my only hope. Every step jarred my broken wrist, and I realized the pained "hew, hew, hew" sounds were coming from me. I forced myself to run. Branches slapped my face, but I was hardly conscious of them. Footsteps thudded behind me, and I tried to go faster. I glimpsed the house. The road was just beyond—

Ham's hand landed heavily on my shoulder, and as he spun me, I raised the slat and brought it around as hard as I could. It glanced off his shoulder before smacking his jaw with a crunch that jerked the board from my hand. Splinters dug into my palm. I didn't wait to see if he went down, but whirled and ran for the street again.

"Amy-Faye! Where are you?"

Brooke's voice!

"Call nine-one-one," I shrieked, hardly recognizing the hoarse sound coming from my mouth as my voice. "Get the police!"

I was at the yard. Halfway across it, I risked a look back. Ham had reached the edge of the woods, blood smearing his face. WWKMD? Chase him down and tackle him. The hell with that. What did Kinsey know, anyway? She was fictional. I turned and kept going across the yard. The street came into view, our cars, Brooke on her phone, and Lola hurrying toward me.

"Amy-Faye, whatever happened to you?"

I fell into her kind, capable, strong arms.

"Your throat!"

"Ham—"

I whipped my head around, suddenly afraid to see him plunging across the yard, a threat to me and my friends. I scanned the tree line, but he was gone. Relief cascaded through me and left me so limp I slumped to the ground.

"Brooke's calling the police," Lola said, squatting to put an arm around me, "and an ambulance. Come on, let me help you to the car."

Brooke ran up to us, fell to her knees, and hugged me tight. "I got your message about the ashes, A-Faye, and I actually walked out on lunch with Clarice to join you and Ham and Lola. Tell me you're okay."

I managed a nod. "Never better." My voice was a raspy whisper from a horror movie.

Brooke gave a watery giggle and said, "You sound like Clint Eastwood." Then we were all laughing for no reason I could see. It hurt but felt good at the same time.

They helped me up and both of them put their arms around my waist to support me to the open door of Lola's car. "Did you see—?" The pain in my throat stopped my words, and I put a hand to my neck.

"Don't talk." Lola pulled a survival blanket from her car's trunk and wrapped it around my shoulders. Only then did I realize I was shivering, even though it wasn't cold. "The delivery guy arrived just after you left and off-loaded my order quickly. I figured you and Ham might still be here. Did he—?"

I nodded. "Murdered Ivy."

"Poor Ivy," Brooke said, sensitive mouth trembling. "Thank God you called us, or he might have killed you, too."

"Thank God you came," I croaked.

We were all quiet after that, waiting in silence until an ambulance screamed into view, followed by Hart's Tahoe, lights strobing.

Chapter 28

I was at the clinic getting my wrist wrapped in a cast when Hart and a couple of officers apprehended Ham Donner. Thank God. I couldn't believe I actually went out with the guy once. What did that say about my judgment? I felt truly sad for Ivy and hoped she hadn't had an inkling that her own brother had poisoned her. In fact, I hoped she hadn't realized she'd been murdered at all. What a hideous thing to think about as you're dying. Although the doc said the wrist was my only serious injury, I was shivering uncontrollably when my parents arrived at the hospital to take me home with them. Popping a couple of the pain pills for my throbbing wrist, I flopped onto my old bed and slept straight through to the next afternoon.

Mom set aside her reading and reviewing to field phone calls for me. I slept in my old room, surrounded by my favorite childhood books and stuffies, while she gave friends the bare bones of my ordeal, brushed off reporters, and told Detective Hart he could come by at three o'clock to do his official interview. She woke me in time to get ready, found a plastic bag to tie around my cast while I showered, and helped me dress in a slouchy T-shirt and jeans. My body was splotched with large bruises from the fall, and I ached in strange places. She did my damp hair in a loose braid, bringing back memories of elementary school, when she braided my hair most mornings before my sisters and I walked to school.

"There," she said, planting a kiss atop my head. "Did I mention I'm darned glad that Ham Donner didn't kill you?"

I shook my head.

"Well, I am." She heaved her bulk off the bed and offered me a hand up.

"Me, too." I hugged her.

The doorbell rang. Mom opened it and introduced herself to Hart. "It's a nice day," she said. "Maybe you and Amy-Faye would like to sit out here." She gestured to the veranda and we obediently settled into the flaking Adirondack chairs. "I'll bring you some tea." She disappeared.

Hart scanned my face. "You don't look too much the worse for wear. How long do you have to wear that thing?" He nodded at the cast.

"Could be six weeks." I made a face.

"You were lucky."

I nodded.

"Can you tell me about it? We're charging Donner with his sister's murder, and also with attempted murder. You. I need a statement. How did you end up in a tree house with the guy?"

Pleased that Ham was going to have to pay for

what he did to me, I told Hart everything I could remember. "He said he killed her because she didn't have faith in him, because no one in his family believed in him," I finished. "Have you ever heard anything more pitiful? I mean, what a dumb reason to die . . . for not wanting to fund your brother's crazy-ass schemes for alligator-wrestling attractions and edible crepe paper, although I guess it was really about not feeling valued. He must have spent years and years building up resentment. It's so freaking sad." I remembered his earlier words about how murder is almost always sad, and fell silent.

"It is sad," Hart said. "I'm sure the prospect of inheriting Ivy's house and money also played a role. He gave us a full confession last night, actually proud of how he pulled it off. He got the oleander idea from a movie, if you can believe it."

"Yeah, I figured that out. I actually saw the DVD cover in his room when I went by after Ivy died. *White Oleander*, right? I think I saw it a few years back. Michelle Pfeiffer was the baddie. So I guess this means Clay Shumer is off the hook?"

"For murder. He'll still have to face charges related to the gambling. As will many other folks, I suspect, by the time we're done decoding that entire logbook."

A neighbor's dog barked. I wondered where Mom had gotten to with the tea and figured she'd picked up a book, begun reading, and forgotten it. "So what about the fire? Clearly, Ham didn't do that."

"As you suspected, it was arson. We confronted

the cop on duty when it happened—Officer Ridgway—and he broke down pretty easily and admitted to setting it."

"But why? Was he a gambler?"

Hart shook his head. "No. But he's got debts, and his wife just had twins. Apparently he's been accepting bribes from someone he wouldn't name—"

"Whose name rhymes with 'Widefield'?"

"Possibly. Anyway, he's been on someone's payroll as an informant. He calls a number—a pay-as-you-go phone we can't track to anyone—and leaves a message when he comes across anything interesting. He called after you turned in the ledger page. He received a big bump in his illicit paycheck for trying to scare you off the case, and then for getting rid of the ledger page. He resigned this morning, two seconds before the chief could fire him."

"Will he go to jail?"

"Up to the DA, if she wants to prosecute. She might offer him immunity if he'll give up the name of the person he was working for. Personally, I'm not sure he knows it. Oh, and guess where he lives? He and his wife rent a cottage on Udo Yasutake's farm. The beehives are practically in their backyard."

I chewed my lip. The whole thing was very unsatisfying . . . If Widefield was behind it, I didn't want him to get away with damaging my business and scaring me half to death. If I'd caved when Ridgway left the threatening note, we might never have found out who killed Ivy.

Hart put a hand on my arm, the one not covered with plaster. "Leave it, Amy-Faye. Do not approach Widefield about this. You know what they say: Some days you get the bear, some days the bear eats you, and other times—like this—you and the bear go your separate ways."

"For now, maybe." I cocked my head. "You and your bear analogies . . . anyone would think you were born and raised in the Rockies."

"Hey, we have bears in Georgia, too, you know." He gestured to my cast. "Are we still on for the wedding this weekend?"

"Oh yes," I said hollowly, giving only momentary thought to making my wrist an excuse for not showing up. "Wouldn't miss it."

Chapter 29

The morning of Doug's wedding dawned clear and bright, but a thin scud was overhead by nine o'clock, and when I left for the ceremony, the sky was a uniform gray with a sharp breeze blowing. I grabbed a cardigan to wear over my sleeveless spring green dress with the wide white belt and flared skirt. It had a fifties vibe that flattered my small-waisted figure. I'd have felt a bit snazzier without the clunky cast on my left arm; it wasn't exactly the accessory I'd had in mind when I picked out the dress. I met Hart—looking handsome in a gray suit with a white shirt and flowered tie—in the gazebo parking lot. He kissed my cheek and I smiled at him, pleased to see him and oh so happy not to be witnessing Doug's marriage on my own. We walked up the slight incline together.

"Going to rain," he observed.

"I don't think the ceremony will take too long." Reverend Ramona, who was the officiant, had a reputation for keeping her services brief. I'd organized one wedding, where the bride went into labor the morning of the ceremony, that Reverend Ramona completed in five and a half minutes. *No lie.*

We mounted the steps of the gazebo, which was decked with pink bows and flowers, just as I had planned it. I figured Lola and her crew had been here since dawn to get ready. White folding chairs were set up on either side of a central aisle, with far more people on the groom's side than the bride's. People I took to be Madison's family members sat in the front row, conversing quietly among themselves. Pachelbel's Canon in D played from the portable stereo system.

Brooke, gorgeous in a coral sheath and a matching hat, waved from a row halfway back on Doug's side. Lola sat beside her, looking tired but satisfied. Neither Maud nor Kerry had been part of our high school crowd, and they weren't here.

I hugged Lola and then leaned across her to hug Brooke before introducing Hart to them both.

"Gorgeous flowers, Lo," I said. I sat on the aisle with Hart between me and Lola and Brooke on Lola's far side.

"Thanks," she whispered. "They'd better get a move on—it's going to rain."

I started to shrug my way into my cardigan, and Hart held it for me, his warm hand brushing the back of my neck. "Thanks."

While Lola, Brooke, and Hart made "get acquainted" talk, I couldn't help but run through my mental event to-do list, noting that no one had bothered to put a runner down on the center aisle. Flowers, music, ushers with matching boutonnieres, videographer—check. No guest book for attendees to sign, and no table for presents. I noticed two people with wrapped gifts on their laps. I shook my head. The guest book would be at the reception site, but some guests from the ceremony wouldn't go to the reception. Two bridesmaids huddled near the gazebo entrance, clearly wishing they had jackets to put on over their strapless pink dresses.

The festivities began with Doug's parents and then Madison's taking their seats in the front row. A moment later, a smiling Doug, handsome in a dove gray morning suit with tails and waistcoat, took his place at the front beside Reverend Ramona in her vestments. He exchanged a joke with his best man and then threw his shoulders back, facing all of us. The crowd hushed and I could hear the wind soughing through the pines. It made a plaintive sound, or maybe that was just me taking the perfectly ordinary sound of the wind in the trees and making it fit my mood. The bridesmaids processed with two groomsmen to the strains of the Cure's "Lovesong." I pinned a smile to my face as a white limousine pulled up. This was it.

The chauffeur, portly in a gray uniform and cap, got out. Instead of opening the passenger door so the bride could make her entrance, he climbed the gazebo's steps and shuffled down the aisle toward Doug. *Oh no*. I could tell by the way Doug's face went blank and rigid that he knew right then, that he didn't need to read the note the chauffeur handed him. The chauffeur, having delivered the envelope, beat feet out of the gazebo and gunned the limousine out of the lot. The music cut off as Doug pulled a folded note from the envelope and scanned it. Everyone was watching him. Madison's mother half rose but resumed her seat when her husband tugged on her hand. Doug lowered the page, swallowed, and then looked out at all of us.

"Well, folks," he started, then paused to clear his throat.

My heart ached for him.

"It looks like there's not going to be any wedding. Sorry. Um, there's still quite a spread at the Club, so you can adjourn straight there. Don't want it to go to waste just because . . . because, well."

"Oh nos" and "I can't believe its" bubbled up from the congregation. Someone started crying. I distinctly heard the word "bitch" but couldn't tell who said it. Doug ignored everyone, striding down the aisle without looking right or left, wrenching at his ascot like it was choking him. I saw the grief in his eyes as he passed. A couple of people reached out to him, but he shook them off. Moving ever faster, he clattered down the stairs and then stopped, scanning the parking lot. His shoulders slumped.

He didn't have a car! Someone had brought him to the park and he had expected to leave by limo, popping a champagne cork in the back with his new wife on the way to the reception. I rose.

"Amy-Faye—" Lola's voice held a caution.

I looked down at a startled Hart. "He needs me," I said. "I have to."

Only vaguely conscious of Hart's nod and Lola's and Brooke's worried faces, I hurried after Doug. Touching him lightly on the elbow as I drew even with him, I said, "Let's get out of here."

He faced me, but the blind look in his eyes made me suspect he didn't even process who I was. No matter.

"C'mon." I headed toward the van. He followed me and climbed in on the passenger side. I was cranking the ignition, thankful the cast was on my left arm, when the back door slid open and Lola and Brooke piled in with a rustle of stiff fabric. The door thunked closed.

"He's our friend, too," Brooke said, meeting my gaze in the rearview mirror. Lola put a comforting hand on Doug's shoulder, but he didn't react.

Most of the wedding guests were gathered at the gazebo rail watching as we peeled out of the lot, spiriting the jilted groom away from their prying eyes. I didn't know where we were going and I didn't think Doug cared. We quickly caught up to and passed the lumbering white limousine, which should have had a license plate reading "2DTHOTZ," and then banked around a curve and lost sight of it. Just as well. We drove through Heaven, past my office, city hall, the marijuana store Rocky Mountain Higher, my brother's pub. The silence inside the van was fraught. No one knew what to say.

We flashed past a sign for I-70 and Doug suddenly said, "The airport."

His voice sounded stiff, rusty, un-Doug-like.

"The airport?" Lola queried gently.

"DIA. I've got tickets to Bermuda—might as

well get my money's worth." He laughed harshly and pulled two ticket folders out of his jacket's inside pocket. "Anyone want to go with?"

I sucked my breath in on a thin whistle. Before I could even think about doing something stupendously, unutterably stupid, Doug was tearing Madison's ticket into confetti, rolling down the window, and letting the pieces trickle through his fingers into the slipstream. The wind ripped them away.

I took the turn that would put us on I-70 heading toward Denver International Airport.

"Road trip," Brooke said softly. After a beat, she continued, "Remember the time we drove to Lake Powell for spring break and stayed on that dumpy houseboat that smelled like cat pee? Was that our sophomore year or our junior year?"

"Junior," I supplied.

Lola jumped in to remind us about Troy falling overboard and asked Doug if he remembered what he called the virulent green cocktail he invented on that trip.

We continued east, bathing our hurting friend in good memories, reminiscences of times that had nothing to do with Madison, as we sped toward the airport and a plane that would take him to a solitary honeymoon. I suspected even a supersonic jet couldn't outdistance his pain, but maybe a week on his own would help him come to terms with Madison's desertion. At any rate, the best we could do was remind him that we'd shared good times together before Madison, and hope he got the idea that there could be more good times, eventually, post-Madison. Doug didn't say anything, but it seemed to me his shoulders relaxed infinitesimally as we drove farther east, and his face lost its carved-from-granite rigidity.

"Acid Rainbow," he finally said, startling us all to silence. He cleared his throat. "The cocktail. We called it Acid Rainbow. Maybe we can mix up a batch when I get back. Crème de menthe and grenadine—"

"And pineapple juice and rum," Brooke put in.

"It was nasty," Lola said. "I'm pretty sure that's why I don't drink."

I smiled and let up on the accelerator a bit. No point in getting there too fast.

Read on for a sneak peek at the next novel in Laura DiSilverio's Book Club series,

The Readaholics and the Poirot Puzzle

Coming in December 2015 from Obsidian.

Choosing a book for the Readaholics to read is a tough task, and the five of us who make up the book club take the responsibility seriously. Usually. There was the one time we wrote the titles of books ranging from *Gone Girl* to *The Moonstone* on slips of paper, taped them on my folks' garage door, and threw darts to pick a winner. Margaritas were involved. (Trust me, the garage door, unpainted since Fleetwood Mac hit the top ten, and liberally pocked with woodpecker holes to start with, was not greatly harmed by our selection process.) Only Lola managed to get a dart to stick. Did I mention the margaritas? Her dart picked Elizabeth George's *A Great Deliverance*. And there was the time, at least two years ago, where we decided (I don't remember why) that we had to find a title that started with "Q" and found ourselves reading an Inspector Rebus novel. But mostly, we take the task seriously.

Which is how I ended up having a conversation six weeks ago with Brooke Widefield, my best friend, whose turn it was to pick a book. We were sitting in my sunroom, almost uncomfortably warm with the sun streaming through the panes, which I had Windexed to streak-free perfection only that morning. The celadon green tiles gleamed, and the plants (chosen with much help from Lola, who owned a plant nursery) stretched greenly toward the sunlight. I'd had an event that went late the night before, Friday, and I was makeupless with my copper-colored hair in a ponytail and wearing a faded University of Colorado T-shirt and shorts that had fit better five pounds ago. Brooke, of course, as always, looked exquisite, mink dark hair curling over her shoulders like she had just finished filming a shampoo commercial and green eyes emphasized by taupe shadow and mascara. Her crisp red capris and denim jacket could have been featured in a magazine spread about how to look chic rather than sloppy running weekend errands. I was the "before" photo and Brooke the "after." I'm used to it.

"It's hard to find murder mysteries without murders in them," Brooke observed facetiously. "But since Ivy, well, I'm not in the mood to read anything too realistic."

Ivy Donner, one of the Readaholics and our friend since high school, had been poisoned in May, and we were all still reeling. I found myself agreeing with Brooke that we didn't need a police procedural or urban noir book for next month.

"There are lots of books without serial killers or gore," I said, taking a swig of my diet soda. "Tons of 'em. Really, when you think about it, books with brains caked on the walls and criminologists deducing the killer's identity from blood-spatter analysis are a relatively modern development. What about something more old-fashioned, something pre–*Girl with the Dragon Tattoo*?"

"Dick Francis," Brooke mused, "except sometimes he kills off horses, and I can't take that."

Brooke had a soft heart for animals and volunteered at the Heaven Animal Haven, the no-kill shelter here in Heaven, Colorado.

"Dorothy Sayers?"

She wrinkled her nose. "After reading that one about the bells, I'm not much of a Sayers fan. Boring. I'm more in the mood for something along the line of Nancy Drew."

"I don't think the others will be too *keen* on that," I said. "Get it? Carolyn Keene?"

Brooke groaned and tossed a throw pillow at me.

"I guess that's why they call them *throw* pillows," I said, catching it.

"Stop with the puns already," she said, "or I'm leaving." She made as if to rise.

"Fine, fine." I held up my hands in surrender.

"What about Agatha Christie?" she said. "We haven't ever read one of her books."

I thought about it. "I guess you're right," I said slowly. "I guess I assumed everyone had already read a lot of Christie, since she is the queen of mysteries." I paused for a beat and decided to confess. "I've never read a Christie book, though. Don't toss me out of the Readaholics."

"I've read all the Miss Marples." She put down

her diet soda, being careful to place a coaster under it, even on the glass table. "I've never tried any of the others, though."

And that's how we came to be reading *Murder on the Orient Express*, the book jouncing on the van's passenger seat as I headed for my brother, Derek's, pub. I'd finished it the night before and was looking forward to the Readaholics' discussion tomorrow. I tried to anticipate everyone's reactions, but the only one I was sure of was Maud's. Our resident conspiracy theorist would be wholeheartedly enthusiastic about the book because it contained a conspiracy. I smiled to myself as I parked the car in the gravel lot. I had found the whole conspiracy thing totally unbelievable. Twelve people working together to kill one man? Puh-leeze. Murder conspiracies didn't work, not in real life.

We've all heard the advice about doctors not performing surgery on their own family members. It's against the Hippocratic Oath, I think, or maybe the American Medical Association bans it. The same should hold true for event organizers. If there were an event-organizer governing body, I'd be happy to propose a bylaw that made it unethical to plan parties for family members, especially brothers. Under that rule, such an act would be punishable by having to listen to an endless loop of John Denver's "Rocky Mountain High" or taking a cross-country road trip with said family. In a VW Beetle. With no air-conditioning. In August.

I looked at Derek and said in my reasonable voice, even though my day's supply of "reasonable" was about exhausted, "You can't invite more people. The fire marshal's max capacity is two hundred twenty. We've already invited three hundred, not counting the people who will come because they read about the opening in the *Heaven Herald* or from a friend. Even though a fair chunk of the invitees won't be able to come, especially the ones from Denver, you're asking for trouble by sending out more invitations this late."

We were sitting in my brother's ready-for-grand-opening brewpub, Elysium Brewing, on the outskirts of Heaven, Colorado. The building had originally been a factory—shoes, I think—and the designer had kept an industrial vibe with exposed pipes and the original brick walls. They contrasted nicely with the new fittings installed late last month. On a sultry August day, the narrow windows were open, and brilliant sunshine lit up the booths with their orange leatherette upholstery and made the woodwork gleam. When I'd heard the pub's decorator was going with orange, I'd been skeptical, but against the dark wood and the bar's brass fittings, it looked really good, especially in the evening under the soft glow from the antiquey-looking pendant lights. From where we sat in a corner booth near the kitchen, I could barely glimpse the patio, where Derek envisioned selling a lot of brews on long summer evenings, and the wide staircase that led to an open area with eight pool tables and an auxiliary bar on the second floor, offices on the third floor, and a rooftop space, which would eventually be a venue for private functions. A humungous stainless steel vat with tubing spiraling around it took up a large chunk of space. It sat in a glass enclosure so Colorado's craft beer enthusiasts could watch the brewing process in action. Whoop-de-doo.

The janitor mopped his way past us, leaving an odor of lemon cleanser, which temporarily overpowered the hoppy beer scent that pervaded the pub. Derek ran a hand through his short hair, which was a deeper auburn than my coppery locks. It stood on end. "People won't all come at the same time," he argued.

"I know, but trust me when I say that guests with an invitation in hand are going to expect to walk right in, not have to wait in line until the place empties out enough that there's room for them." I'd owned my event-organizing business, Eventful!, for four years now, and I'd learned a thing or two the hard way.

"But we've got to invite Gordon's doctor sister, Angie, and her husband, Eugene—he's an accountant— now that they're back in town. Their daughter—what a tragedy. And that guy who's running for state senator against Troy Widefield—not that I want him to beat Troy, but—"

A tattoo of stiletto heels on the stairs and raised voices interrupted us. "—what the judge has to say, Gordo," a woman's voice said. "You can't just not pay Kolby's college tuition. The semester starts in a couple of weeks. He's—"

"He's twenty-four and a useless parasite," came Gordon Marsh's voice. "I paid for his first attempt at college, and I don't feel I owe him another go-round. I gave him a job here, and that's more than he deserves. I'm damn sure he drinks or spills more beer than he sells."

"He's your *son*!" The speaker, a slim brunette, came into view. In tight jeans, a Western shirt that strained the pearl snaps across her chest, and carefully feathered hair, she looked a decade younger than the fifty-two or -three she had to be.

"Don't remind me," Gordon growled. He appeared on the stairs above her and followed her down, his heavier footsteps in contrast to the angry tapping of her heels. Derek's partner in Elysium Brewing, he was in his early fifties with a full head of dark blond hair sprinkled with gray. His tanned face had its share of lines, and he carried a little extra weight around his middle, but he was still a handsome man. He reminded me of a younger, blonder James Brolin. He had a reputation as a player, though, with a philosophy of love 'em and leave 'em. Lots of 'em, if rumors were correct. I was sure he thought of himself as a "stud." He'd tried his pitch on me when he first went into business with Derek, but I was having none of it. Sure, I'd gone out once with a guy who turned out to be a murderer, but I had to draw the line somewhere.

I'd asked Derek why he'd partnered with Gordon, and he'd told me Gordon was an investment genius, head of his own venture capital firm, GTM Capital, with a knack for underwriting start-up bars and restaurants that went on to be hugely successful. He had a unique hands-on approach to his projects, where he or one of his senior staff "embedded" with the company they were underwriting until it was well and truly launched.

"I need him. Don't piss him off, sis," Derek had said, stopping short of suggesting I date the man to keep him happy. He knew how that was likely to go over.

"You'll be hearing from my lawyer," Susan Marsh said, eyes narrowed to slits. "You can't do this to Kolby."

"The hell I can't!" Without warning, Gordon swiped a beer mug from the bar and hurled it in Susan's direction. It missed her by a good three feet, hit a booth, and shattered on the floor.

Derek was on his feet immediately, making calming gestures as he approached his partner. "Whoa, big guy, no need for this." He stood between Gordon and Susan, which made me nervous, but Gordon didn't seem inclined to launch more missiles at his ex-wife.

Susan, eyes big, scuttled out of the bar, but not without stopping to snap a picture of the broken glass with her phone. For her lawyer's use, I imagined. I was so startled by Gordon's sudden fury that I stayed seated, not sure whether to call the cops or let Derek handle it. The two men talked for thirty seconds. Then Derek clapped his partner on the shoulder and returned to me while Gordon headed up the stairs to the roof, shaking a cigarette out of a packet as he went.

"What was that all about?" I whispered.

Derek shook his head. "I don't know. Gordon's been edgy lately, losing it over the least little thing. When we first started putting this deal together, fifteen months or so ago, he was brusque, sometimes rude, but you could always see where he was coming from, you know? I mean, yeah, he was out for number one, looking to structure the partnership contract in his favor, but that's just business. When I didn't lie down and roll over, he respected it, I think. I mean, our contract's fair." He ran a hand through his hair again. "Lately, though, sis"—he gave me a serious look—"I don't know how much longer I can put up with it. If I could afford to buy him out, I'd do it tomorrow. He's rude to the employees—that's why Sam quit—and he busted a crate of hops the other day when the delivery truck was an hour late. If he behaves like that around customers . . ."

I could see worry in the deep line between his brows and the way his jaw worked. I reached over the table to punch his shoulder. "Hang in there. Maybe it's the grand opening that's got him on edge. Hopefully, he'll settle down once we're past Friday night."

"Yeah, maybe."

He didn't look hopeful, and I got the feeling there was more he wasn't telling me. I didn't have time to draw it out of him, though, since I was on the verge of being late for a client meeting. "Hang in there," I repeated, sliding out of the booth as gracefully as I could in my tan pencil skirt. "I'll be back at five."

I'd agreed to take a few shifts behind the bar until Derek could find a replacement for Sam, the bartender who'd left in a huff after a run-in with Gordon the day before. I'd put myself through college bartending, among other jobs, and I wanted to help out because Derek had begged me to and because I, like my folks and sisters, had a fair chunk of change invested in Elysium Brewing. I'd even persuaded the Readaholics to put off our discussion of *Murder on the Orient Express* until tomorrow night so I could work at the pub this evening.

"Thanks, Amy-Faye. You're a lifesaver."

"I'll add that to my résumé." With a smile and another shoulder punch, I left him sitting in the booth and headed for the parking lot and my van.